# THIS REDHEAD

## The Dialogues

# THIS REDHEAD

## The Dialogues

JOHN D. BEATTY

·JDB· Communications, ·LLC·

JDB COMMUNICATIONS, LLC
WEST ALLIS, WISCONSIN

JDB Communications, LLC



1st Edition Paperback ISBN: 979-8-9860169-0-0
1st Edition E-book ISBN: 979-8-9860169-1-7

## *Also from John D. Beatty*

*Crop Duster: A Novel of World War II*
*Sergeant's Business and Other Stories*
*The Liberty Bell Files: J Edgar's Demons*
*The Past Not Taken: Three Novellas*

**The Stella's Game Trilogy**
*Stella's Game: A Story of Friendship*
*Tideline: Friendship Abides*
*The Safe Tree: Friendship Triumphs*

*For Kelly*

*who rented my spare room...*
*this is just a story...sweetie*

# On Style

*This Redhead* consists only of *external dialogues* between two characters, Blondie and Red. There are no non-verbal narratives nor any *internal dialogues*. There are *no* quotation marks for what they say; just those in *their* dialogs, nor "he said" nor "she sighed" nor "they cried" tags. You will read of no facial expressions that they don't *talk* about, no un-*noticed* reactions or un-*vocalized* thoughts. Further, you won't see many *proper* names; mostly nicknames and the odd title. The *italics* are for emphasis. Conversations are naturally paced; some spoken phrases or sentences *invite* response, and are marked by (...). I generously use these ellipses for pacing...and *those pauses*... we're not even *aware* of.

Most of the story takes place in either a two-bedroom, two-story, bath-and-a-half townhouse on a quiet rural/suburban street, or in a neighborhood tavern. The buildings in the neighborhood are close enough together that the comings-and-goings of neighbors are not a mystery, nor are *some* of their *other* activities.

There are no scenes set; no transitional segues described other than in their dialogues. Story breaks and chapters *may* move from one location to another—and you'll *know* when they are important—but just as often, they merely mark the passing of time.

*This Redhead* will require more of *your* imagination than any other story you have *ever* read. You *should* provide missing elements out of your experience. The interior layout of rooms, how crowded the bar is, or any other visual elements...make them up as you see fit. As their dialogs are very personal to them, so too will the scene settings become personal to *you*. You might place Red and Blondie in your kitchen, in your neighborhood watering hole, or in the room where you had a memorable romantic encounter.

It will surprise you at how absorbing a reading experience *This Redhead* will be.

# This Redhead...

*Hey, there, cowboy...*

Hi...

Want some *company...?*

O...*K*...

Crowded...*ain't* it...?

Well, it's New Years...*most* bars *are* crowded on this *auspicious* day, yes.

Aus...uhn, *yeah, sure...so*...make some *room* at the bar, *here*...

O...*K*...

You're kinda slow on the uptake, cowboy...

What do you mean?

You haven't even asked me my *name*...

I'll just call you Red. You should be *used* to *that.*

*OK*...yeah...I *am*...

Take my stool...you're *half* on it, anyway. I *sit* most of the day...

*Thanks,* Blondie...*you* should be used to *that* moniker... *yours* is *ash*-blonde...

You're welcome. *Actually,* yeah, I am...

You *know* I'm trying to pick you *up,* right...?

Um...*I've* never been...*not...exactly...*

Never been picked up before...?

*My* experience with *pickups* starts when *I* ask 'can I buy you a drink,' and ends with, 'sure, but I'll *drink* it over *there* while you're *here...*'

*That's* funny. How about *I* buy *you* one *and* stick around to drink *with* you...

O...*K*; thanks, sounds...*OK...beer*, please...

Welcome...*I'll* have *another* of *these...*so...

Your hair's *pretty,* like *copper...*

I'll *have* you *know* that we redheads *rinse* our *hair* in the *blood* of *those* we *vanquish...*

I'm quite *sure* of *that.* And you have a*d*orable freckles...

*Each freckle* is the *soul* of a *defeated* enemy...

A *seasoned* warrior with a *sweet* smile and *dimples...*

Ah, *hah...you* don't *scare* easy...

I have *little* experience with *being* picked up, so, *should* I be...?

Um...should *I* move on to a guy with *more* experience...?

*If* you are so inclined.

Say *what?*

If you *want* to... *if* you're *not* up for a challenge...

*Huh.* I'll work on *you* 'cause you *interest* me...how many girls kissed *you* tonight...?

*None.*

*Huh?* You *didn't* get kissed in a neighborhood saloon at midnight on New Year's Eve...?

Um...I wasn't *here* at midnight, but... ever played spin-the-bottle?

Sure...

Remember what happened when the girl *wouldn't* kiss the guy?

Um...*that* never...

In *my* neighborhood, she paid the guy a *nickel...*

*OK...*

By the time *I* was fifteen, I had *enough* to *buy* a *car*...so, no; *I* didn't get kissed tonight.

Now, *that's* funny...can't understand *why* every girl *in* here didn't *try*; you're *cute*, if a *bit* on the thin side. Bet you can *dodge snowflakes*...so, what do you *do* that you *sit* all the time?

I'm a writer.

Now *that's* exciting...might I have *read* anything you've *written?*

If you've operated or serviced process equipment or haul trucks, you *might* have...

*Eh...*what's *process equipment?*

Machinery that processes fluids or fluidized materiel for manufacturing and containerizing, like beverages, peanut butter, ice cream, stuff like *that.* Most of *my* equipment makes beverages, but I *just* did a paint blender...

Glad I *asked...*I *think. What's* a *haul truck?* Don't *all* trucks *haul* something?

Off-road dump trucks; mines use the *largest* of 'em, but I've never done one *that* big...what do *you* do, Red?

Ah-*hah!* He shows *interest* at last! *I* drive a school bus...do you *like* what you do...?

*Yeah...*is driving a school bus nine months out of the year *your* dream career...?

Wow! From com*plete* disinterest to talking about *careers* in *less* than five minutes! That's a *personal* record, Blondie...

Congratulations, Red...I guess...

*Drink* up; we'll go somewhere where we can *talk* about *what* you *write about...*it'll *have* to be *your* place because *mine's* my sister's basement...unless you pre*fer hot-sheet hotels...*

Ever start a conversation with a guy who you *didn't* want to get into bed ten minutes after you met him?

We haven't hit *five* minutes yet, so *we* don't count... Blondie? *Hey!* Hello! Over *here*, cowboy...

I'm *with* ya...

Are you *fading* on me...wanna...?

I'll take a pass...

Not interested in *me*...or in *girls*?

I need to know more *about* the women I have *relations* with. OK, *you're* cute, and you have a *gorgeous* smile, and *beautiful* hair, and you *may* be a *lot* of fun, but all I know about *you* is what you *do* five days a week *and* that you live with your sister...

Thanks for *that*...I *guess*...

*Anytime*, Red. I have more *respect* for *women* than *that*... see, we should need *more* out of an *intimate* relationship than a few minutes of *wham-bam-thank-you-ma'am* heat and friction, if you *follow* me. It's *empty*; sex *shouldn't* be *like* that. Guys could get the same *physical* pleasure from using Mother Thumb and her Four Daughters; *you* know, *rubbing one out*...you *get* me?

I *think* I do...*that* sounded downright *poetic*...ya *know*, I could get *used* to talking to you...

Girls who flirt in haste oft repent in leisure...

Flirt? *Hell*, I'm trying to *pick* you *up*; not wasting *time* in just *flirting*. But you *interest* me; I *learn* stuff just *talking* to you and I *like* learning. You *live* around here...?

*Around* here...I *work* not far away...

How come I've never seen you *in* here before? *I'm* here a *lot*...

This is my first time *in* here. About midnight I just started *driving* and *found*...

Where'd you *come* from, originally? You *didn't* grow up in *this* 'hood...*hey*...

Just debating if I want to *say*. I don't often throw caution to the wind.

What's the harm in knowing where you're *from?* It's not like I'm gonna TP your *house...*

That *does* seem unlikely...OK. I grew up in Motown.

*Motor City...*

That's *it.*

What brings you *here?*

Work.

Want another *drink...?*

No, thanks. I don't *drink* much...

Why *not?*

My *sober* brain says 'leave the lady alone.' My *drunk* brain says 'I just want to hold her hand!' And I keep getting my *hands* slapped...

*That's* funny! Want to get *out* of here, grab a bite to *eat?* It's pretty *noisy* and *you interest* me. The pizza joint across the parking lot is open...c'mon, Blondie; I'll *buy* you a late supper...

We'll *split* the check...

Eh, *OK...*

That *guy* over there...with the beard holding the blonde. He keeps *glaring* at *you*...and *me. Who's...?*

Let's just *go, cowboy*...got a *joke* for ya: A guy walks into a wedding reception, goes up to the bartender and asks, 'is *this* the *punch line?'*

The...*yeah, heh...*so, a rabbi, a priest, and a minister walk into a bar. The bartender looks up and says, 'is *this* some kind of *joke?'*

***

Yeah, *that's* good, Blondie. Here's *another* one: A polar bear walks into a bar. Bartender says, 'what'll ya *have?'* Polar bear says, 'I'll have a gin............and tonic.' Bartender asks, 'what's with the big pause?' Polar bear holds up his arms, says 'I dunno. I was *born* with 'em.'

*Heh-heh.* OK, Red, *here's* one: An *Irishman* walks *past* a bar... hey, it *could* happen...

*Ha!* OK: Guy walks into a bar and yells, 'all *lawyers* are *assholes.*' Guy at the end of the bar says, 'I *object* to that remark.' The first guy says, 'why, are *you* a *lawyer?*' Second guy says, 'no, I'm an *asshole.*'

*He-he-he!* OK...um...*OK:* A *dyslexic* guy walks into a *bra...*

*And...*

*That's...it...*

*Huh?* I *don't...*

OK; *never* mind...

*No!* I *want* to...guy walks into a bra...

*Dyslexic* guy...

Dis...*what?*

*Dyslexic*...gets his *letters* mixed up...dyslexia's a *learning* disability...

So...he walks into a bra ...oh, *I* get it; a *bar* ...yeah...*heh...*

Explaining a joke is like dissecting an animal; you might *understand* it but the animal *never* recovers...

Yeah, I *guess...you* need more meat on your bones; a strong *wind* could blow *you* away...

I've been *sick.*

Ah. *Good* pizza here.

The *pizza's* fine.

You didn't *like* it?

I don't often think that the words *good* and *pizza* go together.

You *ate* it, cowboy...

I decided I *was* hungry and *this* one ain't bad...

Glad you approve...*cozy* booth...

*Right* by the kitchen door; gets *all* the traffic *and* the heat... did you use *me* to ditch Beard?

I *came* with him, but he'd been *canoodling* with that *bleach-blonde* since we walked in...

You were trying to make *him* pay attention to *you* by picking *me* up?

*Kinda*...you know a *lot* about people...

I know a great *deal* about people, but I'm *told* I'm a social cripple.

*Long* story...?

*Long* story.

Huh. Maybe I'd want to *hear* it sometime...

*Why?*

You *interest* me...

Can't *imagine* why. After tonight, we'll *probably* never *see* each other again.

It's a woman's prerogative to change her mind. You should know *that*...

I've *heard* it, but I try not to be guided by slogans.

*Deep*, Blondie. What if *I* decide that the unpolished *gold* of a guy like *you* is *sexier* than the gloss of the *lounge lizards* and the glare of the *knuckle-draggers* around *this* neighborhood?

*That* bit of philosophy means you use your *head* for more than keeping your *ears* apart...

What you *said*...I *want* your *number*...

Six.

And...there *should* be six *more* digits...

You aren't *getting* them.

You *sure*...?

Meaning no disrespect, but no.

You *got* a girlfriend? Your *friend* gauge on full?

No and no.

You're *not* interested in *starting* something?

You *realize that attitude* is why there's so *many* single mothers whose only relationships are with their kids and their poor decisions, right? You *settle* for strangers, only you don't *know* what *losers* they might be. And when they *take off* or you *kick* them *out*...

You *are* a philosopher, Blondie. Yeah, *that's* pretty true in a *lot* of cases. But *I* want to *get* to know *you*...

Why? You've got *Beard*...

*He's* screwing Bleach-Blonde by now...

Not much of a boyfriend.

He *never* was...

But you *still* consider him to be your boyfriend?

I've *been* considering him since high school...but he and I are *done*...

And they say *I'm* socially stilted.

*I* haven't said that; you're pretty OK with me...

*YOU* made the first move.

Good point. I think they're trying to close up here.

When they turn chairs over on tables, yeah, that's *usually* a good sign.

So, this is *it* for *us*, then?

Safer for us *both*...

Why? I find you *interesting* to *talk* to...

You have a *weird* sense of interesting, Red.

My *sister* reminds me of *that* all the time...

Just...*trust* me. Tell you *what*: if we run into each other again, OK, we'll see. *You* live around here; *I* live somewhat *near* here. It *could* happen...

What if I was to give you a kiss? You don't *like* it, just *give* it *back*...

*Good* try, Red. That line *ever* work...?

On guys I *know*, yeah, *all* the time...

You don't *know* me...

I *want* to...

Still haven't said *why*...

I just *do*...just *pucker* and *lean,* cowboy; I *promise* I *won't* bite...but you *might* change *your* mind once you...

*Sorry* to disappoint, but...*just* out of curiosity, do your *bra* and panties *match*?

Do my...*bra* and *panties...match...huh*?

*So long,* Red, and thanks for the...the....

Company?

Yeah; company.

You're *welcome*...hope to *see* you again, and *soon*... *bye,* Blondie.

Ya never *know,* Red; ya *never* know...*bye.*

# Rents A Spare Room...

<hr>

*Hello?*

*Hello...oh, hi...*you're a *guy!*

Let me *check...yes,* I *am...thought* I was. Now that *that's* settled, *what...?*

I was calling about the furnished room. Is it *still* available?

It *is.*

Ad didn't *say* it was with a *guy...*

Newspaper didn't *say* it *had* to...

Guess *not...*

Is my *Y chromosome* a *problem?*

Your *what...?*

The gene that *defines* me and most *other* mammals as a *male...*

Oh...it's not a problem for *me.*

Then *what...?*

*Never* mind...where *is* the place?

It's at...

Ah! I *know* where *that* is, just a few streets from my *parent's* place...

You *know* the neighborhood then. Do you want to *see* it?

*Yeah...*

*When?*

How about *ten minutes...?*

Ah...*sure...I'll* just...

Great! Do you *mind* renting to a woman?

*I* don't mind if *you* don't...

I'm *on* my *way...*

I'll be *here.*

***

Hi...*oh,* it's *you,* Blondie!

*Hi,* Red; I'm still *me.* I didn't recognize your voice on the phone...

I didn't recognize *yours,* either. I *knew* we'd meet again, *cowboy.*

*Did* you? Huh...well, *I...*

You *look thinner* than you did *New Year's*...didn't think *that* was *possible...*

Renting myself out as a skeleton to a night-school anatomy class...still *interested* in...?

You? *Yeah... you're* interesting and *not* a creep...

I try *not* to be *too* creepy... but, the *room,* Red, the *room...*

More than I was a *minute* ago...it's *in* the 'hood; the rent's *reasonable,* so...*yeah,* sure; I'm *interested* in the *room... too. Let's* have a *look...*

While *you're...out* here...c'mon; I'll *show* you the *layout* of...

I *know* the neighborhood. *I* remember when *all* this was farmer's fields...

*That* patch over to the west still *is; feed* corn, I think. When the *wind* is right *once* in a while...

You can *smell* the *shit* after the farmer spreads it...

Yup. Gotta *love* those honey wagons...

Yeah...oh, *hi!*

Know *him?*

A teacher in my high school.

He lives in the *next* building, kitty-corner across the sidewalk. *Four-plex* they call these: four townhouses to a building. *These two* units share a sidewalk and a driveway with *those two* in *that* building to the north. Over *there*, to the south, are two *more* units attached to *this* one.

Ah...

*And* we can hear Neighbor-Behind's toilets flush...

Uh-huh; kinda *used* to *that*...

OK. So, *I* use the garage closest to the road; *you'd* use one of the parking spots closer to the building. The neighbor be*hind* us uses the *other one*. The *mail box*, for whatever reason, is *across* the *street*...have you lived around *here* long? *Hey!*

All my life...who's that *you're* waving at?

Next-door neighbor. He's *also* the landlord...

*You* rent here?

Yeah. He owns *this* building *and* those on either side.

Handy...

Especially when something breaks. That green space back *there* we call the *common*. It's shared with everyone on this side of this circular street.

That's why they call it a *circle*...

*That* explains it...c'mon *in*...the kitchen's *right inside*; that corner by the window *there* is *supposed* to be a *dining* room, but I parked my desk and some bookshelves *there* when I decided to *rent* the *second bedroom* out...

You've got a *lot* of books...

Books are my *quietest* and *most constant* of friends; they are the most accessible and wisest of counselors, and the most patient of teachers.

*That's* pretty smart...who *said* it?

Some *smarter* guy than me. Outside a *dog*, a *book* is man's *best friend. Inside* a dog it's too *dark* to *read...*

*Hah!*

There's *more* books in the basement and *my* room...OK, here's the *living* room; *fake* gas fireplace in the *corner...* *coat* closet; not much to *see* there...*half*-bath *there*, right opposite the stairway. Basement's down *that* way; the room's *up* the stairs...and there's *Kitty* in her favorite spot on the landing... say *hi*, Kitty...

You *have* a cat...

If *that's* a problem...

No; just never *lived* with a *cat* before...*hi*, Kitty...

Not much *to* 'em. Feed 'em; make sure they have water; change their box regularly; give 'em some expensive stuff for hairballs; clean up the hairballs they bring up, anyway; scratch their what*ever* when they *present* it...

Beautiful *black*...and green eyes...he doesn't *like* me...

*She* doesn't *know* you...cats get the *exact* same look on their faces whether they see a *moth* or an *axe-murderer* ...though *this* look *might* be because it's close to dinner... *meow*, yourself, cat...*hard* to say, because *you're* the first visitor she's ever *had* here...

Not much of a *social* life, cowboy?

*Not* so's you'd notice. I *got* her from a woman at work whose kids became allergic to her. I *think* I brought *her* home so I'd have a girl waiting for me every night...

*That's* funny...

*That* was before I discovered while dogs think of us as part of their *families*, cats regard us as their *staff*...

Heh-heh-heh...

Follow *me*...*Kitty* will just...*cry* plaintively and *glare* at *me* because I haven't *fed* her yet.

Kinda *steep* stairs...

Yeah; the *movers* noticed that, too; called it a *carpeted ladder*...here's the *full* bathroom to the *right*. The water pressure ain't *bad*, but the water's *hard*: we're on a shared well. And it's a *tub*, not a *stall*. There's *my* room...*that* is the room I'm renting out...and *there's* the linen closet right next to it. We can lock all but the linen closet door...

Huh...the room's *bigger* than I imagined...*little* closet... west-facing window...*perfect*.

I can't say *what* the square footage is; maybe a hundred fifty. *My* windows are west and north...

Is the furniture included in the rent?

The *bed* and *dresser* are. The *curtains* are up to you; put up more rods if you want. *I* pay for the utilities except for water; that's included in *my* rent. The phone *line* in here is separate from the one downstairs and in *my* room...

*My own phone number* at last! That's a *dial* phone?

Use your *own* if you want. Unlimited *local* calls on my plan, but *not* long-distance. We'll *discuss* the bills as they *come*...

Not *much* long-distance; only my gramma lives outside the 'hood.

I'd be a *full-service* landlord if *that's* what you'd want to do...

*Careful* with the *service* cracks, there, bub. There's a *sitcom* like this.

*Two* gals and a dweeb, yeah.

You watch it?

I've seen the ads, but I don't *watch* sitcoms.

You *have* pay TV, though. I recognized the *antenna* outside...

In the living room and in *my* room, yes. You can watch it downstairs, unless you want to shell out a hundred bucks or so to connect it in *your* room...

Naw. The nearest laundromat's...

I have a washer and dryer in the basement...your rent *includes* the use of *those*...

A *washer* and *dryer* on-site? *Plus,* my *own phone number* for the first time in my life? Blondie, *you're* the man of my dreams!

This is business, Red, *not* romance.

Get a *clue,* Blondie! Can't you *tell* when someone's kidding?

Sometimes; *not* with people I don't *know.* Are you still driving a school bus?

Naw; I got *tired* of seasonal employment.

*How* would you pay the *rent?*

I'm tending bar where we met...I *know* just about everyone between the freeway and the lake, and *they* know *me. That* makes bartending *easy* work...

But you're willing to move in with a strange guy?

*You're* not as strange as *some* guys, and you're *not* the *first* guy I've rented a room from; everybody in the 'hood knows *that. When* can I move in?

Let's get a few things straight. *Don't* piss off the neighbors and clean up after yourself. You pick guys up for a one-nighter, you *don't* bring 'em *here*...

I'd *never* do *that* with a guy I'd *just met*...

Our New Year's encounter suggests...

*That* was the *first* and *last* time I *ever* tried to pick up a stranger...I was so *pissed* at Beard that night, then you *gave* me your *stool*...

I was being polite to a lady who was already pushing me *off* it...

*Lady?* How *old* do you think I *am?*

Right around *my* age, mid-twenties...

You're *good,* Blondie...

To continue, *guy*-friends are OK *if* I meet them *first,* but I *won't* have strangers tramping through my *home*...so, do you *want* the room?

OK, let's be straight, cowboy. We may sleep headboard-to-headboard, but you're *not* my *type;* we're not *involved,* and I *don't* need to *approve your* lady-friends...

Not to worry about *that*...

Why *not?*

The difference between me and a calendar is that a calendar *has* dates.

*That's* funny...

I've got a *million* of 'em....

Like...?

A guy at the bar says, 'I slept with my wife before we were married. Did *you?* The other guy says, '*I* dunno; what's her *maiden* name?'

*HAHAHAHA!* That *IS* funny!

I'm here in*def*initely.

*Hah!* OK: do you *swim*, cowboy?

Yeah; I go to the pool at the high school a couple of times a week.

Me, too...maybe we could go *together* sometime...

Um...

I *have* a *bikini* and I'm *not* afraid to *wear* it...

You *know*, a bikini covers *ninety percent* of a gal's body, but *guys* are *so* polite they *only* look at the *ten percent* it *covers*...

*That's* actually *funny! When* can I move in?

After you cross my palm with silver...

After I *what?*

Pay me first and last month's rent *in* cash *in* advance.

Ah! Yeah...OK...let's...*here*...you...*are. That's* what the *ad* said, right?

Yes, it *is.*

I've got *stuff* in my car. I'll bring more *and* some *furniture* later.

Um...*decamping* from...?

Nothing *bad*...

I'll give you a hand...*and* your keys...*after* I answer that phone...

***

Put my coats in *this* closet?

Sure. *That* vacuum cleaner tucked in the back is for living spaces. I've got a shop vac in the basement for bigger jobs.

Can I put this...*here?*

A *plant?*

*Green*, it has *leaves*, it's in a pot full of dirt. Yup; *looks* like a *plant* to me. The corner by the fireplace...?

*Try* it. *Kitty* will be curious, *might* chew some leaves. Keep it watered so she *doesn't* use it for a litter box. There's that *hook* up in the corner; previous tenant hung a big rubber tree there, Landlord said...*may* be better if I made a *platform*...

Lot of *trouble*...

*No* trouble...light chain; sheet of plywood; four eyebolts... I'll get the chain tomorrow...

OK; *thanks*...I can use the *kitchen?*

The only place that's *only* mine is *my* bedroom...

I'll *remember* that...huh; fridge has...*English* muffins, *cottage* cheese, milk, *orange* juice, *chocolate* bars, *veal* patties, *cold* rice, *head* of lettuce, *various* lunch meats, *white* bread... cereal, rice and peanut butter in the cupboard...not a *lot* of *real* food, Blondie...

Need to get to the store. What's *your* work schedule, if I might ask?

Sure; *not* a secret. When I *open* at *three*, I get off by *nine*. I get off at midnight when I go in at *five*. When I go in at *nine*, I'm there till last call and cleanup. I get *most* Sundays and Mondays off, unless there's a *real big* game. *That* OK?

That's fine. I just wanted *some* idea...um...*about* the phone...

Yeah?

You *heard* that conversation...

*Enough* of it, yeah...

Unless you *want* to talk to my bill collectors, *don't* answer *my* line...

You, ah, get a *lot* of them?

When *my* phone rings from five to ten in the evening, it's *usually* somebody wanting money I ain't *got*...I *owe so* much I could start a *government.*

Ah-*hah*...listen, ah...we don't *have* to be *friends*, but *this* will be a *lot* more *pleasant* if we're both *friendly* and *discrete*... *your* business is *yours*; mine is *mine*...

Yeah, OK, but I've never *done* this kind of thing, so...

I *have.* There'll be *some* adjustment, but...we need to get *used* to each other...and *you* need to put the *toilet seats* down...

I've *lived in* the *company* of women before...I was *just* about to make some *dinner*...

*I* have a *cramming* group, *then* I have to go to work, *then* I have a date, *and then* I have a macroeconomics midterm tomorrow...*rain check?*

*You're* in *school*...?

Community college, yeah; business courses...I *gotta* run...

*See* ya, Red! Good *luck* tomorrow!

Thanks! *Later*, Blondie.

***

Oh, *morning*, Red.

*Morning*, Blondie. *You're* up early.

Weekdays, yeah.

Ah.

*Good* date?

It was *OK*. What do you *DO* that you have to get up *so* early in the morning?

Enjoy the quiet of the sunrise while I think about the possibilities of the day and the phone *isn't* ringing; exercise on that bike in the basement; read the paper; watch TV news to find out what *isn't* happening...*good* night at *work?*

*Good* tips, but just *another* game night. Anything *special* in the newspaper?

Um...Politicians making promises they have no intention of keeping ahead of their conventions. President Peanut Farmer's complaining that he didn't see the commies invading the *graveyard of empires* before it happened...

He didn't *see* those so-called *students* taking over the *embassy*, either, the *clown*. I *think* this is in the same precinct I voted in *last* time. You registered to vote?

Sure. You don't *vote*, you can't *gripe*.

Exactly.

Want to read the paper?

I'll read the funny papers and the business section *after* I take a shower...

*Shower?*

Any *idea* how *dirty* a saloon is to work in?

No, though I *bussed tables* for a while...

*Trust* me, I *need* a shower. Mind if I have some of your coffee after?

Help yourself.

 If I *don't* see you later...*ciao!*

*Arrivederci!*

***

Oh! You're still *here?*

I don't *go* to work until eight-thirty.

Ah. Mind if I *join* you while you eat breakfast? *I'm* just having *coffee.*

A freshly scrubbed girl is *always* welcome in the morning.

Not sure if *that's* funny or not...

*I'm* not either.

Do I make you uncomfortable...a *girl* in your place, I mean?

I'll get *used* to it.

When do *you* get home?

I work nine-to-five, so *about* five-thirty.

We'll miss each other sometimes, then.

Probably...

Then we *won't* be in each other's way and I won't *embarrass* you with the *scanty* costumes I wear to *work*...like *this* morning...

And *I* won't embarrass you when *I*...

Cowboy, I'm long past *that*...

*That*...?

Getting upset when guys *stare* at my chest.

You're the first non-family girl *I've ever* lived with, so for *me*...

*Don't* tell me you're a *virgin*...

I *won't*, but if *you're* gonna go *that* far, are *you* as *yet* to be deflowered?

To be de-*what*?

Is your *maidenhead* intact?

My...*oh*, no...*this* is 1980...

I *heard*...

Virginity is like a balloon: one *prick* and you're *done*...

*Heh-heh*...

Sex is like *potato chips*; just *can't* stop with *one*...

*HA!*

I'm *on* the *pill*, so don't *worry* about...

*That's* none of *my* business.

Maybe *yes*, maybe *no*; *some* secrets between roommates aren't *that* secret...*by* the *way*, I *have* a better coffee maker than *yours* at Sister's place. Mind if I bring it over?

As long as we don't take up the whole counter with coffee pots. Just...I'll clean *mine* up and put it under the counter. *Mind* if I ask...um...with all that hair...you *don't* wash it every day...?

Ah...no; about every *six*...*wash*; *braid*; *stack*; *twist*; repeat... *you* could use a *better* haircut...

I cut my *own*...

I can *tell*. My *sister* is a hairdresser, but she cuts men's hair, too; she'll do it *cheap*...

I'll *think* about it...

*I* should get some sleep. My *exam's* at *one* and I *open* tonight.

Should *see* you tonight, then.

Yep... ah, I have one of those adjustable showerheads with a *hose*. Can *we* put *it* in the *shower?* Don't need any more than a pair of *pliers*...

Might take *more* than that to get the old head *off*...

No; *I've* done it before...*please*...

I...um...*don't*...

It's a *lot* easier to get clean with *it*...*pretty* please? Doesn't *take* but a few *minutes*...*massage* settings and *everything* ... feels *so* good...

You got something in your *eye*, there, Red?

Batting eyelashes don't *work* on you, cowboy? C'mon; I'll cook *dinner* Saturday night...*please*...?

Well...

*Pretty* please with *sugar* on top...and I wasn't *wearing* a *bra*... What...?

My bra and panties *couldn't* match New Year's Eve 'cause I wasn't *wearing* a bra...

*Oh...yeah...ya* know, when they *do*, it's because she *wants* to get *lucky...*

*Heh*-heh...so...*showerhead...?*

Well...*OK...*

*Thanks...see* ya, Blondie. It's *on* the *toilet tank...*

But *you* said....ah, *yeah...see* ya, Red...of *course...*

***

*Hey!* You're *early!*

A *little...*

*Missed* you last night...

Busy. What'cha *watching?*

Just an old movie; seen it a *hundred* times.

I'm for a shower. Back in a tick.

***

Hey...*thanks* for changing the showerhead...

Hey; welcome. You *washed* your hair...

Yeah...that *OK?*

*Just* an observation...you *don't* blow-dry?

At the *end. First,* I *have* to...

*Whip* it...*towel* it...*brush* it...*like* you...*are doing...*

Yeah...*mind?*

I'll *get* used to it...

Right...this is an *OK* movie, but I'm not sure *I'd* see it a hundred times...

Eh, I like the dramatic exchanges. The lead actor's especially good.

I've seen him in *other* stuff...

Probably a *lot.* He's *quite* prolific; a *world-renowned* thespian...

But...he's a *guy...*

25

Yeah...*oh! Thespian*, not *lesbian*. A *thespian* knows The Bard's plays by heart. They're a dying breed.

I learn something every time I talk to you...just *hair*, Kitty; no need to *bat* at it...

A toy is a toy...your hair has become a *toy* of *opportunity*...

My...she *got* that *elastic* I lost yesterday...has more *fun* with 'em than I *do*...

*Could* be...

I met Landlord's wife this afternoon...

*Yeah...?*

I was out in the sun and she came over...she's in real estate, you know...

I *knew* that...

She introduced herself and asked if I was the young woman *you'd* been *seeing*...Neighbors-Behind *mentioned* me...

Ah...you *didn't...?*

I told her I was renting your spare room; she thought *that* was...*progressive*...

Yes, she *would...what...?*

She said my *hair* was *beautiful*...

Ah...

Have you *read* all these books?

Um...some of 'em *several* times. *Some* of 'em are reference books...*boy*, you can change subjects *fast*...

Yeah...I want to read *this* book if that's OK...

OK. But you *might* like...*this* one better.

I'll read *both*; decide for my*self*...

There's *more* in the basement if you're interested in *really* dull stuff.

I can barely read the *titles* of some of those down in the basement...I *saw* your AA diploma in *engineering technology*; did *you* go *part*-time?

I went to a community college for a two-year, *full-time* program.

What's *that* involve?

Learning how they make stuff, how it *works*. *Half* of it was learning to draw mechanicals and schematics.

*That's* why you have the drawing board?

Yeah. Had to get *it* to do my homework...

*Those* drawings on the wall...*stunning*.

Thanks...

*That* how you got to be a *writer*?

I kinda *backed* into it; think I'm a good *describer* of things. Engineering techs are being replaced by a *glut* of engineers on the job market; I picked the *wrong* degree. I don't think *anyone* sets out to be a tech writer. There's not much *formal* training for it...

Sounds like bartending. There's schools, but that kind of training's *not* required. What kind of outfit do you *work* for now? I see a lot of *ad* brochures sitting around...

It *started* as a business-to-business marketing firm, but hired *me* as a tech writer because their biggest client needed manuals. You *like* tending bar...?

I like the *money*. The *side* stuff, not especially...

Demeaning...?

Well, my tips go *up* the more *skin* I *show*...

Hence your *outfits*...

Hence...what's that *mean*, anyway?

It's a contraction for 'for that reason...'

Ah; *yeah*...part of the *price* I pay...

You *know* that the men you serve will *pay* for a *glimpse* of your...*assets*...which will increase your *tips*...give 'em a *show* if it makes you money...

As a *liberated* woman, I should *resent* your *sexist* attitude, cowboy

As a liberated *man* and your *roommate, I* need to tell you I *think* those kinds of outfits *feed* that sexist attitude. You can't have it both ways, *little lady...*

*Little lady?*

If I'm a *cowboy,* you're a *little lady...*

Huh. At least *you've* got the guts to *say* it, cowboy. Not every guy *does.*

We *can't* share space if I have to hold my tongue all the time.

No; don't; you're...*refreshing...*I'm *not* gonna become a *saloon stripper* like *other* barmaids have...

Nobody said you *should.* I'm going to observe that you're showing *your* stuff to guys you mostly *know. That* could be humiliating...

Not...especially. *Some* of 'em have seen *more* than...

A college friend and I saw a girl he dated in high school up on the stage of a titty bar once, strutting *her* stuff...

Like that *song...*

Yeah. *She* seemed OK with him seeing *more* of her than he did in high school when we talked to her after her set. For *him,* it was weird. *He* felt embarrassed.

For *himself* or for *her?*

*Both,* I think. Anyway, *she* said she was just doing it for pocket money while she was in college...

Well, *I'm not* gonna start to *pole-dance...*

Up to *you...*

*Yep...*I'll finish drying my hair...

*I'm* going to knock off. 'Night.

'Night.

***

Morning, Blondie.

*Afternoon.* Good *night?*

Was *OK*...wanna lay out in the sun...*join* me?

I don't *do* the sun much; I burn too easy...but *thanks*.

You think *redheads* don't? Baby oil; sunblock; *repeat* and *reapply*...

Pass, thanks.

*Your* loss...

***

You got *some* color, Red.

*Loads* of vitamin D. I feel *great*...your *phone*...

Uh-*huh*...you didn't go out to get a *tan* in *that* getup...

Shorts and t-shirt's enough to soak *some* rays. Besides, I don't want to *shock* our neighbors with a *scanty costume* so *early* in our relationship...

Haven't exchanged more than pleasantries and the occasional wave with most of 'em. I've only ever said *hi* to the woman across the walk that *you* chatted with. Do you *know* her?

She was a year ahead of me in school. She has an order of protection against her ex-husband; *big* custody issues with their little boy.

Where'd you hear *that?*

Sister's beauty shop is next to the sheriff's department, hears *all* the local gossip...you're *not* gonna *answer* your phone...?

It's the finance company; they call on *Tuesday* at about this time...you met our Neighbors-Behind, I heard...

Yeah. *They're* nice...

I don't *know* them well. We share a lawnmower and the garage—separated by a bare stud wall—but that's *it*. *They* moved in about the same time I did. She's trying for a baby...

How do *you* know?

Every few weeks she shouts *'let's make a baby'* over and over while their headboard bangs against the wall.

Something to look forward to...*phone* stopped...

Yeah...

What's the *finance* company want...?

Money...I'm *behind*...*way* behind...

Oh...*listen*: I can't *stand* to hear a phone just *ring*; always feel like picking it up, *mine* or *not*...I have an answering machine upstairs that I'm *not* using...it allows you to pick up *during* the recording so you can *screen* your calls... *want* to...?

Um...you *sure* you're not using it?

Yeah...*and*, ah, *Dad* wants my moped out of their garage... can *I*...?

There's room in our garage in front of my car if you want to keep it there.

I'll bring it over with the furniture; I'll get that answering machine *now*.

***

*Here's*...and a *new* outgoing tape...

*This* is an expensive one...*two* tapes...

*Dad* gave it to me; *I'm* not using it.

I'll...plug it *in*...*here*.

Should *I* record the message? The collectors might be confused if they hear an unfamiliar voice...

The collectors won't *care*...no; *I'll* do it, thanks...

***

What'cha *doing*, Blondie?

Writing an article...

About *what*?

*This* one...paper-making machinery and processes in the last century.

*Fascinating...*

*Uh-huh...*hope the *editor* thinks so and cuts a *big* check.

I'm *serious. I* think that kinda thing's *interesting...what?*

Just...I *never...*women don't usually think *that...*

Well, *I'm* not just *any* woman, *cowboy.* Get *used* to it...

With pl...

*Pleasure?*

Why *not, little lady?*

*You're* not my *type;* remember. How long have *you* been here?

Since March...

So, you rented *this* place, then placed an ad for a furnished room...?

In *May...*the April utilities bill was almost *double* what the landlord *said* they would be.

No calls in *June...?*

I placed a *roommate ad...*

And *you* got calls from *gay men...*

Yep...how was *I* to know? Then I changed the ad to a *furnished room for rent* and you were the *first to call...*

Live and *learn...*does Landlord *know* you're renting a room?

I told him. You *met* his wife...

Did you *say* you were renting to a *girl?*

His wife will *probably* tell him...

Yeah. Where did you live before?

You know that high-rent slum over by the mall? Every other night over there, there'd be some kind of ruckus, and they raised the rent more than it was *worth* without security guards. *Here* at least I have a *garage* and a *basement* and some *peace*. You want a dinner salad? I was *just* about to...?

Sure; *OK*. Got anchovies?

There's bait shops by the lake. Go ahead and *get* yourself some...

So that's *no* to the anchovies.

Definitely *no*. I'll put *lots* of things on my dinner salad, but *bait* ain't among 'em.

*I* need to change for work. Back down in a few.

*** 

*Great* salad, Blondie...

*Glad* you liked it...

This is a nice, *cozy* kitchen...

August heat notwithstanding, yeah...air conditioner can't *quite* keep up...needs coolant...

Not...with...*what?*

Notwithstanding; in spite of; despite...

Oh...the table by the window's a nice touch...want to go *swimming* Monday? *Adults only* from six to eight...

I know; yeah...I *should*...

Looking forward to seeing *you* in a *marble bag, cowboy*...

A...*what?*

That's what girls call those *little* swimsuits...

Ah...looking forward to seeing *you* in a...*never* mind, little lady...

What?

You *said*...a...*well*...

You'll be out of *luck* on Monday. Not *that* kind of *adult* swim...

*Rats*...

*Heh-heh.* OK, Blondie; pla*t*onic roommate. Remember a couple weeks ago when I wore that white halter?

Yeah; I saw...a *lot...*

A *lot* of *what?*

Of...of...

Of *me?* Just *say* it, cowboy. I can *take* it...

OK: that top's *practically* translucent and *very...*

Trans...*what?* And...*very* what?

Translucent: semi-transparent, allowing *light,* but *shapes* are indistinct, though in *that* case it was *tight* enough to show how *big* your...*um...*are...

My...*nipples...?*

Yeah...

*Part* of the idea, but it *concealed* what it *had to...*

*Cover* is *not* the same as *concealment,* Red.

But I *was legal* because I *was covered.* Don't need a cabaret license for *shapes. You* were red-faced because...

I could *see too much...*Red, I admire the female form as much as the *next* straight guy with a pulse, but...

Admire...?

*Yeah.* Wear a G-string around sometime and I *might* put a *dollar* in it...

*Those* things are uncomfortable...

You've *worn* one?

*Sure.* Anyway, I wore *that* outfit three nights in a row and made *over* fifty bucks in tips *every night.* The *previous* three nights I wore just a jean shirt and a bra and I didn't make *twenty* in tips *any* night. And they were *all* crowded, busy game nights.

So, they tipped based on what you were *showing, not* on what you *weren't.*

Yep.

Did anyone notice you wore the same thing three nights in a row?

They didn't *say*...

That's...I *want* to say *too bad*, but I *can't*. You're a *beautiful* girl; got an *impressive* figure...

Im*pressive*, huh...*how* impressive...?

*Well...well-proportioned...um...*

*I* think my *thighs* are *fat*...

Those shorts are too *small*; makes 'em *look fatter*...

Explains why my *feet* turn a little blue when I wear 'em...

I *can't* be the only guy who's ever told you that...

In *fact*, you *are*. Anyway, I'm *done* with *that* experiment. Now...do me a *favor*? I want you to *evaluate* what I'm...

O...*K*...

*Don't* get any ideas...

I'll *try* not to...

I *mean* it...

O...*K*! I'll keep my mind *completely vacant* of ideas...

*Let* me take this...*shirt*...off...now, *this* is what I'll be *working* in tonight...*tell* me what you're *thinking*...*think* and *speak* like a *regular guy*...

In *very* crude terms, then...

*Just say* it...

I've got to get at *least* an *idea* what you...

*Just*...

*OK!* The short, crude, *barfly* version: *nice knockers, toots*.

*Knockers*, yeah...*I'll* have *you* know they are *fantastic* breasts... there's *another*...

*Long*, intellectual version: you've got a *balcony* I could do an *aria* from and *cleavage* that would throw an *echo* like a *mountain canyon!*

A *balcony*...huh...um, what's an *aria*...?

A solo *song*; part of an opera or another, longer work.

A *song? Wow*...and *echo* like a *mountain canyon?* I should *try*...hello...

You *asked*...

I *did*...is *that* what guys think of when they *ogle* a woman's chest?

It's what came to *this* guy's mind when I was *told* to *inspect yours*. The *balcony's* a line from a comedy record from the '60s. The *mountain canyon* is my original...

Clever...

Kidding aside, Red...that's a *pushup* bra?

*Poor* girl's pushup; a cup size too small. Let me take *it off*, change my *shorts*...see what you think *then*...be *back* in a flash...

Figure out how to put a bra *on* without taking your *top off* and womankind will flock to your feet...

It *can* be *done*, just too much *trouble*...

Take your *word* for it...

Depends if you're a *turner* or a *reacher*...

A...*what?*

*Turners* hook their bras in *front* and *turn* them around; *reachers* hook in *back*...

Ah...*which* are...?

That's for *me* to *know* and *you* to *find out*. Besides, *why* put one *on* when it's already *off*...coming *down*...

*You* just wanted to...

Are you *ready?*

Sure...

*Ta-da!* How about *now?*

A *slightly* smaller balcony; *little* less *interesting* cleavage...

But...

But...without a bra, you create a *different* profile...more... um...

More...*nipple*...?

Yeah...

*Stop* staring now, please.

OK.

Maybe I can get the tips *this* way with*out* being *squeezed*...

Do you really *need* a bra of *any* kind?

You're the *first* guy—first *person*—who's *ever asked* me that. I only *need* one to create a *look* or for more *formal* occasions... or around *Mom* or *Dad*...

*Ah...*

How about the *rest* of this outfit? *Too* risqué? *Just...grin* away, but *tell me...*

OK...with *your* legs in *that* skirt, you'll get *big tips*...

You *like* legs, Blondie?

I *do*, yes, especially *well-sculpted* legs like *yours*...

I *asked* about my *outfit*...

Yeah...I've got *belts* wider than that *skirt*. And *go-go* boots...?

These kicks set me back *two hundred bucks* at the vintage store...

You overpaid.

That's what *Sister* said when I *got* 'em...

You should heed her advice.

Does it look like I'm *trying* too hard...?

Trying...*what?*

To *look...what* am I trying to look *like...?*

A *pretty barmaid* angling for *tips* in a neighborhood saloon...?

*That's* it...yeah...

I think the boots would be a mistake behind the bar, frankly...*otherwise...*

The boots *would* be uncomfortable for more than a few hours, yeah.

I have a Round Table meeting tonight.

Round *what* table meeting?

Civil War Round Table. Meets downtown on Tuesdays once a month. I'll be getting in after ten.

I'm getting in after *one*. Have a good *meeting*, Blondie.

Have a good *night*, Red...

***

You *swim* well, Blondie. You *practice* much?

I swam on a team as a kid; liked the exercise.

So, what do you *think* of me in a *tank suit...*?

I think you're a *beautiful* girl in *anything*.

And you're a *good-looking* guy, in a marble bag or anything *else...* but *you* need to put on some pounds. Gals don't know if they should *love* you or *feed* you...

*That's...*

I'm due at *work* in...*ten* minutes...

On *Monday...*?

*Big* game...need *half* a *tick* to get *changed...*

*Hey...*don't...do...*that...*

*What...*?

*Half*-strip on the stairs...*like you just did...*

I'm in a *hurry* and you didn't see anything but my *bare* back...

*Still...*

Get *used* to it, Blondie; you *live* with a *girl* now...*skirt* or *shorts*, cowboy...

*Skirt* or...*why* ask...?

Who *else...*?

*Skirt*...little lady...in *this* heat...

*Skirt* it *is*...*bare* midriff or...?

What*ever* you...

I'd *prefer*...

Better *not* at *that* saloon...

Naw; *no* cabaret license...I need to *eat* something or I'll *pig out* on chips and peanuts...*what's* in the *fridge*...?

Got...cold chicken and hard-boiled eggs...lunchmeat...

Chicken or eggs or oversized hot dogs...? Chicken...yeah, *chicken*...

Want to *heat* it *up*?

*Cold's* fine...I'll be *down*...in...now...how about *this* outfit?

You *are* quick...*white* tie blouse, *no* bra, *shorter* skirt than... you got *underwear* under...?

*Yeah*...see?

*Oh*...here's *my* tip...

Here's *mine*: *stop* thinking what *you're* thinking because living with *me* ain't what you *think*...

I'm figuring *that* out...

Come by the bar tonight; I'll buy you a drink...I'll take a *thigh* and a *leg* to go...*see* ya, Blondie!

I'd take *your* thigh and leg...

*What* was *that*?

*Never* mind...*see* ya!

***

*Glad* you came. *Our* stool's empty. Beer?

OK. Sounded like you had a *reason* to ask. Not *too* busy tonight...

Just the usual payday pals leveling up their tabs and paying off their bets...

*Somebody's* trying to get your attention...

Yeah; I'll be *back*...

***

*That guy's* a good tipper...been *trying* to pick *me* up for a *week*...now he keeps looking at *you.*

*Know* him?

From school, but *he* went to a *different* school after 9th Grade. He's kinda creepy *and* out of work.

*Not* a good combination...am *I* a *beard* again?

You *mind...?*

*Maybe* not.

*Might* be more convincing if we *flirted* a little...

What about the *rest* of the bar...*and* the neighborhood...?

Yeah; *bad* idea...those *guys* you were talking to; I went to *school* with them.

Yeah? Didn't talk about *you* at all.

What *did* you talk about?

They seem concerned about Mom Across-The-Walk...

Concerned...*how?*

*They* think a divorcee with a little boy is ripe for the attentions of *real* men. *They* wanted to know if *I'd* given her a thrill.

Assholes. What did you *tell* 'em?

I barely *know* the woman; left it at that...but how would *they* know where *I* live...?

Because *they* know where *I* live *and* that I'm renting a room from *you*...so, *are* you *working* Saturday?

Yeah. Some research down at the main library.

What are you researching?

Harvesting machinery. Big Boss wants to pitch a farm machinery outfit on a heritage theme. I need to look into how it *used* to be done.

Sounds...different. Why do you call him Big Boss?

Because he *owns* the joint, stands about six-eight, *and* I work *directly* for a *much* smaller guy who also works for *him*. How late are *you* working?

Another hour...

I'll stick around for your *creep's* benefit...

I'd *like* that...and *not* because of Creep...

Yeah...?

*Yeah...*

***

*Thanks* for hanging out...

*Not* a problem. Want a snack? Your *mail's* on the ledge...

Thanks...want *food and* a shower...

***

*That's* better. *This* outfit OK?

It's a *ratty* robe...

*Guess* what's *under* the *robe*?

Not *much* gauging by what I *saw* as you came down the stairs.

Wanna *see* how high my legs *go*, since you *like* them so much...?

*I'm* gonna say they go...*all* the *way up*, but I don't want to degrade you.

*Not* degrading...not *really*...

You don't think that skin mags and skin flicks degrade women?

Yeah, but being comfortable in my home and *playing* with the *cute* guy I *live* with *isn't* degrading...what'cha watchin'?

Movie. You sure have a *lot* of hair to pile on top of your head...

I haven't *cut* it for *years*; nearly at the crack of my butt; getting *tired* of it...want chips? Beer? Soda?

40

Thanks, no. You're *not* working, Red...

Being *polite.* I want *something*...not a full meal. Can I have one of your candy bars?

OK.

Some of *this*...brown stuff on rice...?

Jar gravy...go ahead...

Dad wants to bring my furniture *and* my moped over Saturday morning...*finally.* OK?

Fine. I'll be back early afternoon. Let's watch...

***

Red?

Mm?

You fell asleep...

*Huh? Oh*...is it *morning?*

Nearly midnight.

Guess I was *tired...comfy* sofa.

I, ah, took the *liberty* of covering...your *robe slipped...*

*Ratty* old thing...yeah...*like* what you...?

*I'm* knocking off. See you tomorrow.

But *did* you *like* what you *saw tonight...?*

As a *gentleman,* I *didn't look...*

Sure; *pull* the *other* one...*see* you *later...*

***

*Hey*, Red...that's *it?* A coffee table's *all* your furniture...?

And that side table over *there.* It's all stuff my *dad* made.

Handy guy; *good* work...

We put my *end table* in the basement 'cause there's only room for it up here next to *your* sofa, and I didn't want to muscle in on *your* space...

What's this *my sofa* stuff?

*You* sit on it. *I* sit on the...

*Corner* and *center* units. We can reconfigure this conversation pit any way *we* see fit...*want* to?

Um...O...K...your *phone*...

If it's *Saturday*, it's the *hospital* wanting money...the machine...three rings and...*yup*, the hospital...

*Good* machine...

Yeah...*here*...let's...shove *this*...*here*...*this* can go... *here*...one of Kitty's felt mice...

*Where* would *I* set a drink...what's the *hospital*...?

I was *in* there for a while; still *owe* for it...OK...here...then, *here*...then your *end table*...

*That's* in the middle of the *room*...

But *that's* how it...

*Hold* on. Let's stick *this*...what*ever* ya *call* it...

Ottoman...*there* goes *Kitty*...

*With* her mouse...otto-guy...in the *corner*...

Over *there*, it...

But *other*wise, *everything* sticks into the *room*...*damnit that* won't...

*Almost* blocks the stairs...*shit*...wait; *stop!*

What?

*Before* we get on each other's nerves, let's sit down and *quietly*...

My parent's *loudest* fights were over furniture arranging... *except* for all the others...

Then let's *not* do that, Red. *Pull* your jersey *down*, please...

OK...*Better*...?

At *least* you're wearing pants...of *some* kind...

My *teddy shorts* are for *your* benefit...

Thanks so *very* much...

Welcome...*such* a guy...

Yes. We are *calm* now?

Yeah; an unanswered *phone* gets on my *nerves*...

Just *imagine* what it does to *me*, knowing who's on the other end because of what *day* it is. OK. This *short* section...here... now the pit *frames* the fireplace...table in *front* of the useless thing; TV on top. The coax stretches... yup. Now; *one* corner unit, then an *armless*, then *another* corner. Now, the TV is in *front* of us. *This* is what they designed this expensive stuff *for*. Move the ottomans into the middle when we...

One *cozy* piece of furniture. *Kitty*...there she *is*...looks *very* *proud* of her mouse...

Yeah. *You* can sit on *any* side or end you *want*.

When *you're* on it?

I *don't* have cooties, and I *have* had all my shots...

Wouldn't *that* lead to places where we've said we're *not* going...?

It would if we *want* to *go* to those *places*. C'mon, let's get *your* end table out of the basement...yeah, it matches your *other* furniture. It matches *nothing* of mine, but they match *each other*. Right...*here* on *this* end...

My desk and chair are upstairs...

Does it all *fit* up there? That room's *big*, but not *that* big. *Gotta* be crowded.

I don't want to muscle in on your living room...

*We* just rearranged *OUR* living room, Red. Let's have a *look*...yeah, OK; desk would *fit* better in the living room corner. You can look out the window from there, *too*. Feels all *crammed in* like this...

*Your* desk is in front of the *other* living room window...

Yeah? So?

*That* starts to look like...*doesn't* it...?

So? It's *your...*

Let's just keep it *this* way. Besides, for doing *homework,* I don't *need* the distraction of the TV, whether it's on or *not.*

Resisting the *siren call* of the *boob tube;* good. Let's call our *décor* contemporary chaotic.

Yeah, *heh.* Dad saw your workshop; says he wants to try picture framing sometime. Where did *you* pick it up?

I worked in a frame shop when I was in college. Decided I *enjoyed* doing it; folks say I ain't bad. It's easy if he can make furniture like *this...*

These frames in *here* are *all...?*

Yep...

*Beautiful* work. Can you frame some of *my* pictures?

Sure...

I've gotta get to *work.*

You gonna wear more than a *jersey* and some *teddy-what-evers,* Red?

*I* want *huge* tips...

Go to work like that and you *might* get *busted.*

Naw, but I'll throw *something else* on *just* for *you...*

Just don't take your *jersey* off *before* you...*get* to the...aw, *jeez...landing...*

Get *used* to it, Blondie...you *live* with a *girl* now...

As you *delight* in *reminding* me, Red...I saw *more this time* than a platonic *roommate should...*I *think...*

What's *better:* my beautiful *face* or my sexy *body...?*

Your *sense* of *humor...*

***

What's with the *look,* Red?
You're *weird.*

*I'm* weird? *You half*-stripped in *front* of me yesterday...

*That* was just *me* going *upstairs* in a *hurry*...nothing I haven't *done* before...

*Maybe*, but *I'm* weird? Why?

You're a *guy* who *doesn't* watch sports. Weekends *this* time of year are for guys to sit around and watch baseball.

I'll watch if somebody else is watching and I want to hang with *them*, but I don't go out of my way. Life is too *short* for that.

No team spirit?

Pro teams on TV are mostly out-of-towners who don't represent a community any more than the people on a military base do. They're paid to play to make money for the sponsors.

Don't they build *community* spirit?

*Only* as long as they make money *in* that community. Pro team owners get cities to build and maintain their home venues. The teams have as much stake in their communities as any *other* business, but *only* for as long as they make *money* there. As soon there's no more money to be made, or *another* city makes them a better offer, the team's gone. Colleges get the Association and the alumni to do the same.

*You're* a killjoy...

Just a pragmatist. I don't actively prevent anyone from doing anything they want to do or enjoy. Don't get me wrong; I *like* the *games*, but what TV has *done* to them makes them filler for ads. I just don't watch college or pro sports as a preference. If you *really* want a taste of community spirit, go to *high school* games.

So if I wanted to watch a big league baseball game *right now*, I *could*?

Sure. *I* want to do some framing.

***

Hey.

Hey. Good game?

A *little* exciting, yeah. I don't *watch* sports a lot except at the bar.

I see. There's a new action movie on in a few minutes if you're interested.

Maybe. *What* just happened?

What d'ya *mean?*

Just *now;* with us?

You mean...oh. *You* watched a baseball game, and *I* went downstairs and finished this frame for you. Now, pick a mat and I'll put it together...

OK...*that* one. *Beautiful* work.

Thanks; I'll...

Should we *talk* about this?

About *what?*

What happened with *us* this afternoon?

Nothing *happened,* Red...we're roommates...

*Housemates,* if you want to get *technical...*

As you *say*...we're just getting used to each other... *comfortable* in each other's...*you* live here. *I* live here. We share *space,* not *lives.*

Are we *friends,* at least?

We *can* be friend*ly,* sure, if you *want*...don't complicate it... now, I'll *just...*

Ask a *stupid* question...

*Not* stupid. We hadn't defined *us* yet...*I'll...*

*Us?* There's an '*us?*'

There's an '*us*' for *you and me,* for our *neighbors,* for the *checkouts* in the supermarket, for the *mailman.* We have relationships with people we barely *know* and with people we know *intimately.* They're all *relationships*...now, if *I* can...

Not the way *most* people think of it...

It's the most accurate. *And* fair...now...

For a killjoy, you sure make a *lot* of sense...

Two mutually exclusive concepts, Red...now if I can just *finish* this before that *movie* comes on...

Ya know, I really *like* to see movies in the *theater*...

But *this* one's not *in* the theaters anymore...

C'mon, Blondie; let's go to the discount theater and see what we can *find*...

Sunday is the *one day* all *week* the collectors don't call...I *kinda* like...

*I'm* buying...*and* dinner after...

I'll *change* my *shirt*...put this together *later*...that movie will rerun...

***

*Great* old movie I've *never* seen, Red; thanks.

Welcome. You *like* old movies? Here's *your* dinner...

Thanks...yeah, *here* it is; have some *soy* sauce. I *do* like movies, yes. I've seen so many by myself I'm not *used* to sharing the experience, let alone getting takeout *after*.

Not a lot of buddies? *Here's* hot mustard...

Great. A *few*, but not *movie* buddies.

Dates?

Very, *very* few lately.

Why?

Money, partly...

*And...?*

I've *got* my reasons.

I want to *hear* them sometime.

*Why?*

You *interest* me, Blondie.

*Why?*

I *dunno*, yet. Let's just *eat* and watch *this* one. Beer?

Sure...

# Gets To Like...

<br>

*Shit...Goddamnit!*

Problem, Red?

*What* gave me away?

You're *redder* in the face than usual and you *threw* your purse on the kitchen table, which *startled* Kitty, who just *bolted*...

*Sorry*, Kitty! The cops busted my *idiot* of a *brother* again...

For what?

Dope. Sister didn't *have* many details.

He's done this be*fore*, I take it?

Yeah; *more* than once as a juvenile. But *now* he's *twenty*...

It gets worse. How many brothers have you *got*?

*One's* enough. What're you...*more* articles?

Gotta make *more* money *some*how...here's *Kitty*...she *probably* wants to *eat* again...she *had* dinner and brought it up as soon as she *ate* it...

I'll...

No; *don't. Feed* her more than twice a day and she *pukes* more...

But she's *crying*...

*Might* need to know you're not mad at *her*. Scratch her ears, give her some catnip and hairball stuff...I *gotta* finish this...

OK...*c'mere*, baby Kitty...*have* some nice catnip...*purr-purr*...*mean* old *Daddy's starving* you...here's *this* goop...*lick-lick-purr-purr...that's* better...*I'm* for a bath and bed. 'Night.

'Night.

***

Morning, Red. *You're* up early after a late night.

Morning. I didn't *sleep* well; need *coffee*...what'cha watchin'?

The Sunday Morning Congress...

What's *that?*

Blowhards in and out of power on the network interview shows telling us how wonderful *they* are, how brilliant *their* solutions to *our* problems are, and how *evil* the *other* guys are.

Oh...can I read *this* book? I've *heard* of it...

You should read the one *next* to it *first*...

Why?

The author *wrote* it first. And, it helps to make the *second* one make more sense. Did you *finish* the other ones?

I put *them* back; *interesting*. Want *breakfast?* There's a tube of cinnamon rolls here. Scrambled eggs?

Sure. Red...if you wanna *talk* about your brother, I'll listen...

Not *now*...wanna watch a *movie* while we eat?

*Just* what I had in mind...these clowns will never say anything *worth*...

*Movie* this afternoon...?

Sure; OK...*what* are we going to *see*...?

Doesn't *matter;* I just *love* sitting in a dark room, *watching* the screen *with someone* I *like*...

***

*That* was a *very* strange movie, Blondie.

Some of 'em are. *That* one, though. Not sure *why* it got an Award.

Maybe the audience liked it?

The Awards are a popularity contest among members of the Academy. Hard to say *what* criteria they use, but audiences don't have *anything* to do with their decisions because the big-money blockbusters don't often win anymore.

*Huh...*

I used to think of the Academy as a mutual admiration society, but *now* I think they pick *one* to punish the *other* producers for not picking *theirs* before. They only show *most* of the movies that are *nominated* on the coasts around the holidays so they'll be eligible...

Sounds complicated...

The politics of money and entertainment...

I suppose...Labor Day Sunday we're throwing a *big* party at the bar. *You* should bring a date...

I've got a *better* chance of finding a *sasquatch* than I do finding a *date*...

*He-he!* How about I ask a couple of *my* friends, give you a chance to check *them* out while *they* check *you* out...? Blondie...? Hel-*lo, Earth* to *Blondie*...!

I'm *thinking*...

What's to *think* about...?

The *last* blind date I went on I got *food poisoning*...I took it as a *sign*...

Don't *be* that way...the two I have in mind are *cute*; the brunette's got *better* legs than *I* do; they're *longer*...

*Hard* to imagine...but...

The *blonde's* a *small* girl, but they're *both* fun...c'mon, *cowboy*; lighten *up*; *live* a *little*...

Just don't fill them with expectations of spending Labor Day Sunday with a *wild stud*, little lady...

I'll tell 'em you want a *relationship* of at *least* an *hour* before...

*Red...*

OK, a *week* before *intimate relations* begin.

If it'll make *you* happy...

*They'll* make *you* happy, cowboy...so, a guy came into the *bar* the other night, asked if we had any *helicopter* flavored potato chips. *I* said, 'we only have *plane...*'

What did he *hit* you with?

***

God*dam*mit!

What *now*, Red? And good *evening...*

*Dammit shit hell!*

No *hello* then. How was *your...?*

*AUGH!*

*Good* to know.

*AHHHHHHHHHHHH!*

Just *don't* throw your purse *through* a window...

*DAMNIT TO HELL!!!!*

And tearing up your *shirt?* That's new and *very* risqué. Let me *know* when you're *done.*

*SHUT UP, ASSHOLE!*

Right...OK. *I'm* hittin' the sack. Make *nice* with *Kitty* when you're done...*you* know the drill. 'Night.

*SHIIIIIIT!*

***

Red?

*Mm...*

You fell *asleep* down here.

*Shit...morning...*

Morning. Your *shirt's...*

*I did that...?*

52

*I* didn't. I brought your *robe.*

Thanks...*t-shirt's* ruined. One of my *favorites*, too... *damn...*

*Coffee* will be ready in a few minutes...

I'll take this rag *off...*

*I'll* turn *around...*

Whatever *tickles* your *pickle*, cowboy...nothing you *didn't* see *last night...*

You *know* I don't *look...*

When boobs *flash* before your eyes? Yeah, *sure...*

Well...I picked up the *contents* of your purse from ...well, all *over everywhere.* I put it all on the kitchen table.

Thanks...*shit*, what a *mess* I made...

Your lipstick and your compact *shattered; I* can't fix them.

*Thanks...*Blondie?

Yeah?

Sorry I called you a...

I've been called *worse.* I'm headed for the kitchen. Biscuit? Fresh out of a tube?

Yeah, *sure...*

***

Here's the *biscuits...and* some *honey* and *peanut* butter...

Thanks...*shit...*

I'm all ears, Red...*c'mon...*

Idiot Brother got busted *again.*

Only *family* can incite *that* much rage. *Second* time in...?

*Two weeks...*

For *what?*

*Holding* about three *kilos* of blow for his *moron* half-a-dealer buddy. Moron's God-knows-where and the cops want Idiot Brother to flip on him.

How do you *know* all this?

A deputy Sherriff I went to school with came by the bar, brought me home.

I *wondered* where your car was. Your brother's *how* old?

Twenty...

And *already* he's a *major* dealer?

Not *dealing*; holding...

Doesn't *matter* with *that* much weight. Will he *flip*?

Anyone with *half* a *brain cell* will. That *don't* include Idiot Brother...

Does he do *anything* harder?

He's not *that* brave. This is his *third* drug charge; *second* as an adult, but *this* one's a felony, not just a *joint* or a *lid*...

Sorry.

*Don't* be. My family's *almost* had *enough* of him.

Almost?

Dad's...*Dad*. He bailed him, *but*...

So, he's back home?

Mom *won't* have him back; he's staying at Sister's. Sister laid down the law. He steps out of line at *her* place and she'll *kill* him...he needs a *job*.

What *can* he do?

He's *real* good at getting *high*. Too lazy and too scared of his own *shadow* to keep a *real* job...Blondie, can we continue this conversation while I soak in the tub...? Curtain *closed* if *you*...?

'K...*no* flashing tricks...

*Killjoy*...

***

You settled, Red...?

Yeah; *come on* in...have a *seat* on the *stool*...

'K...anytime you're *ready*, Red...

*Give* me a minute to *just...*

Sure...*take* your...

*Ahhh...*

Just...

*Why* is my family like this? I mean, I *had* a *fun* family once. Now, we just go from one *crisis* to another, mostly around Idiot Brother or Sister's *loser* of a *husband*, who can't keep a *job, either.*

Maybe *brother* isn't *sitting well* in *your* lodge.

I'm *serious...*

I *know.* There *was* a guy who *felt* like a brother...*once...*

What happened to *him?*

He died.

Sorry...*hold* my *hand?*

*That* means...?

My *arm's all* you'll *have* to *see,* cowboy...

OK; *give* it *here...*what happened that your brother turned *into* an idiot? He wasn't *always...was* he...?

We had fun together until Sister was about thirteen and she didn't *want* to play with *him* anymore. She still did *girl* stuff like hair and makeup with *me,* but *not* riding bikes or baseball with *him...*

She became a young woman. How old were *you?*

Eight.

*You* were still *kids* as far as she could see. Brother was *how* old?

Three; we're all *five* years...oh, *I* get it. Yeah, *maybe...*ever *do* this, Blondie?

No; never...

Me neither...kinda nice...

Yeah...your brother...

Yeah...somehow, he never quite fit into any molds. He knows about cars, but doesn't spend the time to learn how they tick. He likes airplanes, but there's nothing he can do with them except *talk* about 'em. He's good at math, but anything to *do* with education after junior high, he just... wasn't interested.

When did he *start* getting high?

Young; *twelve* that I *know* of. Sniffing glue, the *idiot*, probably fried more than a few brain cells by the time he got to high school...God must *love* stupid people; he made *so many*...this water's getting cold. I'm going to rinse off with a shower...

I'll get *going*...

Stay a *little* longer, Blondie? Meet me downstairs?

*Don't* come down naked...

You *are* a killjoy, Blondie. But I *will descend* the stairs *slowly* so you can *admire* my legs...a reward for being my...my...

*Yeah*, yeah...

Blondie, you *are* a killjoy. Why?

I've seen humanity at its absolute worst. I had to study human depravity to stay alive. *That's* made me a pragmatist, and thus a killjoy.

Huh...

What?

Just...*huh*...

***

You *look* better...

I look *fabulous*. And I'm *fully* decent with underwear and everything...*slow* enough...?

*Not* what I meant...*yeah...beautiful*...

Think I don't *know* that? Anyway, thanks for *everything*... this skirt's *cold*...

*Looks* cold, even in *August*...that *shirt* looks familiar...and *not* a tie-blouse if I remember...

I *borrowed* it; picked it out of the *dryer*, OK?

It looks a *lot* better on *you* than it does *me*...

You *would* think so, *wouldn't* ya? *You* have to go to work?

I've *been* at work, helping a friend...

We're *friends?*

A *non*-friend would sit *outside* the tub, holding your wet hand...?

I know a *dozen* guys who'd *kill* to be in your place, but *they* ain't...

OK, so we *aren't*...

No; sorry...*yeah*, we're *friends*...

I should *hope* so. I *should* get to work. I can beg off with a morning migraine *once* in a while...

Blondie...*before* you go...can *you hold* me for a minute?

The closest *I've* had to a *girl*-hug for *years* has been static cling.

*Heh-heh*...then...how's...*this*...?

*Very*...warm...*and*...oh! You *surprised* me.

Just a peck on the cheek, cowboy. My way of saying thanks to my *best* landlord ever. Making up for *last night*.

You don't *have* to. You working tonight?

I'm closing.

See you tomorrow, then.

You'd *better*. And *thanks again* for *everything*.

✳✳✳

Hi.

*Evening*. Ain't *seen you* in...

A *couple days; two finals* this week; *lots* of cramming. Can I borrow some eggs until I get to the store?

Sure. You're *late* tonight, if your calendar on the 'fridge is right?

Yeah. Gonna make coffee.

*I'll* have some of that.

Sure...Blondie, I need an escort for a *cousine's* wedding...

*Cousine?* That's *French?*

Mom's family keeps *boy* and *girl* cousins separate that way. There's nobody *else* I'd want to take to a *family wedding* who *hasn't* said *no* already.

I'm *flattered* to be your *last* choice.

You *should* be flattered but don't *be* like *that.* I'm *serious* and I *don't* want to go doe...

Go...*doe?*

Female deer? Opposite of stag?

Never *heard* that. When *is* this shindig?

Next month, the 20^th, a Saturday. The guy I *asked*...never mind...anyway, I already told *Cousine* there'd be *two* people; they'll *pay* for the *plate* now if I *bring* a date or *not.* I'll have Sister give you a trim...

Well...are you *part of* the bridal party?

No; I'm just one of the *swarm* of cousins and *cousines* attending *l'affaire. Pretty* please?

White tie?

What's *that?*

Formal; *tux* and all that.

Knowing *Cousine, she'd* have jeans and t-shirts, but my aunt wouldn't *pay* for the party at the golf club if they did *that.*

Golf club?

*Old* money in the family and plenty *of* it. *Please? Pretty, pretty* please with *sugar* and *cinnamon* on top?

*Charming* smile, Red...but, if you *ask* like *that...*

I *also* have *charming...*

*Legs*, yes, I *know*, so you can quit hitching your *shorts* up. *OK*; as long as I *don't* have to *dance*. *Kitty* dances better than I do...

*Just* one dance with *me*...for a *haircut*...

*How* long you gonna hold those *shorts* up *that* high? I can *see* your...

*Pretty* panties...until you *agree*...

*OK*, Red...now *drop* those shorts; you'll catch a *draft*.

Not in *this* heat...which re*minds* me: here's *half* of September's rent. I'll get you the *other* half on Tuesday.

Thanks. *How* did a discussion of *dancing* remind you of your *rent?*

I *sometimes* *dance* around my landlords on the *rent*...my pay *can* be spotty.

Thanks for the warning...*and* the...the...

*Show?*

*View* of your *very* attractive legs...and what's *under*...

I'll give *you* a show *anytime* it's *warm* enough...ya know why *flamingos* lift one leg?

Um...*I'll* bite...

Because when they lift *both*, they *fall down*...

*Paha-heh-heh*...

***

*Hey*, Blondie! *Like* the *view* from down *there?*

Ah...*yeah*...sure.

*Slow* enough for ya?

*Fine*...

What *is* it about *guys* and women's *legs?*

*No* idea. I think men are *more* interested in women who are interested in *them*...

*Well, cowboy*, I *am* interested in *you*...

Any idea *why?*

*You* gonna *make* the party today? Got those two *knockout* girls I told you about *lined up* to meet ya; *better* legs than *these.*

Hard to imagine after that *grand* staircase entrance. Now, *why...?*

So you *like* the shorts, but how about the rest of the outfit?

*Lovely*; just *lovely...why...?*

Can't *see* any...?

No *color...shapes.* Not gonna get an answer about why you...

*Nope...*

A*bout* today; I have to *work* some...

They *make* you work on *Labor Day Sunday?*

*I'm* a little behind...

C'*mon, live* a little; get *lucky*, maybe. The party *starts* at noon...

Ah, *what* the hell...*yeah*, why *not?* See you about *two, roomie...*

***

*Three* beers and *three* shots, Red.

Coming *up*, pal. How's it *going* with...?

Fine. Ponytail can't stop *giggling* at *everything.*

You're probably the most *decent* guy that she's *met* in *years*, and the *first* from outside the neighborhood...

Thought it was just *me...*

Nope. Legs is *sweet* on you already.

You can *tell...?*

Yup. *Love* is in the air, *cowboy...*

Nitrogen, oxygen and carbon dioxide are in the air, *little lady.*

You *romantic devil...*and you wonder *why* you *don't* get *dates...*

No, *I* don't wonder. Gotta get *hot dogs*, too...*hand* me a *tray*...?
*Here* ya go; *good* luck, Blondie.

***

They...*left?*

Yeah. Said they have to *work* in the morning.

Get their *numbers?*

Yeah. Gave 'em *mine...*

Got some *sugar*, too, *didn't* ya? I *saw...*

Yeah.

*Pony*tail was disappointed that she didn't get *hers* on the *lips...*

*Legs* didn't either...

Avoiding com*mit*ment?

Or herpes...

They're *not...*

Probably not, but I'm *not* taking *any* chances right now... been sick e*nough*...that woman at the end...on *our* stool, the one with the...*the...?*

Ginormous balcony? *Her* legs are OK under those jeans, not that *most* guys look *below* her *boobs...*or *above* 'em...want an introduction...?

A guy either picks the *right* one in high school or he wades through a sea of single moms, divorcees and *embittered* women later. *Which* is she?

Two *kids*; two *divorces...*

*Yeah*...probably *bitter* as *basil*...my *lot* in *love* life...

A word of advice from your *favorite* woman of the world?

Yeah, sure...

If you're not *looking* for Miss Right, but will *settle* for Miss *Right Now*, buy *her* a drink and that *ginormous chest* will be *yours* till *morning...*

And...so...she's *loose*...?

As a *kite* in a *whirlwind*, pal...

And she's *not* a friend of yours...?

*Uh*-uh...

So, *you* don't *care* if...?

*Uh*-uh. *I* have a date tonight myself. *Go on* over for a commitment-*free* night; *get* your *ashes hauled*...

*Well*...

*Don't* overthink it and *go get laid.* You should learn *not* to *think* once in a while, when your *urges*...and don't *try* to tell me you don't *have* 'em...

I just...*yeah*...O...K...*send* her a couple shots of what*ever* she's *drinking*...

On the *way* and on *me!* Go *get* her, tiger!

***

Blondie! Didn't expect to see *you*...

Yeah, *well*...raiding the refrigerator?

Grabbing one of your chocolate bars. Didn't *go* well with Chesty?

Well, I walked her home...

*Want* something...?

No, thanks...she paid the sitter...

How old *are* her kids?

Ten and five; they were in *bed* when we got there. We *talked* for a while and we *started* to make out in the living room and Ten-Year-Old went into the kitchen and poked around in the refrigerator before he came into the living room. 'Mom, we're out of juice,' he said. Didn't even *look* at me...

Used to *strange men* in the house...

That's what *I* figured. Chesty went into the kitchen, and *I* felt...

Like a *client*...

There it *is*. I made my excuses and...

Did you get her *number* at least?

Yeah. Don't *know* if...

Get past *first base*...?

A *little over* her shirt; she *took* her bra off before we...I see *you* did, too...

My landlord is not *supposed* to notice *that*.

It's hard for your *housemate not* to notice *that* when you are wearing a *men's*...um...

*Wife-beater* shirt.

Yeah. *You* look better in one of those than *guys* do.

*Thanks*...

That *jiggle* was gratuitous...

Gra...*what?*

Gratuitous: unwarranted; un-called for; unneeded.

You didn't *like* my little *show?*

How could I *not*...I *have* a pulse, Red. Look, *you're* a...

*Beautiful girl;* you keep *saying* that. I *like* to show *how* beautiful I *am*...

Red, your landlord/roomie doesn't *need* peep shows...

Blondie: just...*enjoy* my *company and* my *playing,* OK? Get *used* to...

*Don't* you resent showing *me* more than you do your *customers*...?

If I *did,* I wouldn't *do* it...OK?

OK; OK...so, *your* date was a *bust?*

He was *all over mine*...

*Heh-heh*...

Then *his* roommate interrupted. *They* got into it about a bill *one* of 'em didn't *pay. I* wasn't *in the mood* after *their* little *pissing* contest, so I came home.

Well, we *both* struck out...want a slug of schnapps? I *keep* it for...

A consolation drink? Sure...

*Here's* to...

*Next* time...

*Next* time.

*Mm.* You don't *drink* that much, Blondie. *Seriously,* how *come?*

Well, here *lately,* because it's irritating...

To *what?*

My kidneys and other *connected* parts.

Why?

I...had a nasty infection *recently*...rather *not*...

Uh-*huh*...Blondie...?

Huh?

Another *shot?*

Yeah.

*Schnapps* or...?

Just the *schnapps*...Red...*oh!*

*Just* for *you, cowboy.*

You *don't* find flashing me degrading or objectifying, like they say on TV?

*Not* in *private,* and when we *both* need cheering up. *That* OK?

That's...*oh*...fine, Red. Ya know what did the girl said to the tattoo artist before flashing him, don't ya?

No, but you're gonna *tell* me...

*Tit* for *tat*...*another* slug of schnapps.

Another *shot,* Blondie...maybe *that'll*...know what *toys* and *boobs* have in common?

Sure; another *shot*...no; *what,* though I can...

They were made for *kids*, but *men* end up *playing* with 'em...
*here...*

*Yeah? How* about...*these?*

*I'd* play with *your* sweaty boobs if you *let* me, Blondie...

Like *yours* don't *sweat...*

Girls *glisten*, Blondie; they don't *sweat*...but *yours* make *me*
wanna...

Jiggle...

Jiggle *juggle...*

***

Blondie? You *OK* in there?

Yeah; *I'm* fine. Go back to *bed* or whatever...

Look at your *clock*, pal. It's *nearly* ten in the morning. Just
*wondered* if...

*Oh...ugh.* I'll be down in a minute.

***

Hi.

*Hi!* Coffee's fresh.

Thanks. You're...embroidering...?

*Cousine's* wedding present quilt that Sister *made* and I'm
*decorating... and* a skirt for my niece. Want to *finish* both
before next week when I start *another* two classes. I fed
Kitty; *she* wouldn't shut up...

Thanks. What're you taking *next...?*

Microeconomics II and business planning I. You sleep *late*
after a *few shots?*

I couldn't *get* to sleep until nearly dawn. Took a *pill...*

Oh...are *you...?*

I'm *fine.*

You *sure?* You *look* a little raw.

I'll *be* OK, thanks.

I do *neck rubs*...

I don't *doubt* it...

C'mon; can't *hurt*...have a *seat* here...

OK...ah...*mmm*...ah...*oh, yeah*...*very* nice...

You're *very* tense...

Yeah...I...*am*...tense...*mmm*...

Blondie?

Huh?

I'm having a guy over for dinner next Sunday...

Ah...OK. Dinner and *more*?

Just some takeout and conversation...

*Mm*...takeout for a dinner guest?

*He's* bringing it...

Know *what*? *I'm* gonna call Ponytail...she said *she* gets every other Sunday off...as if to *say*...

Yeah; she *was*...and you *just now*...

Call me *slow*. I *used* to have a *handle* on life, but it *broke*...

Heh-heh...*I* want to get some *sun*. You paying bills this afternoon?

In*ev*itably; *then* I'll listen to the answering machine...

I'll give you *another* neck rub *after*. Catch a movie tonight?

*Maybe*...see how I *feel*...

OK...*I'm* for the sun...

***

You're *warm*, Red.

You're all *tense* again, Blondie, watching *me* on the *lawn* while you're paying *bills*...

With money I *ain't got yet*, *post*-dating the checks and filling in the zeroes on the account line to *slow* processing while listening to *politely* aggressive voices *enquiring* as to *when* they can *expect* money I ain't got...*mmm*...*expert* hands; *warm*...um...

Belly...

*Very* relaxing...

*Close* your *eyes*...relax...*shh*...

*Mm*...

*Keep* your eyes *shut*...

*Why*...?

*Just*...

OK...what's *that?*

My *shirt* over your *face*...please *don't* look around...

*Why*...?

You'd get a *face*-full of my *balcony*...this chair's *higher*...

'K...*feels* like...a *bare*...

*Chest*...

*Yeah*...on my *neck*...

You're *supposed* to feel like you're in the *womb* again...*do* you...?

Since I can't *possibly* remember, *how* would I *know*...?

Yeah; I thought *that* was dumb...feel *better*, anyway...?

Uh...*huh*...Red, I *like* you *and* whatever *perfume* you're...

Sunblock, shampoo, deodorant, and soap; *maybe* fabric softener; *no* perfume...

Come to *think* of it, I haven't seen *any* anywhere around...

I don't *like* it...*cologne*, sometimes...

What's the difference?

Perfume's more concentrated; *stronger*...

Be *that* as it may be...your *t-shirt* over my face is a *little* stifling...

OK...*better*...?

Uh-*huh*...I've got a road trip starting tomorrow. Trying to drum up business...you gonna give your *hands* a rest...? *Red?*

Huh?

You just gonna stand behind me with your *hands* on my *neck and* your *chest* on my...?

*Huh...?*

As much as I...um...enjoy your *tender* ministrations...

Tender mini-*what?*

Things done to *care* for...someone...

Ah...did you call Ponytail...?

She didn't...answer...*mmm*...Red...you...want to *eat*...?

*Oh...dinner...?*

I've got a chicken marinade working...when you...get...*done*...

Movie tonight?

We'll see...*Red*...you...?

*Done*...

***

*Great* chicken, Blondie. You're a better cook than *Dad* is...

Thanks...I guess. Your dad didn't get the cooking bug?

Not really....ya know *what?*

Huh?

*We're* gonna *pass* on the movie out tonight; *you* look tired...

Doesn't keep *you* from going...

I'd rather *not* go alone...we'll find *something* on pay TV.

***

Blondie...? *Hey*...Blondie...

Huh?

You fell asleep down here.

Oh...*time* is it?

I *just* got back from *work*...

Oh...*how* was...?

*You* should get to bed. Want *help?* You seem kinda *out* of it...

Took something for a toothache...*ugh*. Guess I was tired.

C'mon; let's get you to *bed*...

***

Hey, how's the toothache, Blondie?

Faded, thanks.

Calling your *dentist*...?

No *money*; no *dental plan*...

Oh...sorry. Anything *I* can do? String on a doorknob...?

Too much expensive dental work...

*That* might *explain*...

Yeah...how's *school* this semester?

*Ugh*, the econ teacher's a *Nazi*.

Some are *like* that...that's a *different* kind of...*not* overalls... *halter*...something...

*Jumpsuit*, they call it; denim...

Never *saw*...any *support* in that...um...?

*Just* the halter's *tension* between the waist and neck...

And *tension* it's *got*.

*Mom* stopped in the bar last night and *she*...

*OW!*

What's...?

*Toothache* again...

Want some aspirin?

No; won't help. I've *got* some stuff for it.

Same *stuff?*

Yeah...

Go to *bed* first...

*Not* at six in the afternoon...

Go sit down. I can try a neck rub...

Worth a *try*...at least I know you won't try rebirthing me in *that* outfit...

Well...

*That's* OK...mm...nice...

Tense...just relax...think of something *nice*...

Yeah...

*What* are you *thinking* of...

A *pretty girl* rubbing my *neck*...who just dropped her *jumpsuit halter* over my face...

Not *rebirthing*, but...

A bare *belly* on my neck...*mm*...we're on the *first floor*, Red...

Yeah...but...*see* the *petals*...?

The...*what?*

These stick-on things over my...just *look around*...go on...

*Oh*...ah...*your* solution to the *see-through top* issue...?

Not hardly; this *denim* is *irritating* to *delicate* skin...now: think of something *else* nice...the object is to *relieve* your *tooth*ache...

I know...you're dis*tract*ing, anyway...

That's *something*...how's the toothache...?

Um...*better*, actually...mm...your *bare belly* does the trick...

Good...

Just hope I never piss you off so much you want to do a *two-handed throat massage*...

I wouldn't *like* that...sometime I'm gonna *let* you...

*Look up*...

Uh-*huh*...got to get to *work*...

*See* ya, Red.

In the *morning*, Blondie...

***

Morning...

*Morning*, Red...so, I *caught* Ponytail finally...

*And...?*

*And*...she wants to get together at the student union Sunday afternoon...

She *is* a student at the *university*...

About to finish a BA in liberal arts...

Huh. She *is* pretty smart...

And *eager*; I hardly got as far as 'want to get together...' before she said 'when.' How was work?

Good, actually. This outfit got me *almost* as many tips as that one *you*...

Huh. It *looks good* on you.

Warmer in the air conditioning than those skimpy halters and peek-a-boo skirts, too.

Ah...back to Ponytail: how is it you *know* those girls...?

I know Ponytail from the neighborhood...*and* she dated Idiot Brother for about five minutes before she wised up.

Ah...*Legs*...?

*We* go back to *grade school*. She was right next to me at commencement and right *with* me at the bottom of our class. She slings drinks at that saloon down the road from *ours*...

*And* she puts out...?

*Don't* be so *crude*...but, *yeah*, *sometimes*, according to the gossip...can't *say* that about Ponytail...though I *doubt* you'd be deflowering *her*...

Good to *know*, Red...

So, gonna call Legs, too?

Yeah...then there's the eternal problem of *cash*...

Huh...*well*...

*Just* pay your rent on time, Red. Don't *think* in other terms...I'll *figure* it out.

I have *the rest* of the *rent...my* date will be here about two this afternoon.

*Thanks*...good *luck*, Red...

Good *luck*, Blondie...

***

*Hey*, Blondie! How was *your* date?

She's young; fun, but *young*. Plays *pool* like a *shark*.

*Some* girls are better at that. Boss *talks* about pool tables sometimes.

*You* play?

Not much; no *good* at it.

Someday, *you* and *me*.

*Maybe*...

How was *your* date? He *seems* like a nice guy.

He's just come back from the Wild Blue Yonder.

Any possibilities with him?

*Maybe*...you gonna *call* Ponytail again?

*Maybe*...*some* women...more *work* than *others*, ya know?

Yeah...so are some *men*.

Then *again*...

If you can't *be* with the *one*, Blondie...

There's *that*.

Give her *that chance*, pal. Swimming tomorrow?

Yeah; I'd better.

72

***

Hey...

Hey, *yourself*...you *look* puzzled, Blondie. Burning *more* midnight oil...

I *am*. Got *this* in the mail today...

*'Dear...as you are aware...your credit rating...a new program... an authorized agent will contact you within thirty days if you choose to take part'*...sounds like a *fortune teller*...

Doesn't sound...*right*. Ever *heard* of this outfit?

Um...sounds *vaguely* familiar...lemme see the *envelope*...

Here...how was *your* evening?

*Long*...there's a *postcard* in here...the cheapskates want *you* to put a stamp on it...they *stamped* the envelope, too... postmarked from The Big Apple...

Lemme *see*...return if I want to *take part in the program*... PO box in The Windy City...

***

Hey, Blondie...

Evening, Red...sent that *postcard* back the other day...

Yeah...? *I* need a shower...talk *while* I'm...

*O...K...*I'll...

Sit on the *landing* until I get *in* the shower *and* when I come *out*, if it'll...*prude*...

Yeah...all...*right*...*flasher*...

So, you *mailed* the *postcard*...

Right...got a *call* this evening...guy said he was *with* the program, said they're working up a figure to *take care of* my *debts*...

Uh-*huh*...

I asked if he had any *idea* how *much*...

Yeah...?

*He* said *pennies on the dollar* in *easy monthly payments*...I nearly shat my pants...

*Yeah?* I'd *believe* it...

Yeah...like this *enormous weight* lifted off my guts. *I* said...

I'm getting *in*...

'K...

Yeah...so, *pennies* on the *dollar; colossal weight*...

Right...so I asked when he'd *know*; when would the calls *stop? He* said *by the end of the month*...

Well, *that's* something...

Yeah...

*Pah...just* a minute...

*Maybe* I should...

*No*, it's OK; rinsing my *face* off...but you're not *convinced?* Hand me that *big-tooth* comb by the sink?

Sure...I *dunno*...something just *feels*...wrong...*here*...

Thanks...feels *off?*

Yeah...*too good* to be *true* usually *is*...know what I *mean?*

Yeah...it *does* sound weird...want to *wash* my *back*...?

*Not* today...

You don't even *have* to *look*...

How would *that* work?

I can *make* it work...

I'll bet...*pass*, Red...

*Your* loss...so, what are you gonna do?

I dunno...I *gotta* do *something* about my bills or I'll...

Want to *join* me in here...

*Pass*, Red...

I can take your *mind* off...

*Red*...

*Don't* say I didn't *offer*...

I won't...you shut the *water* off...?

I don't need *that* long...let me dry off and I'll meet you downstairs for another neck rub.

OK...

You can *leave* now unless...

OK...

Blondie, you're *thinking* too hard...either *come in* or...I'm getting *cold*...

See you downstairs...

***

*There* she...is...sweatsuit and all...

You think I'd come down here in my *altogether*?

Kinda...robe, anyway, after *those* invitations...

I *didn't think* you'd take me *up* on 'em; just rhetorical...

Rhetorical *invitations*...never *heard* of...*rhetoric* is a tool of persuasion, Red. Rhetorical invitations doesn't make *any*...

OK, *unserious*, then...sit *back* here...relax...

Mm...nice...your hands smell like...

Soap; lotion. They get *rough* because they're *wet* all the time. You were *saying* about...?

Yeah...just doesn't seem...ya know, like there's gonna be some nasty little clause lurking in the shadows that gives them the rights to my first-born...at this point even if there's a *chance* this guy's on the up-and-up I'll *take* it...had a nightmare the other night about falling in a *pit* lined with my *bills*...thought I was *suffocating*...

Sounds *terrifying*...

All I could *hear* was those voices from the *collectors, saying 'when can we expect payment'* over and *over*... *that's* your...

This *sweatshirt's* very floppy; can just wrap it around your head...*don't* look up...

I *won't*...until you say I *can*...

You...*can*...feel *better*?

Yeah...boy, is it *dark* with your *hand* over my *eyes*...

***

Want some *dinner* after a *long, hard week*, Blondie? I'm *closing* tonight.

I was *just* thinking about that. What have you got in *mind*?

I've got pork chops, spinach...

I was *going* to start with rice.

You *always* start with rice.

It's easy and quick.

That's what the *box* says. *You* start the rice; *I'll* start the pork chops and spinach.

Want a salad? There's hard-boiled eggs in the 'fridge...

There's *always* hard-boiled eggs in the 'fridge...

Easy and quick.

You're big on easy and quick. Why *is* that?

Just don't like to spend a lot of time cooking during the week. I'm *not* very *good* at it.

That beef last week was *fabulous*. Your *mom* cook?

*Step-Mom* does; *she* taught me. My *mother* died in childbirth.

Oh. Sorry. I didn't mean to...oh, that *rebirthing...sorry!*

It's *OK*, Red; you had *no way* of knowing and I never *knew* her...

You don't *talk* about your family. Got *pictures*?

In the basement.

Why are *they* down *there*?

I see them when I have something to do with my hands and my mind...we've *got* a minute or ten; c'mon...

***

*That's* my step-mother, married my father when I was eleven months old. She was *also* my mother's *foster* sister. That's my *father*; *killed* in a car accident when I was three; don't *remember* him, really...don't *have* any of *my* mom...

Who's *that?*

Girl from high school. Her yearbook picture...

You still in touch?

She died in '76; leukemia.

Sorry...she meant *something* to *you*, though.

My heart belonged to *her* for a while, but she was *never* someone I could call my own.

Why *not?*

*I* dunno...

*Those?*

My step-brother, step-sister and *second* step-father. Step-Sis is *our* age; a *fun* girl...we lived in the same *house* until I left town. Step-Brother's older, has a wife and three kids; I don't *know* him well...that's *his* family. Let's go back *up*...

***

I *talked* to your stepmother on your phone when you were on the road. The phone rang; the machine picked up, and *I* heard a *woman* say her name and ask if you were *there*...I figured it was personal, *not* commercial...

Yeah; she *said*...what's *your* take on *her* reaction when you said that you *just* rent a room?

She said *oh*. Don't know if that was a *reaction* as much as it was just...*oh*...

Doesn't your women's intuition or feminine insight read more into *that?* I mean, there's *oh* and there's *OH*, isn't there?

*Why* is it guys think estrogen gives *women* some kind of *sixth sense* about *other* women? She said *oh*, as in *that's nice to know*. That's all I *can* read into it.

And you talked *about*...

She asked how long I'd *been* here; *I* said since July. I said I tend *bar*; I go to *school*...that's *all* we talked about. What did *she* say about our little conversation? After all, you *lived* with her most of your life.

She was surprised, but that's all *I* could get. I adore the woman, but frankly, sometimes she's too much the lawyer.

And you want *me* to do better? I've never *met* her...

I guess not. You made your introductions; she's satisfied with that.

Yeah...you on *good* terms?

Sure. We talk regularly...

Grandparents? Aunts? Uncles?

My father's father *was* in Motown; he died two years ago; his *mother* died before I was born. I have an aunt—Dad's sister—and an uncle; five cousins I *barely* know. My mother grew up in foster care; no idea if *she* had any family.

You in *touch* with your father's family?

Turn the pork chops...Dad's family was estranged from him *before* he died; not *sure* why...

You had *two* step-fathers?

Step-Mom married Step One when I was five; she'd been trying to get by on her salary as a public defender, living in a downtown apartment *about* the size of the downstairs here. Step One was a big-firm attorney, well off, helped Step-Mom start her *own* practice; lined up partners and clients. Suddenly, we had money and moved into a big house in the suburbs.

Sounds *great*...

Yeah, except he was *controlling*; he cut us off from *everyone*. Like all control freaks, he only let us have *his* friends, *his* business associates. I had a curfew, had to do homework from *this* time to *that*—even in the summer.

*Jeez*...

Step-Mom could only have a social life that was connected with *his* or *her* law firm or *their* country club—*nothing* outside. They *always* seemed to disagree on *something;* even the most trivial stuff, like how flowers were arranged in a flowerbed... he improved our lives, even if he *is* a rotten bastard.

*Some* people are alive *only* because it's illegal to *kill* them...

Yeah...I never *met* any of *his* family, ever; can't say I ever saw a *picture,* even.

Why did they divorce if he *was* such a *generous* asshole?

From the time I was *six,* I saved *most* of my allowance and my odd-job and bottle-collection money for a new bike, in the meantime settling for whatever Step-Mom could *find* for me to ride.

You were enterprising...

Yeah. When I was thirteen, Step-Mom took me to the cycle shop and made up the difference for a *new* ten-speed. I rode it to all the hangouts, showed it to my friends, got all the *oohs* and *ahs* I could.

A *reward* for hard work...

I rode home and Step One took a hatchet to the *wheel spokes,* then said, 'now *beg* to fix it.' Step-Mom pitched him out *there* and *then,* got a *bundle* in the divorce settlement for mental cruelty, got him to put *me* through whatever college I wanted to *go* to.

Served him *right.* What are you going to tell Step-Mom about *me?*

The truth, if she *asks.* I don't know *if* she'll ask...

She's not nosy...?

I think she wants to see me paired off like *any* mother would; might imagine that's who *you* are...

Do you *want* to be paired off someday with *someone?* Not *me,* of course...eh, pork chops and spinach are done.

*Not* you, of *course,* but if the *right* woman comes along and I can *afford...rice* is done; let's *eat*...how about *your* family?

I know about your parents and your brother and sister. What about the rest of your familial menagerie, including the mess of cousins and *cousines* I'm going to meet on Saturday?

Well, all my family but Dad's mom live within an *hour* of here...

That's why you're still *here*...

I guess. Both Mom's and Dad's families are *very* prolific. Between five uncles, three *great*-uncles, seven aunts, *nine great*-aunts, and a mess of *second* and *third* marriages, I have dozens of *first* through *fifth* cousins and *cousines* on *both* sides of the family.

Something to look forward to. *Great* pork chops...no, Kitty; *not* for you...

What's your *current* step-father like?

*He's* OK. Step Two owns a plumbing supply house; was one of Step-Mom's first clients. His son sent me *some* of the pictures I have in the basement; I don't even *own* a camera...wanna see a *movie* after dinner?

***

*That* was an experience, Red. *Thanks* for *dragging* me *kicking-*and-*screaming* to your family event. Get the mail?

Yeah; you pro*test*ed, all right; *grinning* all the way. Here's *your* mail, unless you want to be 'occupant' or 'our neighbor' today.

Pass...not con*vinc*ed, huh?

Nope...*thanks* for being my date...

More *bills* and *junk*...and...*huh?* I was your *date?*

What *else* would *you* call yourself? My family *approves* of you.

I...ah...I *guess*...your *family* approves of me...?

They *do*...that garter came right *to* you...

That *was* weird. Those *other* guys looked disappointed.

Who *were* they?

Some are *engaged* to *cousines*; some are cousins; the rest are just *dates*.

Who was the girl I *had* to dance with, took the *picture* with? The one who caught the bouquet?

A *cousine* engaged to *one* of the guys you disappointed. You *dance* a *lot* better than *Kitty* does...better than *most* of the *guys* I *know*...

I'm out of practice...*Step*-Sis taught me all I know...

How did *that* happen...?

The evening Step-Mom and Step Two announced their engagement, she told me she was going to dance as *much* as she could at homecoming *and* that *I* was going to dance as much as *she* did. Taught me to box-step *and* waltz that *night*, by the *club pool*; there was a dance ensemble out on the clubhouse terrace...

I can *see* it now: *her* in a floor-length gown and elbow-length *gloves*; *you* in your *white bucks* and *pink carnation*... *hair* slicked back...

*Not*...really. She was in one of those floral print mini-dresses...

With the matching *panties*...?

Yeah. *I* was...

Catch a *glimpse* of 'em, did ya?

More than *once*; it was a breezy and *hotter-than-hell* night and...*what* the...? *What* are you *giggling* about...?

Just imagining *you* with a girl you *just met*, *dancing* in the dark...*you* get embarrassed when I don't wear a *bra*...

*That's most* of the *time*, Red...heh-heh. Yeah, I *was* pretty young at that age...

*This* I believe. *Never* mind; go ahead... *you* were...*how* old?

Sixteen and *awkward*...*she* thought it was funny, too, because I *was* so awkward, clumsy, and I turned red whenever I...

Brushed her *softer* parts...?

Yeah. But she was patient, taught me that dancers *have* to watch each other's *eyes* at *first*...asked if I was *that* dorky on *purpose*...

Dance *is* foreplay...

She *said* that...*I* never understood it...

You get it *now*?

No.

Too bad...I've *got* to get *out* of this dress; let's go *up*...

Right behind you...you're *very elegant* in that dress...*fits* like a *glove*...

Basic black; the *only* color of dress a copperhead *needs*...

That *chain*; accents your *color* well. You don't *wear* jewelry much...

I don't *have* much and I don't *care* for the costume stuff. Un*zip* me...

I *zipped* you, so...here...*just*...*wait* till you...*close your door* before you...!

Too late, *date!* You live with a *girl* now...

Nothing I haven't *already* seen...

With *your* dancing skills, you could have *any* woman you *want*...but you're *overqualified*...

Huh? For *what*?

For women nowadays. You're a *super*-nice guy, bright and funny when you *need* to be, but you won't hurt a fly. Gals in 1980 want dangerous, rough, *screwed-up* guys they think they can either fix or tie down. Trouble is, *those* guys only want gals for *one thing*...*why* I have *no* idea...

It's the Cult Leader Effect. Cult leaders attract the most *vulnerable*, the most *gullible*; so do the *bad boys*...

Something *to* that. Bouquet-Catcher *said* you were super-*cute*...

*When?*

Just before we left.

She was being kind...

She was being *honest*...*I* think you are, too.

*I* don't get it...so, your *family approves* of me?

*They* approve of you as the guy I'm renting a room from and I brought to a family wedding; that's *all* they're seeing you as.

Ah...that's...

That's *all* they know...Sister, though, sees...*else*...

Else...*what? What* else? *How* did we get *else?*

Else...*else.* Cowboy, you're the first platonic *housemate* I've ever *brought* to a family function. All the *rest* have been...

*Else...?*

Yeah...wanna see a *movie* after we're changed...?

Sure. Meet you down *there*...

In a*bout* a *minute*...

I'll *feed Kitty*...

***

*Dumb* movie...know *what*...?

What...?

This is the longest I've *ever* rented a room from a guy without at *least* making out.

Really? You've been here, what, *eight* weeks?

*Ten.* After a *month*, we usually started *something*...

How many *of* them have there *been?*

Um...three...no, *four.* The *rest* were family or women.

How many of *the non-family men* did you end up doing something *more* with than making out?

Um...three...

And how many of *them* did you have *this* conversation with...?

Counting *you*, one...

And we're having *this* conversation...because...?

*Because*...

But you're *not* going to start *something* with *me*... because...?

*You're* not my type...

*So* you *say*. Were *they* your *type*?

Yeah...doesn't mean we *can't* live under the same roof in separate bedrooms...

Right...

The *next* movie's a new romantic comedy with that hunky blonde...like *you*...

You said I was *skinny*...

You were; you've put *some* meat on you since I got here...

Thought you didn't want to *start* anything...

I'm *not*; just making an observation after everything *you've* said about *me*. And I find you *interesting*...

Can't imagine *why*...

*Maybe* with a *girl*friend you'd find *out*...

My love life *lately* has been watching everybody *else*.

Single *can* mean you're just resting your heart for your *next* lover, cowboy.

*Deep*, little lady. Mine's been resting for *years* now...

*Speaking* of *which*, you *called* Legs?

We'll connect *sometime*...

Don't wait *too* long. I see you got *something interesting* in the mail...from a person of the *female* persuasion, by the handwriting...

A thank-you note; she just turned *six*.

And...who *is*...?

Yearbook's daughter. She's with her aunt now.

*What's* she...?

I sent her some money for her birthday.

Uh...there was *also*...

My *other* mail was another *not*-so-gentle reminder I owe the hospital somewhat over *four grand*...

That program...?

*End* of the *month*, he said...

*Sorry* I...Blondie?

Huh?

*I* want to call this an *official* date.

O...K...

So...*I* want a goodnight kiss. I *promise no* tongue. We're *not* starting anything *more*.

Just...so, *this* would be the *else*, with *limits*...

Yep.

*Now?*

*Now.* But I want us to *stand up* for it.

Yeah...now...*oh!* You *surprised* me.

That *was* the idea. *Again*, but this time, *move* a *lip* a *bit*... just...like...*that*...

Yeah...*Red*...you *with* me...mmm...*hey*...?

You have a *very sweet* kiss, Blondie...very...*sweet*...

You're a *nice* kisser, Red...*Red?* You're *zoning* out...and... still...OK; *stop*, now...

Um...*yeah*; sorry...how about a *hug*...?

Oh...*oh*...*my*...*so* warm...um...Blondie...let's *stop* here...

Yeah?

We'd...*better*...

Yeah; limits...

*That* was just so's we...*know*...right...?

*Just* so's we *know*...*right*...'night, Red...

Yeah...'night...Blondie.

***

Morning, Red...*you're* up early for a Sunday...

Yeah...

You *look*...

Like I didn't *sleep* much...*feel* like something *Kitty* brought up...

OK...all the *wedding excitement* keep you...?

*That* too...

C'mon down...but *put* some *pants* on, please...

I'll...*look* at *me*...Blondie, I need to ask a *serious* question, and I want *only* a *yes* or *no* answer...

OK...

Will you *please* have *sex* with me *right now*...?

No...

*Please*...?

No...you *know* what...

*Forget* I asked; I'm *exhausted.*

Forget *what*, Red?

I'm going *back* to *bed*...

***

*Morning*, Blondie...

Red...oh, *shit! Sorry!*

***

*So sorry*, Red...even *not* looking I saw *SO MUCH*...

Not *that* much to *see*...you're *still* blushing...

It's em*bar*rassing...*isn't* it?

Not for *me*; nothing to be embarrassed *about. Coffee* ready?

In the kitchen...but I *surprised* you; saw you like...*THAT*...

You *didn't* surprise me; I *knew* you were *up* and *around*...

You left the *bathroom* door open *on purpose?* I *have* to *pass* it to get downstairs! *You didn't have ANYthing*...

I don't like to *sweat* after a shower and the bathroom's *damp*...

But you take a shower *after work!*

I was too *tired* last night and I'm washing my sheets today...

Well...I'm *supposed* to wear *blinders?*

*No,* silly...this is *my* home, too...now you *know* I'm a *natural* copper...

The vanity's too high to see *that* far...

There's *few* men *worthy* of the *fire* of a natural copper's *privates* and *you,* Blondie, *are one*...it just didn't *occur* to me to *close* the *door*...

It *didn't occur* to you...

I *also* know *now* for *sure* that you are *so not* my type...

What's this *my type* bullshit you're *trying* to...*after* you...?

I'll put it this way: *my* type of guy would have stopped by the bathroom door and *tried* to strike up a conversation... or *tried* to *start* something *else.* I *wouldn't* have left the door *open* if you *were* my type of rude, sullen, dumb-as-a-rock, *grabby* kinda guy that I've known all my life...OK?

After *the question on the stairs* last Sunday...?

*Especially* after *the question on the stairs*...that I asked you to forget...

*What* question? *What* stairs?

Yeah, thanks...

Welcome...*them* you *wouldn't trust*...*me* you *do*...I'm thinking this *type* isn't what you're *looking* for, but what you always seem to *attract.*

You *got* it. Want some breakfast? Got potatoes chopped...

*Why* do you trust *me? Why*...?

Know how many guys have turned me *down* before?

I'm gonna guess...*none*...*and* I'm gonna guess it's because of the *signals you*...

Right...*maybe* that, too...and *before* the what-you-forgot, I almost *didn't* wear my *nightshirt*...

Why *then*...? Why not *before*...?

I've *got* my reasons; let's *leave* it at that. So, breakfast? I've gotta go grocery-shopping later. Wanna come *with*?

Separate carts...

Yeah...

Red...?

Blondie...?

You *do* have a *beautiful* body...

*Thank* you...

I *almost* weakened, you know...last *Sunday*...

I *thought* so. *Two* basted eggs?

***

Geez, the price of milk has gone *up*; nearly a buck and a half a gallon now.

And a dozen jumbo eggs are over *seventy-five* cents. Who was *that* at your register?

A girl in my class in high school. The one at *your* register was a year *behind* me.

Think they know we came in the same *car* from the same *place*?

I don't think there's a corner of this *county* that *doesn't* know that...

That *bothers* you?

Why *would* it? Not like you're the *first* guy I've ever roomed with...

Do they figure we're *doing it* by now?

*Maybe...wanna make 'em right,* cowboy?

Little lady, *you* know *I* need...

Yeah. That doesn't mean we can't *swap spit* once in a while. You know; with *tongue* and *hugging* and *petting* of the *minor* kind...

Thought you didn't want to *start* anything...but *the question on the stairs...*

I *asked* you to forget it.

Forget *what?*

*That* aside, I *still* find you interesting. And I *like* you...we *can* agree on *limits...*

You ever proposition someone you *didn't* like?

No.

So do you *like* me, or *like* me like me...?

*Definitely* the first. The *second*...I'll say *getting there...*

I like *you,* too, but *why* do you find me interesting? Because I don't *try* anything and *I* said 'no'...? Gimmie that bacon... freezer...

Here...*partly* that, but...I just *do...what* makes people *like* each other, *anyway...?*

There's libraries *full* of books that ask *that;* there's *islands* full of philosophers who *can't* figure it out...*I* haven't heard an appropriate answer *yet...*

*I* think it's because personalities *complement* each other; share interests, yes, *but* it takes *work* to make them *mesh...* to *harmonize; synchronize...*and it's just easier for some than others...do *you* like me or do you *like* me like me, Blondie? *Blondie? Hey...*

*Yes,* I *like* you a *great* deal, Red....a *great* deal...I *care* for you as a *friend* and...and...um...

*And...?*

Words *fail* me...your explanation of why people *like* each other...*brilliant...*

Thanks...Blondie, I say this as your *friend* and your *housemate*: making out *might* relieve *some* of your stress...

And *make* a *different* kind... *what* makes you think I *have*...?

Your *neck's* got more *knots* than a *scout's* convention every time I massage it. You're *awake* half the time when I come home late...and all those *damn* phone calls...those dunning *letters*...I see it in your face *damn near* every *night* and every *morning*...

My phone and mailbox...one day they'll *kill* me...

And *every Sunday* after you listen to the machine, you're *so*...

Yeah...Red, I *have* to be honest: *some* nights I *just* want to cuddle with a girl to *try* to take my *mind* off...*then* I remember I don't *have* anyone to...

*Next* time...let *me* know...

*How* would I let you *know*...?

*You'll* think of *something*...*when* was the *last* time you *actually* made love...?

Every time somebody *asks* me *that* I die a little inside...

So...no *answer* for *that*?

Let's finish putting these groceries away...

*C'mon*, cowboy: *when*...?

*I* need to keep moving on my laundry so *you* can...

*When?*

*April '77...OK, Miss Nosy! Any more questions?*

*No*...I also *gotta* do my nails today, and I have a *paper* due, and mid-terms coming up.

I gotta pay *bills*...*research*...*cat's* box...

Blondie...I *want* to be your *friend*...

Red...*I* want to be *yours*...

So, as a *friend*, I'm offering a *little* more *stress*-relieving than a neck massage...with just a *little* tongue?

Lemme *think* about it...

Settle for *that*...here's the *milk*; put *these* eggs under *those*...

***

*So*, cowboy...*offer* still *stands*...

Uh-*huh*...working on your *nails* in there...?

Yeah...*done*...you *want to*...?

You yell at *me* for doing *mine* in the living room...

Your *toenails*, yeah; *that's* gross...*no* response to...?

*I* need to change Kitty's box yet...

*Damnit*; *I* talk about making out and *you* talk about *cat shit*...

You forgot the *piss*. Yeah, I'm *quite* the Romeo...

*YOU...YOU...UGH...*

Red? *RED!* Don't...stomp off like...*that*...*please*...? Red...ah, *shit*...

***

*Hey*, Red...

*Hi*...*warm* in here...

Yeah; you're *undressed* for it...

*My* home, too...

Yeah...*Red*...?

*What*...?

Friends...?

When we *talk* about *anything*, *don't* change the subject to *cat shit*...

My inner coward says I don't *know how* that happened. But, my outer housemate knows I was avoiding an awkward conversation...*still friends*...?

*Friends*...what's *on*?

***

*That* was...

Interesting, Red...

Yeah...*those* look like *my* shorts...

*That's* why they *only* rise above my...

*Pubes*...*no* other guy has *ever* been skinny enough to wear *my* shorts, though those *are big* on *me*...you've gotten *into* my pants *without* getting into my pants...*that's* a *new* one...

Yeah, *heh*...they *must've* been in the *dryer*...that *whatever you've* got on...

*Cotton* and *comfortable* in this *heat*...

What do you *call that*...?

A *jumper*...God *knows* why...

The *material's*...

*Chiffon. You're not* wearing a *shirt* at *all*, you *slug. Women*... that'd include *me*...don't have the *luxury* of going topless...

*That* thing *barely*...

It's *enough* to keep you from being too *distracted*...hi, Kitty... go by *Daddy*; it's too *warm* and we're still *mad* at him... *barely what*...?

*Never* mind...

*What*...?

*Barely* hides your...

*Charms*...more *comfortable* than a *saggy bra*, and *again*, this is *my* home, too...

*OK, OK*...

What *we* wear in the comfort of our *own home* should be bounded *only* by...

Our *modesty*...

*And* present company...*guests* don't *need* a show...

*OK*...there's this new, um, courtroom drama...wanna *watch?*

Sure...want a *beer?* Kitty's *hungry.*

She brought up her breakfast when *you* were upstairs. Getting to be about her dinnertime.

*I'll* get her...

*OK*; beer, yeah...what about our dinner?

Got *dogs, fries* and *slaw*...

*No* work; perfect...I've *wanted* to see *this* one...

***

*Red...?*

Huh...?

*About* your...*offer*...

*Yes...?*

Are you *still offering...?*

Stress-relieving tonsil hockey...?

Yeah...if *that's*...but I got the *feeling* I was *frustrating* you...?

Blondie: you're the *only* guy who's *ever* said *no* to me...

You said that...am I *frustrating* you...?

*Honestly...?*

*Honestly...*

*Yes,* because...I'm *horny*...and *you...you...*

Oh; sorry...and I...*what...?*

Make me *want it...OK...?*

So *this*...um...*tonsil-hockey*...would be for *more* than *my* benefit...?

*Mine* too...if *that's*...

OK; thanks for being honest...I *told* you *before*...

*I* know; *you* need *more* than heat and friction...

But *you don't*...

I don't usually *need* much stimulation, but I'll be*have*...*limit* myself for the first time since *high school*...

OK...

***

Red...?

Right *here*...

Let's...

Kill the *lights...stand* up...*hands* on my *waist*...there...

*Not* like I haven't *done it* before, but *this* feels like Make-Out 101...

*This* is...just *pull* the *string...let* it *drop*...some *skin* to *skin*...

*Mm...not just skin...mm...*

Gimme your *hand*...a gentle *touch*...yeah, like *that*...

I thought *copping a feel* was without the feelee's cooperation, let alone her assistance...and *guid*ance...

*New* experience...

You *like* being felt up...?

By *some* guys...some*times*...

Am *I some guys?*

*Uh-huh...OK*, now, cowboy...*hands* on my *waist* and pucker... mmm...feel *better*, babe...?

*Some...babe?*

Just a *sweet nothing* between the *two* of us. Besides, what *else* would I call a *guy* while *he's*...

This is *starting* to feel like a *dance lesson*...

Dancing *is* foreplay and *so* is...

*Is* it...?

You've still got at *least* three minutes on my *make-out* meter, cowboy...but *that's* not my waist...

You have *very* firm...

Yes, my *butt's* firm...*like* it?

I...

You don't *have* to *squeeze*; you're *not* testing produce. *Now...* *just* a *touch* of *tongue...mmm...oh yeah...*you could break hearts, babe...and you haven't *had* any in *three years?*

I'm single by choice; not always *my* choice, but *still... choice.*

Eh, I've been on the market so long I may as well be on *clearance.*

*You* set the prices, though.

*Rub it in,* pal. So how's my *patented* relaxation technique *working?*

Just...*fine...*

Think of me as the *teacher* you can...*like...a big* hug... very... *mmm...oh...hard* to *stop...*

*Hard* to...feels *too...could get...we better...stop...*

*Please...a little press...into my...oh...!*

Red...*don't...lose* my...

*Don't* fall...

*BALANCE...*

*O...VER...! WOAH...!*

*Ooof...*

*OOOH!*

Oh...Red...you OK...?

I'm...*great...*you?

*Great...haven't* been...*here...for a while...*

Wanna...*wrap* my *legs...ahhh...*

*Long* time since...mmm...that *do it* for *you?*

*Enough...*now get up *off* me...*now...*

Just as soon as *you* unwrap...

The *unwinding* is *always* tricky, even on the *floor...now kiss* me and say...

*Mm...'night,* Red.

*Mm...'night,* babe...

***

*Morning*, Blondie. Must have *coffee...hi*, Kitty.

*Morning*, Red. Early class?

Yeah...*what... what's* with the *look...?*

You. You *say* you're *not* a morning person, but you're *always* pretty in the morning. I *like* your hair *completely* down...

*You...guy...*I haven't even *brushed* it yet. Getting up in the *morning* is the leading cause of being *down* in the afternoon... you *know* that, *right?*

My, *my*, Red; aren't *we* the morning philosopher?

Just not *that* much a morning person...Blondie, are we *OK* after last night?

*I* slept like a *baby*. You?

*I* did, too. I dreamed we went *fishing*, and I haven't *been* fishing since I was a *kid...*

Just the visual cortex processing information to create memories...*I* haven't been for years, *either*. Did we *catch* anything?

Didn't *get* that far, killjoy. I was *asking* about...*us*. Are we still *friends* or are we...

*More?*

Yeah. *Are* we?

I don't *know*. Do *we want* to be?

Ask me *after* I wake up...

*I* gotta get to work...

***

Hey, Red...

Hey...let's *talk...*

*After* your shower?

While I take a *bath...*just *class* today...

***

Blondie, I *don't* want you to get the wrong idea...

*Which* idea would *that* be, Red?

That...what *happened* last night...that *I*...

That we got some *relief* together...and *I* ended up on *top* of you with our pants *on*...?

I didn't *plan that* much...

It *felt* spontaneous...*and* pretty good...

*Yeah*, but...*that* was *just*... I was *super*-ready...

So was *I*... just heat and a *little* friction...

But did that *matter*...with you *literally in my shorts*...?

The only *girl's pants* I've *been* in in three *years*...

*He-he-he*...*don't* make me laugh in a warm bath; I'll *pee*...

Still horny...?

*Not* as *much*...I don't usually *need* much...

*We* OK?

*We're* fine...

'*Night*, Red.

'*Night*, Blondie.

***

Hi...*what's*...*hey*, Blondie; you're *still* up?

Hi...*yeah*, I *am*...

*What*...at *two* in the *morning*...*during* the *week*...?

*Just*...*shit*...

Babe, what's *wrong*...?

C'mere...let me *just* hold...*something warm*...*shit*...

It's *OK*...what*ever* it is...*shh*, now...*shh*...

*Honey*, I...

*Honey?*

If I'm *babe*, you're *honey*...just *another sweet nothing* between the *two* of us...

How can I *argue* with a *crying* guy with his *arms* around my *waist* and his *head* on my *chest*...I thought *honeys* were *blondes*...

*You're* the exception...see that *money* on the desk...?

Yeah...

*Count* it...

Ten...fifteen...sixteen...twenty-five...thirty-five...forty-five...six...seven. Sixteen dollars and forty-seven cents...

That's *all* I've *got* between *now* and the *fifteenth* of the month, and I *still* need gas and groceries...

You paid the *rent* and *utilities*?

Yeah...*and* my credit card—it's *still* maxed out—*and* the *cat's* got *food* and *litter*, but *I'll* be *hungry*...but the *finance* company hasn't seen a *full* payment since...um, *May*...and the *hospital*...since *June*...

Why do you owe the *hospital* so much...relax, babe...

I...just...*can't*...*keep*...*doing*...*this*...

Just re*lax*...shh...*we'll* be OK...shh...

I can *feel* your heart...

I'm *sure* of that...*shh*, now...you're getting my *sweater* all *wet*...

Sorry...

Just...get on *under* it...

*But don't* look *around*...

Gone *this* far; you *can* or *not*...feel *better*...?

Feel *safe*...

Good...I've got *some* of my rent now; I'll have the *rest* tomorrow...*shh*...

*Thanks*...

Sure...oh, I can *spot* you some *groceries, too*...

I'll pay you *back*...

*Mm*...a kiss a day for a *week* and I'll call us even...

On the *lips?*

Nothing *less*, babe...*sometimes* a *bit* of *stimulation*...

You'd trade...?

*Minor* expressions of affection and *little thrills* for groceries...

*Cheap*...

Worth it to *me*, babe...

I don't want charity...

*Charity?* You've got your *head* under my sweater and you're *staring* at my...

No, I'm *not*...I *don't* want to take advantage...

Babe, I'm not *offering* charity and it's *not*...I'm *helping* my *friend*...just go ahead and *look*...

No, I *won't*...*kissing* friend...?

*My kissing friend* in *trouble*...now, *get out of there, looking or not*; your first *payment's* due *now*...

*Before*...?

*My* terms, *not* yours. *Stand* up...

*But*...

*I'll* tell you *when* to stop...now *pucker*...

***

Feel *better* after a few *shots*...?

Feel...numb...pull that *quilt* over...

*That's* the *idea*, babe. Now, put *your head* in *my* lap...just relax and tell me *why* you owe the *hospital* so much...

Last winter I got an *awful* pain in my back. They found stones in my kidneys and my bladder. They got rid of *those* in a tank...

I've *heard* of that...you are *really tense*...

When they *say* that tank's painless, it *ain't*. I had a bruise from chest to knees. It's also ex*pensive*. *And* I got an *infection* that *felt* like it got into *everything* from my *waist* down. I ended up in the *hospital* for a *week*; I could barely *stand*, *and* I was on antibiotics for *a month*...

Ugh...*that's* why you lost the weight...

Yeah; twenty-five pounds in four weeks. New Year's Eve was my first day *off* antibiotics...

*Oh*...

A couple days *later*, there was a *mugging* right outside my apartment door and I said 'to *hell* with *this*' and moved *here*. I bought my washer and dryer, waterbed and the *pit* on credit with the finance company. In March, I got another *infection*, and I lost *another* twenty pounds...

Yuck! Health insurance?

Yeah, but the insurance company *said* the two were unrelated, so I had to cover *two* deductibles, *and* they said the *tank* was *experimental*.

*Bureaucrats*...

They're in business to *make* money, not *give* it away...Big Boss *paid* me while I was out, God *bless* him, but the deductibles and what the insurance *didn't* cover were nearly *half a year's* pay. Then my *car* died a rather *noisy* death right *after* all *this* drama. It cost nearly *two grand* on my credit card to fix and to rent a junker to get around, but I couldn't *afford* a *new* car, or even a good *used*.

Wish I'd have *known* you then; I *know* guys...

I don't *doubt* it...I wiped out my savings to pay the *doctor* and I *still* owe the hospital...I got my first *utility* bill in March, and...

Put an ad in the paper...

Yeah. So now I pass blood every once in a while, and booze is often irritating. I'm *broke*, got *bills* up the wazoo...and the phone calls started a month *before you* walked into my life...*why* am I *telling you* all *this*...?

Because I asked and *I* need to know what we're *up* against...

*We? You* don't...

As long as I *live here*, I *do*...

*You* can *leave*...

I *know*...I don't *want* to...

*Why?*

Your *head's* in my *lap*, this is a *great* location, I *like* you a *lot* and the *rent's* cheap...*that* OK?

That's...*fine*...

Now re*lax*...*four hours* until your *alarm* goes off...*spend* it here...

O...K...

***

Red...?

Yeah...?

I gotta get *up*...

'K...you *OK*...?

I'm...better...you *really* want a part in this *shit-storm*...?

I *am* part of it as long as I live *here*...

When was the *last* time a guy fell asleep with his *head* in your *lap*?

Lemme see...*four hours ago*?

*Before* then...?

*Four hours ago*...

*I'm* gonna get going...you *working* tonight?

Yeah...got two *classes* this morning...

See you tonight...

Don't take *this shit too* seriously, babe; you *won't* get out alive...

Yeah...

You gonna *go* to work? You look a little...

I'll see...Red...?

Yeah...?

*C'mere*...

*Don't* get amorous; I haven't *had* a shower yet...

Just a *kiss*, honey...

*That's*...OK...

***

Hey, Red.

Hey! How're *you?* Did you *go* in to work today?

*Late*, but yeah...I don't know *how* your saloon makes *money*, closing so *early*.

*Most* Tuesdays *are* pretty dead. Boss realized that, even *if* Monday *is* an anagram for dynamo...

It *is*...yeah! Never *noticed* that.

*He* had to explain what an anagram *was*. You writing another article?

Yeah; paper-making through the ages...

Fascinating...anyway, in *this* neighborhood he couldn't justify staying open late Mondays so we get a cleaning crew in now...Tuesdays we close earlier...so...*sit* still...relax...*shh*...

You want to *spill* whatever it is you *want* to spill...while you loosen me...*up*...you *did* bring a *bottle* and *glasses*...?

There's some *changes* with my *situation* coming...changes in the *business*...shh...

That place could *use*...updating...*that's* your...*chest* on my neck *again*...

*Shh*...yeah...Boss is sinking *more* money into his *other* businesses. He said he wants *out* of the saloon-only business...re*lax*...

He *has* more than one place, though, yeah?

Yeah, but the *others* have full-service kitchens...*shh*...

I thought there was more money in booze than food.

There *is*, but food draws steadier *income* and fewer *rowdies*... *shh*, now...he's gonna either *close* the saloon or *sell* it...loosen *up*, babe...

Ah...*mmm*...

You *got* a minute or two to look at some...*stuff?*

*Want* me to *look around* now...?

Go a*head*...

*Magnificent view* of a...

*Lovely* bra, *ain't* it? You know anything about business plans?

A little...Big Boss is walking me through one for *my* department...but *you're* the business major.

Yeah, but *I've* got this *accounting* problem...*you're* good at math.

Yeah, but *my* accounting module was enough to balance a *checkbook* and not *much*...

Pull your *head out* of there so I can take a shower while you *look* at *this*...

***

OK; I've looked. *What's...?*

*That's* a projection for the bar from Boss's bookkeepers, two years out.

Lots of *red ink* there, Red. Business plans make a *lot* of assumptions...

*I* think they're making *too* many. *They* don't *see* much growth...

*They* don't see *any.*

According to my business courses, the bar's got *all* the signs of a *failing* business; aging clientele, increasing isolation, lack of updates...but it's got *all* the things an independent suburban taproom *should* have: a *great* location, good repeat business. I think it *can* have a *stable* future with the right investments and good management...

Yeah, if you say so...what's *this*?

The city is *closing* the *main road* for repairs at the end of *next* year for *about* six months.

The bookkeepers don't see the business coming *back*...

Nope...Blondie, *how* would someone turn this situation around?

Red, how in *Hell* would *I* know?

Just...*think* on it for a minute or two...

For as long as *your chest* warms *my neck*...

I can do *this* all *night*...

Hm...*what's*...county plat map...here's your *bar*...here's the *pizza joint*...

Yeah...

Look *here*...the pizza joint's *platted* lot goes around...yep, over *here*...with an *easement*, *here*, you *could*...see...?

*Huh*...

*That's* not a very...*hard*...*massage*, Red.

*Uh*-uh...I've *thought* about us being *more* than just friends and housemates, babe...

I have, *too*...but...we're *not that* kind of friends...honey...

Do we *want* to be...babe...?

Honey—*Red*—I *won't* turn you into a rent-slut and I *need* your....

I won't *let* you do *that*, babe...can you draw *your* idea up... for *me*?

I'll make a sketch for ya...before...we...go to...bed...

Our *own* beds...

Uh-*huh*...

Thanks.

Welcome.

*Want* to...*this* is a school thing, but...your *labor's* worth... something...

Keep massaging...I'll *think* of something...

Not *that*...

More like another *bag* of *groceries* or...*mmm*...something along *those* lines...

Yeah, *maybe*...along *those* lines...want a *shot*...?

Sure...thanks...then I'll...*oh!* Not *that* kind of shot, Red...

Just a *little* closeup peek under the bra, Blondie.

***

Hey, Blondie! What keeps *you* up all night...as if I need to *ask*...?

Get your *shower*...

***

OK, now *what's*...?

A *guy* came to the *door*, handed me his card and said he represented that *program*...

He had a *figure*...?

I was *told* a check for *three grand* would be enough to cover my bills. *He* said my creditors had all *agreed*...

Sounds...fantastic...

Sounds *too good* to be *true*. *He* said he'd *have* to have my certified check within *three days*. *I* said I'd get *back* to him, and *he* said that it was a *onetime only offer*...told him I'd *call* and he left *after* repeating a bunch of other *threats* to my credit that I'd *been* hearing...*I* couldn't raise that in three *days* or three *months*...

Sounds...lemme see the *card*...*embossed*...PO box...*where* do they expect *you* to come up with *three grand*?

*That's* what I asked him; *he* said I should borrow from *friends* or *family*...*you* got *three grand* lying around?

Ah, *no*, but...Step-Mom...?

When this disaster *started,* I talked to her about it and she... it boils down to *not unless I'm about to be out on the street...* Step Two told me that when I moved out, I was on my *own.* Step-Bro, I guess, took a *chunk* out of him after *he* left...

Oh...

*I* get it; tough love...I *called* and...

No exceptions?

Step-Mom *hinted* that...*may*be...if I had *any* assurance that...

This was *legit*...

Yeah...it *looks* like a lifeline, but for all *I* know it's...

An *anchor*...

And I'm al*ready* drowning...

***

Hey...The Guy was here...?

Yeah...

So you said *no*...and he...?

Came up with some threats I hadn't heard before...like *'we can confiscate your car to secure your debts,* and *there is nothing preventing my associates and me from entering your dwelling and seizing property to satisfy your debts; debts you willingly incurred...'*

Sounds like a shakedown...

Yep. I just told him to do what he *had* to do...and he *left*...

Never hear from *him* again, I'll bet...

I *dunno*...*hope* not...

You *OK*, babe...?

I *will* be...*shit*...

Uh-*huh*...so, a guy walks into a bar and sees a dog licking his privates in the corner. Guy says, '*gee*, I wish *I* could do *that*.' Bartender says, 'you'd *better* try *petting* him first.'

*Hahaha...*

What *three words will* ruin a man's ego...?

I, ah, *don't...*

Is it *in...?*

*HEHEHEHE...*

Why do motorcycle gangs wear *leather?*

*Something* about...

Chiffon *wrinkles* too easily...

*Ha-ha...!*

What's the *worst* combination of illnesses?

I...um...

Amnesia and diarrhea. You're running but can't remember *where.*

HEHEHEHE...

Better?

Better...

# Has Dates and Plans...

*Hey, Red.*

*Hey,* Blondie...

How's *work?*

Fine. Ah, there's a *guy* I'm *interested* in...

Like you find *me* interesting...?

The *other* way. I've known *him* since high school. He came in with some *other* guys a couple of weeks ago. His friends picked up some girls, left him alone on *our* stool. It *still* took a couple nights before we...

Yeah; *one* thing *led.* A *lot* of guys lead with *that...*

*No,* he *didn't!* You think I'm *that...?*

I think you're that *lonely...*

*Huh?* I *have* dates!

You're the *loneliest* person I know...how many guys have you *done it* with since you moved *in* here...?

*Other* than...?

I don't count; I mean *full-on frontal* with *pants-off*...do you even remember their *names?*

I *don't* screw strangers!

That guy you brought here for supper *last* time: you knew his name, but you *didn't* know much else.

I *didn't screw* him...calling me a *slut?*

Calling you *lonely*, honey.

Don't *honey me, you*...I'm *not* lonely...*you*...GUY...I've *got* a *date* tomorrow night. *Don't* wait up. *I'm* for a shower... *you*... *you*...UGH...

***

You *waited* up?

It's not *that* late, Red...from the looks of your *face*, it wasn't *that* great a date.

*Damn.* I *tried* to clean up at the restaurant.

Didn't go well?

Didn't *go* at *all.* We *sat* down, ordered *drinks, then* he said he wanted me for a *friend.*

*Kiss* of *death* without *lips.*

Reminds me just *how...*

*Lonely* you *can* be...

*Yeah*...and how...

Right *I* can be...

Yeah...*don't* be so *smug, you*...GUY...*shit*...are we *friends* who can...with*out*?

*C'mon...*

***

*Morning,* Red.

*Morning.* Ya know, I could get *used* to living here with you...

I think you've *already* gotten used to it.

Can we *stay* like *this...*?

You mean, making out with *bare-chest* hugging and pants-*on thrills,* providing *hands* to *hold...warm* embraces late at *night* while you *flash* me once in a while...can *you*?

Coffee...

It's hot...what's the longest you've lived in the same place since you left home?

110

Um...a *year*? About *six months* with guys...

That's a *lot* of moving, Red.

Plants get pot-bound...

They *do*, yes. You've brought plants into *this* place for the first time.

You *had* plants...and *Kitty chewed* on mine...hi, Kitty...

That moldy bacon in the 'fridge didn't count...*has* she since that first time?

Not since you built that *hanging*-thing. No; I mean that *thing* you have in the downstairs bathroom.

Big Boss gave me that air fern as a joke, said I'd never be lonely as long as I had a plant that thrived on neglect.

So, why'd you put it in the bathroom?

It just *landed* there.

And I've landed *here*.

But you've always lived in *this* neighborhood.

Yeah. This is the longest I've ever lived with a guy without *doing it* for *real*, especially after making out. *That always* led to... but we *did*...

Yeah; we *did*...feel the *need*?

To...*move*; no...to...*some*. Do *you* feel the *need* for... more...?

Not the *need*, no. But when you sit at the kitchen table across from me in a *ratty*, *short* robe, *teddy* pants and a *see-*through, too-*big wife*-beater shirt, it *might* make any *other* guy believe you're trying to pique their interest...

Am I *piquing* your *interest*?

I'm resisting...even after *that*...jiggle...

*Why?*

Look: you *barely* make enough to cover your rent, and I'm *not* a *lot* better off than *you* for cash flow...and I *need your cash*. But you're my *friend* who I *won't* kick to the curb in favor of someone who *can* pay more, and I sure-as-*hell* ain't gonna turn you into a rent-slut even if I...

And you carry me half of *most* months...

*Mid*-month rent is better than *no*-month rent...

*Very* generous...

Generous has *nothing* to do with it. I've come to *care* for you...*too* much to just *bed* you without...*despite* that, I'm not *sure* how much *you* care *back* because *you*...

I *care* for you a *great* deal, babe...but *not* the *way* you *need*...

Good to *know*, honey...

*Welcome*, babe...*babe*; now, *look* at me. *Listen* to *everything* I say, OK?

OK...

Don't *say* anything until I finish...OK?

OK...

There may soon be a *time* when I'll *have* what you *need*. I'm *not* there yet...*nothing* to say...?

You said *not* to...

So...*say*...

I can only *hope*...we care about *each other* by then...

Me *too*...I'm not sure *how* or *why*, but, *babe*, you're turning *me* into a female version of *you*. More staid, more circumspect, more calculating...

You gonna be a blonde, too?

*Never*...*smart*-ass!

OW! *Kick* me in *slippers*...

You *asked* for *that*...and I can't *believe* I used the words *staid*, *circumspect* and *calculating* to describe *myself*...

Congratulations. I have to admit that I *might* become a male version of you; more casual, *fun*-loving, ebullient, carefree...

You don't have the *chest* for a bikini top, and I *ain't* all *that* carefree...

*You* don't have *bill collectors* calling all the time. Which *reminds* me, I wondered: *who* covers your school? Not that it's any of *my*...

My parents; I'm the only one of *three kids* who *ever* got a *single* college credit...babe, if I still *paid* your rent...*could* we...just *sometimes*? I *really*...

You mean, *clothes off*...

Horizontal; *full* contact...

I *need more* than a quickie, honey, especially with someone I *care* about...

You *care* for me...?

I've already *said*...pay *attention*...

Well, it may not be long before I won't be able to resist *your* charms and do *something you*...

I've got *charms*?

You *do*; plenty, cowboy. I don't *make out* with mere friends, let *alone* stuff their *heads* under my *sweater*...or...the *other* stuff we've *done*...

That makes *me what* if I'm not *mere*?

I haven't figured *that* out yet. *More* than just a friend, *much more* than a landlord, *less* than...anything *else*.

I asked if we can *stay* like *this*...can we...?

What if we *didn't*? You said you haven't *had* any in three years...?

*Don't*...please. I'm *not* looking for a *pity-lay*...

It wouldn't *be* pity, babe. When—*if*—we ever *do*, *trust* me, *pity* would be the *last* thing on my mind...so...*no*?

Sorry...besides, *you've* got *all* the *guys*...

*They're* getting *wise*...s'OK; I'll get *over* it...we OK?

*Sure*....*wise* to *what*?

Let's *watch* something...

***

Blondie...what *doing*?

Finishing editing this article...how was *work* tonight?

The usual. May I *enter* the inner sanctum of your den?

It's a *corner* of the *living room*...you never asked be*fore*...

Well, I'm asking *now*...

You're al*ready*...I meant to *ask* you before...what's *this*? I *found* it...

Where'd you *find* it...been *looking* for it.

In my drawer in the downstairs bathroom. What *is* it?

A brow and lash brush; an *expensive* one...been looking *all over*. *Where'd* you find it?

Like I *said*, in *my* drawer in the *downstairs bath*room.

Huh...

*Still* getting *used* to the hairpins and the elastics, the headbands and the scrunchies, the barrettes and the...

I *hang* my *sexy bras* and *lacy panties* in the *basement* now, after you *collided* with them in the shower...

And I collect 'em when I have to make sawdust down there...for *yours*.

No sawdust in the *cups* or *crotches*; appreciate *that*, thanks.

Welcome...*clear* the *crate*, here...*have* a seat...

Thanks...thought you *lived* with women before.

Step-Mom wasn't as profligate with the hair stuff; hers is very *thin*. Step-Sis and I had an *agreement*, and hers is *short*, anyway. You don't *wear* much makeup, do you?

*Not* much more than lipstick and eyeshadow and some *color* for my non-*existent* eyebrows. This brush lets me *shape*...

*I* can *see* your eyebrows.

*Now*; yeah, 'cause I darken 'em, but some *morning*, check 'em out. I don't wear a *lot* of makeup *most* of the time...but I am *now*? Can you *tell*?

Um...I *think*...eyeshadow; a little *something* on your cheeks; lipstick.

Blusher; *no* eyeshadow, just *tired*.

Never quite understood the *why* of makeup.

It makes us *beautiful* for you *guys*.

I think you're beautiful with *or* with*out*...

You're *weird*...

So, your formality means *something's* up, Red. *What...?*

Would you *mind* if I threw a party for Sister *here*? A birthday *surprise* thing...twenty people or so.

When?

Saturday?

*I* should find some place *else* to be?

Why?

I dunno...*family* and...

*Friends*, Blondie; you're in the *latter* category. Besides, I want to show *Dad* our *project*...

*Our?*

Part of it *was your* idea...

O...*K*...

***

Do you even know *half* these people, Red...?

We grew up and have *lived* in the same neighborhood for *most* of our *lives*...

Who's the guy by the door? He keeps *drooling* after you... and *something else*...

The brother of one of Sister's friends. We *had* a *thing*...

He's the *only* one who is interested in *you* because of *you*... *other* than me...

You're...*interested* in...*me*...?

That *OK*...?

*I* have a party...

***

What's...what're the *kids* crying about?

Your brother-in-law's *pissed* at his twelve-year-old daughter and his six-year-old son because they *dropped* some *pizza*...

On the *living room carpet?* How'd anyone *see it?*

He *stepped* on it...he *showed up* drunk, *been* yelling at them since he *got* here...

Typical of the asshole *loser*...he took an *IQ test* and the *results* were *negative*...I'll...

No; *I* told him to *lay off;* pick on someone his own *size.*

*Careful,* Blondie...he's a *mean* drunk...

A *drunk* and *belligerent blowhard bully.*

Yeah, *but*...where'd he *go?*

Outside...

***

*Hey!* What the *hell's* the ruckus out *there*...?

Neighbor-Behind wants to get his car out and Loser's not *interested* in moving *his* car...I'll...

Blondie, *NO*; I'll get *Sister*...

I'll *handle* him...this is *my* home and they are *my* neighbors...

*Our*...but *careful*...Blondie...*careful*...*babe*...

***

Well, *that* was a *great* party, Blondie, *despite* Loser...

We'll have to make it up to the Neighbors-Behind...

Later; *I* need to go to bed...

*I* need to clean this mess up...*Sister's* a lot of laughs.

You had a *long* talk with her. What *about?*

Hair styles...

She clipped *your* skull *once,* all-over *short*...

*Baseball...*

*She* doesn't know *baseball* from a quarterback sneak...

I'm sworn to secrecy about *our* discussions...

*Yeah,* sure...just so's you *know,* Loser is a jealous man, besides his *other* miserable qualities...

When he looked into my eyes and I *told* him to *stop* bullying his *kids and move* his *car,* he saw the *truth...*

What truth is *that?*

Hold that bag up higher. That everyone who knows *him* knows he's a blowhard who *won't* follow through on his threats, made *or* implied.

Yeah, *but...*here's *Kitty,* finally. Everything he touches turns to *shit,* except his kids. But they're Sister's doing, *not* his... it was *them* you and Sister were talking about, *wasn't* it...? Yeah, it *was...*how many more bags have we *got?*

They're *just kids...*we've got *enough* bags; all that cardboard makes us look wasteful. Someday we'll separate recyclable stuff. Kitty, *that's...*OK; it's your *toy* until somebody *steps* on it...toys of opportunity...

About Loser: *how* did you make him see what you *think* he saw?

I just gave him a look, *straight on,* that told him I wasn't impressed...that I see *through* his *tough*-guy façade.

You'll have to tell me *how* someday. You talked to Idiot Brother, too?

Briefly. He's a *kid.*

He's a kid who's been in and out of trouble and got off with probation. Now he's *not* a juvenile and out on *bail.* Might not *be* so lucky this time or *if* there's a *next...*

*When* there's a *next...*

Yeah; you're probably right. Want to finish cleaning up *later?*

Don't want to wake up to *this* on a Sunday. And *I* want to sit down to a piece of cake before it petrifies.

You didn't *get* any?

Didn't get any champagne, either.

It's *cheap* booze, but OK; let's *finish...*

***

*Great* cake, Red. Your *mom* made it?

Yeah. She's always baking *something.* Probably why Dad and Mom are so *heavy.*

Did you *know* your dad's...?

*Not* well, yeah.

Sorry.

More champagne?

OK. About *four hours* to *sun*rise.

If you make any *noise* that wakes me up before *noon,* I *swear* I'll run around the building naked.

*Oh,* yeah, *that'll* stop me. Remember, I've *seen...*

Lighten *up,* babe. *Half* a glass left. *Let's...*

*Pour* away.

I'm *killing* the lights.

*Except* over the stove...

Yeah...*quiet* at *last...*

Just the refrigerator trying to keep up...I *like* that vest...

Thanks; just finished it yesterday...*that's* a *beautiful* sweater...

Step-Mom made it...I'll *pay* for the booze for a while... *worth* it sometimes...

*I* move *we* move this meeting to the living room...

Seconded and carried...

***

Just put our *feet* up...*hey,* Red...

Hey, *yourself...*

Are *you*...ah...*OK*, Red...?

I *will* be...sometimes, putting my head in a lap's *just* what I need...*mind*?

Um...*need* for *what*...?

Keep my brain from going out of control...*hey*, Kitty...

*She* wants in on this, too...ah...Red, I don't *know* much about women's *hair*, but *yours* is very *silky* for its length. *I* always see...

Sister keeps the split ends away with her conditioners; I brush *every* morning, *and* I use *placenta* every other time I...

*Afterbirth?*

*What?*

That's what placenta *is*: afterbirth.

Didn't *know* that. I've been using it for *years*. *Now* I'm kinda grossed out, but I *enjoy* learning stuff from you.

You like learning, *period*...

So what *were* you and my parents talking about in the basement...Blondie...I *asked*...?

I know...just *trying* to...it was *business*; just *business*...

*What* business...?

They were interested in *my* take on your brief presentation...

*What* take...?

What I *thought*, thinking I'm an *adman*...your mother *knows* my outfit, apparently.

Uh-huh...still waiting on your *take*, what you *told* them...

I said for a *school project* it's pretty impressive as far as I can tell, not that I know anything *about* that *kind* of thing... but it isn't *just* for school, *is* it...?

It's the *future*...*my* future...*maybe*...what did *they* say?

They wondered how *you* would feel about expanding the reach of your *family's* business to encompass *your idea*...

They asked *you*...?

They *seem to* be under the im*pression*...your *mom* said 'my *daughter's very fond of you; I can see it...*'

*MOM!* Of *all* the...OK...what *else*...?

Wanted to know if *I* would *help* you...

If *you* would...help...*me*...?

I said I'm a *tech writer* and *half* an *engineer* who *works* in advertising and marketing, *not* a businessman, but that I'd do anything you *asked* of me because I *care* for you...I *didn't* elaborate on *that*...

They *will* on their *own*...*go* on...

I told 'em I'm broke and in *desperate* need of money, that if a new opportunity presented itself, I'd *have* to...

What did *they* say to *that?*

*They* said that *broke* is a temporary condition, but *poor* is a state of mind...

They *would* say something like that...*then*...?

*They* said they'd be grateful for any help I can *render*...

Huh...

Your dad *also* asked why *your* answering machine is on *my* line...said the family *depended* on you *having* one that *you* use...

Uh-*huh*...wonder *how* they...?

They called *your* line, then *mine*...I told *him* you were *lending* me *yours* until I got *another* one...said mine *died* and I get *business* calls...

*Oh*...

I *said* I'd get a *new* one...*soon as I can*...

Uh-huh...

*Then* he said he'll have *another* one sent over Monday... out of the *warehouse*...*Red*...?

*Later*, babe...

*Now*, honey...*stop* kissing my belly...

Babe, I really *can't stand* to *listen* to a ringing phone. Dad's exaggerating; if *I* get *one* call a *week* from them it's a *lot*...

You didn't *have* to *lie* about...

Yeah, I *did*, babe; I *did* because you wouldn't have *used* it otherwise. You were so *miserable* after that *call* I...

It's *my* problem, honey...

It's *ours* as long as *I'm living here* and I *care* about *you*...

You cared...*then*...?

Not as much as I do *now*...babe...?

Huh?

Why *didn't* you give me your number New Year's?

Honestly?

Honestly...

You were the first girl to express any interest in *me* in *years*...I *think* I was frightened...

Of *me*...?

Of the *prospect* of the most *beautiful girl* who'd ever said 'hi' to me—be*side* Step-Sis—seeing *me* as a *failure* 'cause I'm *so* damn *broke*...then *losing* interest...or *worse*...

Worse?

That you *wouldn't* call at *all*...*that* would just make my *empty* nights even *longer*...

Gimmie your *hand*, babe...

'K...ah...you're *not* wearing a...?

*That* make *any* difference...?

No...

*Not* our *first*...just *hold* my...

A-*HEM*...about your mom's im*pression*...?

Yeah, I'll *talk* to her...

How would *she* get the *idea* of that...?

Dreaming on *her* part...

Uh-*huh*; *I'm* holding *your*...

*Platonically*...

Sure; yeah; *that's*...

What it *is*...

I'm *copping* a *platonic* feel with your permission while *you* *platonically* kiss my belly...if *you* say so...

I *say* so...*mm*...*this* feels...

Like your mom has a *correct* impression...

I was going to say *beautiful*...we care for each other, babe, so why *don't* we...?

You *know* why...a-hem...your father *also* asked me if I ever thought of *selling* my frames...*then* he said there's a *market* for custom frames...you *sell* those sports posters and large-format photos you've got on the wall in the bar?

On consignment, yeah...*what* about...?

Do they sell *well?*

Not *real* well, but...*can't* we *just*...?

*No*, honey...I *could* make frames; even with pyrographic names for a *lot* less than *commercial* shops...

Pyro...*what?*

Pyrographic: wood-burned.

Wood-burning. Haven't *thought* of that since I was a kid.

Apparently, your father and your *boss* are friends, thinks you guys should *try* it...

Huh...*yeah*. Can you make a sample?

Yeah.

How *fast*...?

I've got *some* stock...tomorrow...?

I want to *commission* a sample...

On *speculation*...?

What's *that?*

At *my cost*...

Um...how about a *month's* rent...?

*Done*...

I have a *confession* to make, babe...

*OK*...

*You've* been on my mind since New Year's...

Huh...then, so do *I*...*same* confession; *same* sin...you *tired*?

Ex*hausted*...yet...*you*...?

I wait *much* longer and I'll pass out *here*...let's *retire*...

Can *we*...?

To our *separate* beds, honey...

*Why*...?

You *know* why...

*'Night*, babe.

'Night, honey.

***

Afternoon, Red. Coffee's *old*...make *more* if you want... *there's* a frame sample...

Afternoon...*hey*; sample's *great*! I'll take it in Tuesday... what's on TV?

Old movie...that *bikini bra* doesn't *fit* at *all*...

Doesn't even go *around* me anymore...you *like*...?

Sure, but gauging by the polka-dots on it, I'd say the Lads from Liverpool were still together when it *did* fit...

This *was very* stylish when I got it for my *thirteenth* birthday...wanted to show you I *have* one...

Maybe it was stylish and modest *once*, but *now* it's very *abbreviated* on you and it *doesn't*...

Bottom is *long gone*...what would you think of a *crocheted* bralette...?

Well...not sure *most* venues would...what's a *bralette*?

*Looks* like a bra, but it doesn't *squeeze...maybe* just around the house...*throw* me *that* top, *will* ya?

*What* top?

The one I dropped on the steps behind your *head* as I came down...

*Here...*at *least* go into the *bathroom* to change, OK?

For *your* sense of modesty, *cowboy...*but I'll leave the *door* open so we can still *talk...*

About *what?*

Gardening...

Don't know *anything* about it...

You mean there's a subject you *don't* know anything about?

*Many...*shouldn't take *this* long for you to take a *bra* off that's hardly *on...*

*No...*just...re*lax...lean* your *head* back...*shh...*

Um...OK...huh...*oh,* yeah, *nice,* Red; neck massage in the morning...

It's almost *one* in the *afternoon...*

Don't be facetious...

What's *that?*

Never mind...I ad*mire...*your *shirt* over my *face* again?

Uh-*huh...want* a *face-*full of my *balcony?* Just *look...*

Mm...pass...*what* are we *doing,* honey...?

What *lines* are we *blurring,* babe...?

Yeah...*mmm...*

*Just* the lines *we...*

Do I hear your *phone?*

Yeah...*shit...*just...

You gonna *answer* it?

You *want* me to *stop?*

Don't do *anything you don't...still* ringing...

*UGH...*be *right* back, babe...

***

Red?

*WHAT?*

You *OK?* A thirty-second *phone call* followed by ten minutes of *crying*...I *gotta* ask, what's *up?*

*Nothing's* up, Blondie...*not* a *God*damn thing...

Doesn't *sound* like nothing. There's one of those romantic comedies you like on in a few minutes.

I'll be *down* in a *minute.*

OK...I *listen...*

In a *minute!*

***

Red...

*Hi...*

***

Want something to *drink*, Red? I'm going to the...

*Let's* just *watch* this...babe, can I *join you* over there?

C'mere....*take* my hand...*lean* in...c'mon...*shh*, now...*have* a *tissue...*

***

*That* was a weird movie, Red...here's *more* tissues...

Yeah; thanks...

You're weeping for a whole movie and you *don't...?*

Just *sit* here, babe...*please...?*

You *hungry?* You didn't get *any* food today, and it's nearly *three...*

*Not now!*

OK...here's another one of *your* movies...

***

*That* was better...there's...

*Why* do so *many* guys treat girls like something stuck to their *shoes?*

I try *not* to *shit* on anyone, treat *others* the way *I want* to be treated...have another tissue; your *nose...*

Thanks...*why* are *other* guys such *assholes...?*

*I* believe...junior high girls...

*Explain.*

Remember in junior high, when you and your *gal* pals laughed at us because we *smelled* funny, or our *clothes* didn't fit well, or we were so *awkward* around you?

But *that* was the *queens...*

*That* was *training* for the rest of our lives. *Some* guys never quite get over the humiliation and take it out on women later. Understand?

*Maybe... I* never did that...

Not *every* girl did, but *enough* did. Not every *guy* was a target, either, but *enough* were.

You?

*Not* after 9th Grade.

Weird...

Much of my *life's* weird...that *first* movie is on *again* in another hour. Want some *dinner?*

I don't *feel* like cooking *or* waiting for *you* to cook ...

I'll *call* for a pizza *with* anchovies...

You don't *like* pizza...or...

*Want* it or *not?*

***

*That* hit the spot, babe; *thanks.*

Welcome. You *feel* better?

*Much...babe...I need...*

I know *that look...*

*Yeah...?*

Yeah...you never answered my *earlier* question: *what* lines *are* we blurring...?

Just the lines *we* drew...no one *else's*...we've crossed a *few* of 'em already...there's *still many* lines we *haven't* crossed... *babe...many, many* lines...I need dis*t*racting...

Distracting...this is...you want *this* kind...now...?

*Do I...do tell...mmm...*

Red...*honey...I...*

Know what a *garlic seduction* is, babe...?

Um...no...

*Start* by taking off our *cloves...*

*You* start...your *socks* don't count...neither does your *sweater...*

How a*bout...*lie *down...*

So *you* can...?

*Straddle* you...*let* me...

O...K...you're getting *very* familiar with...*that hand...*and you *have something* under that skirt...*mm...*

Yeah...*I can do...this...gently...*

*Ah...*

Oh, *yeah...*so Wife asks Hubby...*mmm...* 'you *ever* seen twenty bucks all crumpled up?' Hubby shakes his head...

Uh-*huh...*

*Yeah...wife* reaches into her *top,* pulls out a crumpled twenty...*mmm...*

*Oh...*

*Yeah,* babe....*then* the wife asks, 'you ever seen *fifty bucks* all crumpled up?' Hubby shakes his head. Wife pulls a crumpled *fifty* out of her *pants...*

A *fifty*...

Wife asks, 'ever seen *ten grand* all crumpled up?' Hubby says, 'no way!' Wife says, 'look in the *garage*...'

*Ppp HA! Ahh...ah...oh...woo...*

*Mm, yeah OH...oh...kiss me...*

*Mm...*

I *needed that*...another *beer?*

You've just *had* your way with *me...kinda...*another beer *won't...*

I *get* my way with you *all* the *time...*just *not...*

Distraction. Blurring those *lines* again, Red...

Ready to *erase* a few...*tell* me you *didn't* need *that...*

I *won't...*

Let's watch that movie again... beer?

Sure, since we don't *smoke*...that *phone* call, Red...

*Watch* the *movie*, babe...

***

Hey, *Red*, *wake* up. Movie's *over*; I'm knocking off. Gotta *work* tomorrow.

Guess I was *tired*.

You nodded off *ten minutes* into the movie. Want to *talk* about that phone call...?

*Maybe* tomorrow. 'Night.

'Night.

***

Blondie...? HEY! *Blondie...?*

Huh? Yeah; *what...?*

Talk *now...?*

*Not* through the door...

Kitchen...?

*Let* me...*ugh*, I get *up* in an *hour*...*meet* you *down* there...

***

You wanted to talk, so *talk*...

OK...first, *thanks* for last night...

For crying on my shoulder, the pizza or another *pants-on*...

For absolutely *everything*...

*Well*, honey, *I* cried under your *sweater*; *you* cried on my *shoulder*; we *both* got some *relief*...*tell* me you didn't get me up for *that*...

*Don't* freak out on me...

*C'mon*. It had *something* to do with that *phone call*...

*Partly*...Blondie, I *think* it's just *possible* that I *might* be pregnant...

Uh-*huh*...I *figured* you *might* be having a *penalty* for *late withdrawal*...

Ha-*ha*...would be an *April Fool's joke* if it weren't *October*...

I'm *sure*...

*How'd* you...?

You *look* like you're *ill* some mornings...no *feminine hygiene* traces in the trash since you moved in...

*Shit*, you're smart...

Folks *tell* me...

Folks are *right*. I'm *bloated* and a *little* nauseated *some* mornings...either *morning sickness* or the *flu*...

If it *was* the *flu*, you'd get *better*...drooling Door-Guy's the *father*? That was *him* who called...he *had* a vacant, open-mouth look of disbelief, so...

I asked him to *call me*. So...he asked if I was *sure* it was *him*. Of *course*, I'm *sure*. What's he think I *am*?

You *know* what he thinks...

Same thing the *neighborhood* thinks...

Yep...have you told your family?

No, and I *won't* until I *know* ...Blondie?

I'm right *here*...

Will *you* go to the doctor with me...?

You don't want *Sister* or...?

My family's like a *party line*; tell *one* and *everyone* knows before *sundown. I* want someone who I *trust, and* who *won't* blab it all over town un*til*...

When?

I'll *try* for today or Tuesday...

Let me know; I'll clear it.

***

*Thanks* for coming *with* me...

Anything for a *pal*...what *now?*

*Now* we put the groceries away...

I mean the *rest. What* do you want to *do?*

Put the *groceries* away, *then* I have to go to *work*...and *wait* for the results...

***

Hey!

Hey. *Busy?*

Just reading...

Chat...?

Sure...

*Pucker...mmm*...thanks *again* for...

Get the *results?*

Yeah...

So...?

*Not* pregnant, *but...*

Heavy *but*, honey...

I gotta go to the *hospital* tomorrow morning...

Need somebody to...?

*Would* you? *Just* a *test*, they said...

Sure.

***

Hi...*hey*; *nice* gown, Red. What's with the *wheelchair...?*

They're prepping me for surgery...can you call *Mom?*

What...*now?*

*Now*...kiss for luck?

Sure...

Call *Mom...?*

***

Hey.

*Hey.*

Thanks for calling my family...c'mere...*come* on...*mmm...*

*Anything* for a *pal*...they don't seem very...ah, *sure* about *me...*

What did you expect? A *week* ago, you were the guy I was renting a room from. Three *days* ago you were talking about our *family business*...today, you sat in *uncomfortable* chairs with them all day. What are they *supposed* to think?

I guess. Your *folks* think *I'm...we're...*

*I'll* clear that up *later...*

You look a little *worn...*

I just had a bunch of *cysts removed* from my uterus...how would you *think* I *should* look?

Ask a stupid question...what *kind?*

*Normally not* malignant, but they *could* be...one was *turning*...

When will you *know?*

Few days...*Mom* had 'em, too, after Idiot Brother was born. My *nieces* and *Sister* are at risk.

One of *them*, huh? Well...

I may *not* be *able* to have *kids*, now...*oh*...

It's *OK*, honey; it's *OK*...*shh*, now...*we'll* be *OK*...

***

You need to *rest*; I should *go*...

Babe, I *might* want to go down by my gramma in the Land of Enchantment for a while.

OK...

*I* just need to *get away*. Come *with* me?

As *what?*

My *very* good and intimate guy-*friend* who I'm *not* sleeping with...not for a *lack* of *trying*...

*But* we...your *family*...?

My family will believe *me* when I tell them what we *aren't*...

How *long* a while?

A week; two.

What would *that* do for those *blurry lines*...?

*I* think *you* need them...

So do *you*...*we* have to *look* like we're in a commercial transaction so *you* aren't thought of as a *rent-slut* who still goes out on *dates*...

Yeah...a trip *together*...

Wouldn't *support* that imagery...

No...babe, Mom wants me to convalesce at *their* place...a *week* or so...

*That's* up to...

*I* want to stay at *our* home; in *my own* bed...

*That's* up to...*our* home...*your* bed you're *renting?*

Yeah...I see it as *our home*, babe...

Those blurry lines, Red; what about *them?*

I'm going *home*...*our* home...blurry lines *stay* blurry...

*When* can I *take* you *home?*

***

Your mom's *not* happy with you...*or* me for *agreeing* to it...

So she'll *call* every morning and every night for a report. *I* need to lie down. Will you just *stay with* me for a while?

You *sure?*

Yeah; c'mon up *with* me...

I'll feed Kitty...

***

Just have a seat on the bed...

OK...so they *weren't* malignant?

No, but the *one* was *transitioning*...now I need annual checkups...

Sorry...did you, ah, *clarify* our relationship with your family...?

I told them we *weren't* sleeping together. That's all they *need* to know.

So...what *is* our status...what *are* we now?

I'm not...*shit*...I *swore* I *wasn't* gonna break down *again*...

C'mere, honey...*shh...shh*, now...*you're* OK...*shh*...

***

Feel better for the cry, Red?

Yeah. Just... *relieved* and sad at the same *time*, you *know?*

I *don't know*, but I can *imagine* that kind of thing is *scary* when you're alone...

Would I have *been* alone if...?

You'd have your family, your friends...you'd have *me*, whatever *I* am.

Could I have stayed here *with* a baby?

Why not?

Hard to make the rent...

We'd work *something* out...

But you *need* the money I pay you...*and* the groceries I *still* buy...

We'd work *something* out.

*Why?* We barely *know*...

You...*you* said 'we'd' figure out *my financial* mess...

Yeah...what does *that* mean to...?

It means I'm *not drowning alone*...besides; I know more about *you* than every woman I've *ever* slept with, *combined*, and I suspect *you* know more about *me* than *most* of the guys you've been dating since puberty.

*Half*-right...I've never seen *you* completely naked...

You've *seen* me in...

That few inches of *marble bag hides* the interesting parts... *and* I enjoy being with *you*...

*Why?*

You saw me *full frontal*...

In a *mirror* in front of a *vanity*...

You would have seen *more* a heartbeat later if you *hadn't* run away...you've been *under* my *sweater*...

*With and* without...

But you *didn't look* when I was *without*...and you *could* have...and you *let* me...

Get *relief*...

Yeah...any *idea* how hard it is to push guys away all the time? How *hard* it is to *limit* intimacy with guys?

No...but I *wouldn't*...

You *push girls away*...

*They* don't *try*...

*You* don't *notice* and *that* has the same *effect*. Every time Mom Across-the-Walk sees you, she practically salivates... same with Gal Neighbor-Behind. *Either* of 'em would give it up if you *smiled* at them.

How is it *you* notice this and I *don't?*

*You're* not on the make, so *you're* not looking. *And*, you don't know how women *think*, their body language...but I don't *really* know what *kind of* lover you are...

You *do...kinda...*that's *less* than half of *any* guy, ain't it?

Yeah, I guess. Now that we're horizontal together in bed, don't you feel the *urge* to...?

Are *you...?*

Not *that*, but I *could*...

I *feel* the *urge* to *comfort* my *friend* in a...um...

*Night*shirt and alluring *plastic pants*...

I was going to say *platonic fashion*...do you *enjoy living* here?

You're my *favorite* housemate *ever*. Do you enjoy *having* me here?

You're *my* favorite housemate ever.

I'm *also* the first and *only* so far...Blondie: *what* the *hell are* we?

POSSLQs.

*What?*

POSSLQs: Persons of the Opposite Sex Sharing Living Quarters.

Where in *Creation* did you get *that?*

Government made it up for the census. *You* kept putting off *saying* so I...

*That's* the only name that *fits*...I'll still *strip* on my way upstairs...

I've gotten *used* to that...I could *even* get used to Ill-fitting tops in the living room and *bare-bottom questions on the stairs*...

I *asked* you to *forget* that...

Forget *what?*

Yeah...you could *see*...?

Yeah; *barely*...

*Very* punny...

*Thank* you...you said you moved out of your house right after high school. What precipitated *that?*

Mom and Dad were...*how* do I say this...at odds over what *Mom* called my *promiscuity*...*she* wanted me to settle with just *one boy*. *Dad* wanted me to have *fun*, but to go to *college*. I *started* orientation, but I just wasn't *seeing* it...

No direction...

Exactly. I was *friends* with an *older* guy who had a house down the street who got me a job insulating ductwork. It was good money for a teenager...

So you could pay your own way...

Right... Sister got pregnant for the *third* time, Idiot Brother got busted and *they* became the focus of their attention; their *bickering* was nonstop. I asked Older Guy if I could rent his spare room...

And you got out from under...

Yeah. *That* was three weeks after graduation. Suddenly, *I* was no longer a problem, and they forgot *why* they were sore at *me*...

*You* were independent enough *not* to fight over anymore...

Yeah; *that* makes sense...never thought of *that* before. Did

Step-Mom fight with your stepfathers about *you?*

Step One, *all* the time...the *bike* was just him declaring he was *done.* Step *Two*...Step-Sis's bedroom was to be right next to mine when they moved in in '71; we would share a bathroom that connected the two. Step Two has a *thing* about *appearances*...

Were you two an *item*...?

Me and Step-Sis? We'd had *fun* at the club together; Step Two just *read* us wrong that summer...

Is she *pretty?*

She's one of the most *captivatingly beautiful* girls I've ever *seen*...present company excepted, of course...

Of *course*...

She's also one of those people who, no matter *what*, gets along with *every*body. We'd known each other from the club swim team, but never *socialized* until Step-Mom and Step Two became an *item*. When they got engaged in '71— the day *before* they announced it though *we* knew it was coming—she changed into a bikini after team practice and we ate lunch from the snack bar together...she'd never *worn* one before and we'd never *spoken* much...

She was *teasing*...

In *her* way...*I* think it was *her* way of telling the rest of the guys on the team *she* was unavailable; paying *sudden* attention to a guy she only knew by *name*...

*Could* be...so...you *never*...

I *thought* about it for a few *moments*, once. So did *she*; she *told me* so. I think that's why we're such good friends: we *thought* about it and decided *not* to *act*; too many domestic complications.

I guess...so...back to your housing situation...

I offered to move into the *basement* if it would solve the problem. Step-Sis said *she* wanted the basement...*then* it became a big *joke.* Still *is* a joke between *us* even after she moved into that room...she moved *out* of the house last year, got an apartment close to campus...we *write*...she's got a *boyfriend* she wants me to meet...dunno how *serious*... Red...*honey*...?

Mm...?

'*Night*, honey...

Mm...

***

Hey! How's work...?

*Hi!* Work's...*work*...*feeling* better?

Yeah...*well*...what'd ya *think?*

I think you've *upgraded* our windows...huh.

Sister *had* the material, filched the rods from the folk's basement. What'd 'ya *think* of it...?

Well...I think it's a definite improvement on the sheers we *had* in the living room...and the *kitchen* window has a *valence* now...huh.

Sister said you wouldn't *notice* that...*and*...?

You moved *my* pictures up from the basement...

I thought they *deserved* better than to hide in the basement... was I *wrong*...?

You hung them with pictures of *your* family...

Uh-*huh*...

Do you *think that* much of me, honey...?

I *think a lot* of you, babe...there's no other guy I *know* who would have done for *me* what *you've* done, including Idiot Brother and Dad...

Some *laundry*, some *cooking*...

My *super-nasty* laundry, babe...nobody *else*...

Your *mom* would have...

*Not* in the *middle* of the *night*, she *wouldn't*...but *you* did...

Didn't *want* to let those stains *set*...

They're not even *your* sheets...

My *mattress*...

Doesn't *matter why*, babe...you got up out of bed and *did* it for *me*...

I *hate* to hear girls *cry*...makes me *feel*...

*Helpless?*

*Useless*...

You *rushed* downstairs and started a load of *laundry* at half past midnight because you felt *useless*...

Say it like *that*, it's *not* so...

*My* way of saying *thanks*, babe...you look *tired*...

Three *hours* of sleep; yeah...

I made calf's liver and onions for dinner, since *I'm* so *damn* anemic...

With *bacon*...?

Is there any *other* way to make it *edible*? Boiled broccoli...

Still *got* hash browns...

Made *more*...

You've been *busy*...

I've been *bored*...*and*...been wondering *why* it's been so *long* since you had *real* sex...

Frankly...*gun-shy*...

Let's get *dinner* on while you tell me *this* one...

Let's...

***

OK: *Why gun-shy?*

*Great* liver...has to do with how my *last* job ended. I'd been there two years before I put in for a management job. Since I started there, this *woman*—a lab supervisor—had been

139

dropping rather *broad* hints about which club she would visit on *this* night or bar on *that* one; the *concerts* she was going to...

And *you* wouldn't *take* the *hint*...

*She* was...not *ugly* or anything; she just *grated* on me. She *smiled* too much whenever she *saw* me; did a little *skirt-lift* whenever she sat down in *front* of me. She sat on my *desk* too often, in skirts *too short* for the office. *I* didn't have that much to *do* with *her* lab...

*She* was interested, but *you* weren't...

Not especially. We ate lunch together in the cafeteria a couple times, *only* because she came to my table about 10 minutes after I'd started... even when the place wasn't crowded. She'd just *plop* herself down and start *chattering* away. I'd *nod* and *smile*...

Tried *not* to engage...

Or *encourage*... I ran into her in a saloon downtown one Saturday night a few months *after* I applied for management...*I* was a *little* plastered and a *lot*...

*Yeah*...?

*Yeah*...so I *settled* for heat and friction...next *day* she calls me, says she wants to *get together* again; I said *no*. Next thing I know, Lab Super told HR that she felt *threatened* by *me*...

Threatened...*how?*

Shit if *I* know...but HR didn't *need* any explanations. They gave me a *choice*: get *fired* for *cause* or *resign*. So, I *quit*... *that* was in May '77. Found out from people who were still *there* that Lab Super had a, ah, *protégé* who *got* that job I put in for, a guy that, ah...

*Took* her *bait*...

*Yep*...

Sounds like you'd have a *legal* case...

Yeah, but if it's *that* kind of outfit, how long would they drag it out? And to what end? Not like I'd want to work *there* again...

True.

So I was out of work for *five months*; put a *dent* in my savings. Then a neighbor said *his* outfit—with *Big Boss*—was looking for a tech writer and I thought I'd *try* it, see if I was any *good*. Never thought of *that* before...

You'd never *done* it before?

I had a one-semester course in engineering documentation, but *that* was as close as I came...

But they gave you a shot...

From the time I walked in, I was the *only* one in the *building* who could read a schematic *or* make sense of the manuals their client needed to update. I started out on contract and they *hired* me a month later. I didn't look *twice* at my co-workers until recently; haven't wanted to risk having somebody *else* take a hatchet to my wheel spokes...

Blondie...babe, *look* at me...stop *chewing...swallow... pucker...*

*Oh...mmm...sweet...*

No *hatchet* when I did that...not even a *butter knife*...

No...but I don't *work* with you...

Yeah, but you've *had* dates *since*, right? I've...

You *have*; and I'm *grateful*...

*We've* even come *close* a few times...

*Very*...

No *need* to be *afraid* to get back out there, *is* there...?

I *am* out there; I'm just not *lucky*...but *you*...something I've *wondered* about, Red...you were ready to move *before* you *saw* this place...what was...?

I was with Door-Guy until June...

There were burger wrappers in your car...you were *living* in it...

Yeah...he got on my last *nerve* and I bailed...saw your *ad* and...

Ah...you *dragged* your *plant* around...?

Yeah. I thought once I got tired of hauling it around, I'd *stop moving...*

*Have* you?

I'm *tired* of hauling it around...

So you'll *stop* moving...?

Either *that* or I'll just leave it *here...*

*Hope* you do *neither...*

I *will* if you *turn me down* one too many times...

Stop *counting...*

*Who's* counting?

***

*Hey!* Anything good on TV?

*Hey* yourself, Red. Not...really...

*C'mon; stand* up and *kiss* me...*mmm...*

How are *you* doing?

*Better*, thanks. You gonna *go* to that picnic on the common at the end of the month? You had *that look* in your eyes this morning...

*What* look...?

That sad, '*I need to get laid and soon*,' look...

And *you* weren't *interested* for once...?

Bad *timing...*

Uh...am I really *that* pathetic?

*Sometimes*...I'll ask my *cousin* if *he* wants to come...

Was *he* at the wedding?

He didn't *make* the wedding...he's a *kissing*-cousin...

Really...*that grin* tells me you *have* kissed him, too.

I know *everything* about him, right down to the mole on his...

That's *nice*, Red. I might ask *Legs...*

*I've* got a *date* after *work* Friday night.

Well, *I've* got one on Friday, *too.*

*Who?*

A widow from Round Table. She *lives* near here; I've been picking her up for meetings.

Ask *her...*

Yeah, maybe...good *luck* if I *don't* see you, honey...

Thanks, babe. You, too.

***

Now, last night *was* weird, Blondie.

It was a *little* bizarre, yeah. OK, she *lives* around here. OK, she's a *widow.* But I had no *idea* she met her husband in your saloon...

*And* that she wanted to stop for a nightcap on the way to *her* place. I *know* her, kinda; she went to parochial schools...

Know what happened to her husband?

You should ask *her.*

But do you *know?*

Um...car accident, I *think.*

I'll ask her next week.

*Another* date, Blondie? Did you get lucky *this* time?

*Yes,* to the first; *no,* to the second. A hug at the door...

*Sweet* hug?

Just the standard po*lite* embrace between *friends* of the opposite sex. But she *asked* me out for fish fry; said she had a prior commitment on the day of the party. How about *you?* How was *your* encounter? Did *you...?*

It was fine, but, no. Didn't *seal* the *deal.* Just couldn't *quite...* ya *know?*

No, I don't.

Yeah, you *do,* but you're too *polite* to *talk* about it. Single *also* means nobody's *cheating* on you.

143

I'll *risk* it.

Yeah, you *might*. I've got a preference for both my sanity *and* my self-respect...*you*, my friend, have single-handedly *restored* my personal dignity...

So, the guys you've been dating all these years *don't*...?

*You* treat me with more respect than every *other* guy I've *ever* dated...

Nice to know...I *get* the self-respect part, but you *don't* go out with the same guy twice in a row...how *come*?

I *haven't* since Door-Guy...

Why *not*?

*I* need a *shower*...'night.

Right...OK...'night.

***

Hey!

Hey...

You *alone?* Where's your *date?*

Took her *home*...

Ah...*grab* a *stool*...beer?

*Pour* me a *shot* of *something stiffer*...

'K...this *short* one's on *me*, buddy.

Thanks...*half* a spoon...and...*WHEW!* What's...*that?*

Absinthe. *This* brand's 179 proof; *Boss* brought it from Spaghettiland. Like?

Can't *tell*...too much like a *hot poker*...I thought that stuff was *illegal* here...?

Good for what *ails* ya, pal; just *don't* say you *got* it *here*... need I *ask* what...?

She paid for *her* half of dinner, then *she* said...just no *chemistry*. She wants to be *friends*.

*My* last date; *same* thing...

Sorry, Red.

*I'm* not. *Alone* is better than *shitty* romance.

How *much* better? At least *then* there's some *feeling*; someone gives a damn if I *live* or *die*.

*I* give a *damn* if *you* live or die, cowboy. And *Kitty* does, too...*you* care about *me*...

Yeah, and thank *God* for *you two*...late tonight?

This place *look* like I'll be late?

Maybe *not*...

Maybe another hour...wait up?

I...*maybe*...

You *should*...got something to *tell* you...

About why *string bikinis* are like *corrupt governments?*

Um...*this* I gotta hear...

People wonder how they stay *up* and wish they would *fall*...

No...*heh*...something *else*...

***

Hey, Red.

*Hey*, babe.

So, what's this *big*...?

That yellow slip in your mail?

Yeah?

Mail-lady knocked on the door, said she had a *registered* letter. *I* wouldn't sign for it; didn't think I *should* have, so she left *that*...

Yeah...from the *hospital*...want their *pound* of *flesh and* their *money*...

Can't you set up payment plans, like they offered *me*?

I *did*, but I couldn't meet their minimums after the *second* go-round...how *did* you pay for *your*...?

Dad...

*Oh,* yeah...well...they're probably telling me I've got *thirty days* or they'll send my files to a *collection agency* and blow my *credit* for the foreseeable future...at *least* I managed to pay my *GP* off...*shit...*

Babe...? *Hey,* babe...

*Huh...?*

C'mere...c'mon...just *wrap* your *arms* around *me...head* down...*shh*...it's OK; *we'll* figure it out...*shh...*

***

*Jerk-Weed* calls *me* a *rent-slut. More* beer...

Right *here.* Which one's *he...?*

*That* Jerk-Weed, from three doors down. He was two years behind me in school.

Why would *he...?*

Beard told Jerk-Weed that I live here for *free* because *you...*

*Why* would Beard *say* that?

Because Bleach-Blonde *lives* rent-free with *him* now...

What's *that* got to do with *you?*

Beard is feeding *that* crap to *everyone* because *I* left the bar with *you* New Year's and stuck *him* with Bleach-Blonde, who ain't much in the up*stairs* department, if you *get* me...

*Ten months* ago and you're just hearing it *now?*

I *think* the story *just* started. *Sister* would have heard it *before...*

If you just left it alone, didn't *talk about it, what* do you think would happen?

Well, the *gossip* would...and my *reputation...but...*

Your *family* knows the truth...*we* certainly do...your rep's what it's *always* been...just...leave it *alone* and it'll die out...

A lie can travel around the world before the truth gets out of bed...

*Yeah,* but confronting *this lie* will give it a substance it doesn't have—make it *look* like there's an element of truth... just...let it die.

I suppose you're right...*Legs* seems to be enjoying herself...

*She's* a barrel of laughs, but she says she has a long-haul trucker boyfriend.

She *wishes* she *had him*...she *certainly* has *eyes* for *you*...

In your imagination...

Not *mine*, pal; *hers.*

I *doubt* it...

*I* don't; even Cousin sees it...

Uh-huh...do you think *everyone* knows you've *done it* with your cousin?

*Idiot Brother* blabbed it all over town a *decade* ago after we got *caught*...

Hence the moniker...you started young...

Yeah...Cousin's *looking* for me over there...

Better go on *over* there, then...

And *Legs* is looking for *you*...

Yeah...*I'd* better go, too...

***

Hey. Was *hoping* you'd stay by *Legs* for...

*Kiss* at the *door, that* was *it*...

Sorry...

Get everything in?

Yeah; *just* putting it *away*...

*I'll* help...where did this chaise come from? Looks *weathered*...

My folks' garage; been around since I was a *kid*...

I'll get it into the basement...

Garage...

'K; in the morning. Is there room in the fridge for this *last* six-pack...?

Yeah. There's...let's *see* here...*two big spoons* of potato salad... *three* buns and...*two* hot dogs left. You *hungry?*

*Gimmie* a *beer;* we can polish *that* stuff off...so, tell me about you and your *cousin...*

Here's a *spoon*...I was *fifteen;* he was *sixteen*...middle of July, and all the families got together for a lakeside party to celebrate Sister's *second* pregnancy...

Lived near a *lake? Boil* those dogs...

On the *way*...our cottage by the lake the family *owns...*

The *cottage...?*

*And* the *lake...*

Ah...so, *wet* bodies; *heat; water; sunshine...*

*You* got the picture...Cousin was picking kids up—Idiot Brother, me, cousins, cousines—and throwing them around in the water. I was *bigger* than most of 'em, so he *had* to *plant* his hand between my *legs...*

Felt *good...*

It felt...*yeah*, a *lot*...went back three, four times...

He was *wiggling* his *fingers...*

He *was*...when the party spread out, Cousin *suggested...* not like it was a *romantic* seduction or anything...

Just *'let's get it on,'* and *you* were *off...*

*Just* like that. We snuck off to the basement...

Separately, of *course...*

Of *course*...I had my *bottom* off by the time *he...*

*Eager*, were you?

*Dripping* like a *percolator*...he got his *marble-bag* off...
And *he* was at *full-mast...*

*He* had a *tent pole*...we got *started,* and after a few *minutes* Mom turned the *lights* on and came *down* the *steps...*

*Whoops...*

*That* party *ended...*

I'll *bet...*have you...*with* him since...?

Have I...*what...? Have* a dog...

*You* know...thanks...

*Say* it...*mustard...?*

Yep...*and* horseradish... done the horizontal hula with him *since...?*

*Hell* no...

Curious: did you *enjoy* it...that *first* time...?

I *think* I enjoyed the *idea* of it more than the *reality*...I *didn't* finish, but it's *different* for girls...

Did *he...?*

Almost *instantly*, but he *kept it up* for *me*, I *guess*...end of the potato salad...now you know about *me*, Blondie; how about *you?* When was *your* cherry busted?

I didn't get *caught* with a *cousin* at fifteen...

So, who *was* it? Your senior prom date...?

*That* was Step-Sis; I went to *hers*; she went to *mine*...

Hers?

She went to a private school, and I was in public...

Ah. So when *was* it? Fair's *fair*, cowboy...

Do we *have* to talk about this *now?*

*Yes!* Fair's *fair*...

OK: my *first* sexual encounter was in college. We sat next to each other in a manufacturing processes class. She had a weird laugh. She'd *just* broken up with a guy she'd been with since junior high; the only boyfriend she'd ever *had*. We had *four* dates; we *did it* on our third. She didn't *mind* that I was...

Inexperienced...

Yeah...*then*, on the *fourth*, she said *I* wasn't *The One*...

*That's* always rough on *guys*...

Yeah...I *helped* her grow *up*, she said...

How *noble* of you...

Wasn't I *just. Thank* you...

OK: did *you...enjoy...your* first?

It was over *so fast* I...couldn't *tell*...

She subscribed to the old saw: by flirting with *many,* you *could* miss *The One*...

What *is* The One, anyway...?

Girl's superstition. It's the belief that there's only *one* guy for a girl...

You *buy* that?

If I *didn't,* I wouldn't have been *cruising* for the past *decade*... but...the other day, a guy walked into the bar and I asked him how it was *going. He* said 'holding my own.' I said, 'holding someone *else's* could get you *arrested*'...

*Heh-heh*...

Seriously, I *worry* about you, babe. You're surrounded by books and papers. Your *love* life...

Sucks *ditch*water, yeah...*you* keep *reminding* me...except for *you*...

*I* don't count...you work in your *office* or *here*. Not *much* of a life...

Life *enough,* honey. Not a lot of *cash,* either. *Most* months I'm *so* broke I can't pay *attention*. Besides, I *have you*. It's been *months* since you bought those *first* groceries for me and we *still*...

Wanna *stop*...?

Do *you*...?

*You*...?

I've come to *like* it...a *lot*...

Me, too...but *I* don't count as a girlfriend; not *that* way. *You* need...

You're *important* to me, Red; I *mean* it...

I *know*, but you're not *living*, Blondie; you're just *existing*.

It's a lot better than *not* existing...let's clean up...*that's*...

*My* phone...*my* machine will get it...

OK...*sounds* like...

*Mom*...*some* shit about Idiot Brother *again*...*shit*...

*Go* on, *get* it...get it *over* with...

***

*Hey*...

Hey...what's *on?*

Old western...what's *up*...?

Well, they haven't *arrested* him again, but he *has* got an *attack* of the *stupides*...

Stupid people were put here to test our anger management skills...

Don't *I* know it...I've gotta go over by the house...

*This* late? Want *me* to come *with*...?

*They're* not *ready* for *that*, babe. *Don't* wait up...hug for *courage?*

*Any* time, Red...

***

Hi...

Hi, Red...*late*...?

Yeah. Start *coffee?*

In the afternoon? O...K...Red...*what's*...?

Can you watch Sister's kids for a few hours next Saturday while we try to talk *sense* into Idiot Brother?

He's resisting giving up Moron...?

Yeah. So *can* you?

Um...are they housebroken?

They're *not* in diapers, but Three-Year-Old needs *help* for the bathroom.

Sister doesn't mind if this guy you *live* with takes her daughter to the bathroom?

It *was* her idea. The kids *like* you, especially after the party; the rest of my family—except Loser—are getting *used* to you...

*Used* to me...you *did* set them *straight* about us...?

I *did*. Other guys I've roomed with *this* long have been...

Ah-*hah*...and they've known *them* from the 'hood....

*And* they *don't* know *you* that *well* yet, but they *know* we're *not*...take the kids to the park for the afternoon...

I have a date Saturday *night*...

With *Legs?*

A woman at work asked me out for drinks. I'm not meeting *her* until 6, so if you're *done* by 5...

I'll make *sure* of it...Blondie, *I* need...

C'mere...

***

*Morning*, Blondie...

Morn*ing*, Red...

How did it go with the kids?

We played in the park. I amused *every*one by trying to get a hula hoop to work, failing abysmally. *Then* we had pizza. Twelve-Year-Old took Three-Year-Old to the bathroom...

Problem solved. How was your *date?*

*Brief*...

You *didn't* get laid...*again?*

She was *quite* up-front about that. She said she may never *have* sex again before *my* first drink arrived...

Wow!

Yeah, *tell* me about it. Before her *third*, maybe ten minutes later, she *loudly* announced that she most *definitely* would have *no more kids*...

*One more* embittered divorcee...

Indeed. She *then* said that I had to catch up. *I* said I wasn't interested in drinking and driving, said goodnight and left...

Shortest date I've ever *heard* of...

I'm mortally certain *I* was there only to keep her from looking like a woman drinking alone.

Sorry, Blondie...

*Why?*

That's just sad for *you*...

*Why?*

Don't you feel the *need* for female companionship?

At this point, I'm *mostly* concerned with paying my bills. For female *companionship*, I have *you*...

*I* don't count, babe; we're *not that* kind of...

You're a *female*; you're in my proximity nearly every *day*; we peck lips at *least* once a day; you *flash* your *damn*-near *everything*. We *hug*; you *massage* my *neck*; we make out once in a while, *and*, when you're *feeling it*, a little *more*. You find me *interesting*, and *like* living with me...that *not my type* bit is wearing thin...*how do you not count...?*

Don't *complicate* my *brain*...

Don't oversimplify *us*...

But don't you *enjoy* sex? Non-committal *romps* once in a while can...

I need *more* than casual, honey...none of my *affairs* have *ended* well...

Now *that* is *tragic*, babe...

Look, you're considering the need for sex from a perspective that's significantly different from mine. You're *used* to having it *more*; *I'm* used to having it *less*; that makes it more important to you. If *you* suddenly had to live *my* sex life... now that *would* be tragic.

Amen to *that! But*...ya know *what*...?

What...?

Our...ya know, when *we*...*you* and *I*...

Relieve *stress*...

Yeah...some of the *best* I ever remember having...

*Really*...?

Really...*heh-heh*...

*What?*

*Somehow*...*funny* how the mind works...*that* reminded me of something Sister told me last *spring*. Twelve-Year-Old was trying on a *very* skimpy bikini...*barely* covered what it was *supposed* to...

If *I* may *say* so, your niece is a very *mature twelve*...

*Tell* us about it. Sister took *one look* and said, 'if I had worn *that* in *public* when I was *your* age, *you'd* be six years *older*.'

*Ha-ha-ha*...

*Suffice* it to say, Twelve-Year-Old did *not* leave with *that* suit...

Yeah, I guess...so this *other* twelve-year-old asks her mom about the hair she's getting in her...

Yeah...?

Her mom just says 'that's your *monkey* growing up...'

Ah, *hah*...

So the twelve-year-old tells her *older* friend 'my *monkey's* growing *up*, getting *hair*...'

Uh...

And her *friend* says, '*that's* nothing; *mine's* eating *bananas*...'

*PWEEW...HAHAHA!*

So, how did it go with Idiot Brother? *Sister* wouldn't *say.*

*Now* you're changing the subject *again...*

*Not* gonna talk about *girls* and their...so...?

He's *stuck* on the idea that *snitching* is...

Would it help if *I* were to talk to him? A private chat with a disinterested third party about life choices and the justice system...*might* help.

Babe, sometimes *you* say the *strangest* things. You *can't* get *laid* in 1980, and *he's* supposed to listen to *you* about important life choices and the justice system?

There's *two* people who *know* about *my* sex life these days, honey, and *I'm* the *other* one, and *that* has *nothing* to do with the *other* stuff. What has your *family* got to *lose?*

***

I give *up.* How did you get Idiot Brother to agree to *that?*

Let me...finish *this*...paragraph...

What are you *working* on?

*Failed* cotton harvesters...there were a *lot* of 'em before the '60s... *aaand...done.*

OK, now spill.

OK, he *said,* his involvement *was* limited to *holding* for Moron. On *that* basis I convinced him that, at his *street-level,* his *code of silence* is *moviemaker bullshit,* a plot device to build tension. Normally, the *big* dogs know trying to control the street-level *rats* isn't *worth* the *exposure,* even to make *examples* of 'em...

Is *that...?*

He agreed he doesn't *know* much because he's not really *involved,* and he's not *important* enough for the goons higher up the food chain to care about what *little* he *knows...*

At least *that's...*something...

It's a *lot*. He *also* agreed that Moron will rat *him* out the first chance *he* gets. *That* leaves him with *two choices*: one *short*-term, one *long*; *both* painful. The *short*-term choice is to give up Moron and get *some* credit for coming clean, for which he'll do *some county* time...

You *think* so...?

Likely; *that* much weight's *got* to come with *some* penalties. The *long*-term will come if he clams up, because Moron will lay it all on him the *first* chance he *gets*. Idiot Brother makes *that* choice and he'll end up doing a *longer* stretch of *state* time...

Huh...how would *you* know about all *this*? You're not in law enforcement and you're *not* a criminal...

*Trust* me, Red; I *know* something about informing on assholes...

And you convinced Idiot Brother...how?

He looked into my eyes and saw that I spoke the *truth*, like Loser did.

I look into *your* eyes, Blondie and...holy *shit*, babe, I could lose my *mind* in those china-blues of yours! But *how* does that *work*...?

I clear my mind of uncertainty...of *all* doubt. If *I* don't believe what I'm saying, neither will *anyone else*...

*How?*

I tell myself that *whatever* the circumstance, *mine* is the *only truth worth believing*, the *only* way forward. That certainty *grounds* me like a *lightning rod*. Without *that*, I'll convince *no one* else; they'll *ignore* my *words*.

How did you get that, um, *talent*?

Can I *just* say that to survive in a *shitty* place, I *had* to develop the talent?

Need *more* than that.

Why?

I have to tell my family *how* you changed Idiot Brother's mind. The whole *mind-control* thing...how *you* got *that*. My family *isn't* gonna...*spill*, babe...

If I *do*, you *can't* share the *details*. I *don't* want people thinking I can't be trusted...about *anything*.

*They* trust you; *I* trust you...*give* me *some* credit...

OK...I spent a *year* in a minimum-security facility, starting when I was barely fifteen. To be accurate, I did eleven months.

*How* did you...*why?* I may not know *much*, but I know that a *year* in *jail* as a juvenile takes *some*...

I *beat* a kid's *head* in with a ball bat.

*Why?*

A buddy of mine lived across the street; a *good* buddy, *good* guy. A *little* goofy, a little *slow*, but, *you* know...

Yeah...

Buddy and I were messing around at the *neighborhood* pool and this bully—*notorious* asshole—decided it would be fun to spray deodorant in Buddy's face.

*Ow!*

He ran up to Buddy, held the can about an inch from his face, and *sprayed* back-and-forth. It happened so *fast*, no one could *stop* it. Then he *tossed* the can away and *laughed* while Buddy was stumbling and crying for help.

*Christ!*

Between the chemicals and the force of the spray, Buddy was permanently, *legally* blind; could see light and dark, but *no* details.

Oh, *wow*...

I *said Bully* did it; so did Buddy. We named everybody *else* who was around when it happened—there were maybe *ten* others—who *saw* what happened, but *they* all turned blind, deaf and dumb.

*Why...?*

Bully's old man said that Bully was *across town* when it happened. Old Man was a *very* influential guy around town, and *no one* was about to call *him* a liar...

*Ah...*

So a month *later*, Buddy took his dad's *shotgun* to his own head...

Shit...

Yeah. I *heard* it happen...

*Oh...*

I saw them from my front lawn as they took Buddy's body out in a blanket; saw his *blood* on the ambulance guy's uniforms. And there was Bully and Old Man, *right* down the street, laughing like it was *all* a *big joke...*

So *you...*

*I* don't remember *much* of what happened next. A dozen witnesses *said* I grabbed a ball bat off a neighbor's lawn, ran down the street and *knocked* Old Man in the head, then took after Bully. Next thing I *really* remember was getting handcuffed, looking down on Bully on the grass...

*Oh...*

Old Man's injuries were minor; Bully was *pretty* bad...

Ugh...

Despite Old Man's influence and friends in high and low places, there were enough witnesses for Step-Mom's law partner to defend me on the grounds of emotional distress and diminished capacity. *That's* why I only got a little less than a *year* in *minimum...*

Where you learned *certainty...*

Among *many* other things, yeah. It wasn't *exactly* a prison; but it *wasn't* a summer camp. There were bed checks every night and work details every day but Sunday. We got counseling a couple times a week *and* group therapy three times, but I could still keep up with school. In *my* units, we *had* to...

Units?

A dorm of sixteen guys; the guys in *my* units were all fifteen or so. Some were there for car theft, robbery, burglary, dealing and the like. There was one *other* guy in for assault like *I* was. *Some* were transitioning from juvie to *real* prison, including a couple of murderers and a rapist. Minimum security or not, there were guys in there who would break your arm because they were bored. But if somebody *saw* it and wanted to get into *another* unit...

*Suddenly* they remembered...

Yep. Some of those guys *may* have been criminals, but there were *damn few* rocket scientists among 'em. One day two guys got some smack in but no *works*. One cut the *other* guy's arm vein open with a piece of glass and *poured* the shit in...

Wow...

*After* he bled out, they asked around what happened and me and *another* guy told 'em what we *knew* because otherwise they'd punish the entire *unit* for it. We got put into segregation...

Segregation?

Single bunk rooms that *don't* socialize with the other units. *That's* where I spent *half* my sentence. *That's* where I learned that the code of silence for *most* guys is bullshit, 'cause the small fry just don't *matter*. I came out a month before I turned sixteen; *six weeks* before Step-Two and Step-Mom got engaged.

*Huh*...what did Step Two think of...

We *talked* about it; I satisfied him it was a *fluke* for which I was punished. Step-Sis *never* mentioned it except in relation to...

Your *lack* of girlfriends...*that's* why she wore that bikini: to show she wasn't *afraid* of you...

Huh...never *thought* of *that*. But...*Buddy* was the closest I ever *had* to a brother. Even after eleven *years*, sometimes I miss him *so* much it *still* hurts...shit...sorry...didn't *mean* to...

Babe, it's *OK*. C'mere...shh...shh...it's *OK*...shh...shh... shh...let *it out*...

***

Hey...

Hey...*hi!* What's with the *leotards* and the...*oh*, you're a *cat*...

*Purr, purr*, cowboy. How you *feeling?*

*I'll* be OK; back on the antibiotics *again*. Doctor says it's *just* another infection...keep getting *kicked* where I already *hurt*...your *hand* is cool...

Your *head* isn't...take some aspirin for that *fever*...

*Yes*, nurse...

*You* held *my* hand; *I'll* hold *yours*, babe...

You late tonight?

*Big* party for Halloween, so *probably*...*sure* you don't want to put in an appearance?

I just ain't *up* for it...have fun, honey...OW! *Whisker* in the *eye*...

Sorry; *price* we *pay* for *kisses*...get *well*, babe...

***

Blondie?

Huh?

Can I come *in*...I'm *just* out of the shower; no *alarm* in the morning; I'm in my *night*shirt...

Might as *well*; you're *here* now...

Can I sit *on* your bed?

Can I stop you...I don't *have* anything *on*...*sweating* like...

Want me to take my *nightshirt* off?

*No*; just...

Gimmie your *hand*...

Where are you gonna *put* it? I'm *not* up for...

Right *here* on the bed rail, with mine...just...like...*that*...the Halloween bash was a *colossal* success. We had bobbing for apples and a costume contest and a hayride...

Glad it worked out...

*Chesty* put in an appearance. Legs and Ponytail were *looking* for you, so were *Sister* and Mom and Dad...*I* missed you, too...

Sorry...*I* need rest...'night...*mmm*...

'Night...*mmm*...

*Red...mmm...honey...mmm...mmm*...

*Five* kisses tonight, babe, so you get better *five times faster.* 'Night.

'Night, honey.

***

Huh...? *What* the...*Red...Red*, honey...

Wha...what? *What's*....oh, *hi*, Blondie; *morning*...

*Morning*...how long have you...?

I've been here for the past few *hours*; wanted to make sure *you're OK*...

You didn't *have* to sleep *here* for *that*...

I wanted to be here for *you just* in *case*...

In *case* of *what?* I've got a *urinary* infection, *not*...ah, *never*... so...Red, are *you*...?

What...?

*In* the *altogether*...

*Look* for yourself, *cowboy*...just *look*...see...?

Uh-*huh*...*night*shirt...

Not *used* to a waterbed...*felt* it every time you *moved*... thought *sure* you were gonna wake up when I crawled *in*... *time* is it?

You gotta *be* somewhere?

Work tonight...but there's something I want you to *see* this morning...

*Not* where the *horse* bit you...

I've never been that *close* to a real *horse*...

I thought girls went through a *horsey* phase...

Not *me*. No; something *else*...

Then let's get *going*...

*You* first...

Why?

Because I want to *see* you in the *raw*...

OK...*happy* now?

You're *very* impressive, *cowboy*...

Get *over* me, little lady...I've *got* to go...

***

OK; what is it you want to show me...?

*This* is *our* final proposal...what I had *before* was just an *outline*...

Hm...I *see*...this...and...this...can all *this* be done...?

Boss's people are *saying* it's *workable*. All we need is *this*... and the *financing*...

*Uh-huh*...*good* plan, Red.

Thanks...*wow*...

Wow...*what*?

I did all *this* in the space of a few *weeks*...

Your business school's paying off...

But *that* was *your* idea...

*You'd* have come up with it, eventually.

*Maybe*...

You're *shivering*, Red...

*This* is *scary*, Blondie...

C'mere...you've taken it *this* far; you can take it *all the way*...

*Only* if...

If...*what?*

*You're...*

If I *can*...what are you *really* asking, Red?

What's for *breakfast?*

***

So, *Twelve-Year-Old* came as a...*what?*

Hippie flower girl. She found a picture of Sister and me in '69...

You were in those *flowered dresses...?*

*I* was; Sister only wore some *flowers* taped to her underwear...

And Twelve-Year-Old...?

*Copied* it with big felt daisies and sunflowers. I didn't think Sister could have been *more* embarrassed when Twelve-Year-Old said, 'but *Mom;* it's *just* like *yours...*'

What did your *folks* think...?

Mom said, 'I *told* you this would happen...' and Dad just shook his head...

I'll *bet*...ah, *shit...*

Your *phone...*

Yeah...the *machine*...and...it's the *hospital...yep;* threatening collection...

Sorry, babe...

Yeah...as if I didn't al*ready hurt* in the...

*UGH*...nothing to *compare* it to...

Lucky *you...*

Want an ice pack...hel*lo*...babe...?

How many gals would offer an *ice pack* to a *guy* for his...?

I *dated* athletes who hurt themselves in *their* nether regions; I *know* some things about *your...*

I'll *bet* you do...

*Here...have* some *frozen peas...what's* the difference between kinky and perverted?

Um... thanks...I *dunno*...

*Kinky* is when you tickle your boyfriend with a *feather*; *perverted* is when you use the *whole bird*...

*That's*...

What are the *two most important holes* in a woman's body?

*Well*, I...

Her *nostrils*...

*He-he*...

What goes *in* hard and comes out *soft and wet*?

Oh, *I* know this one...

Chewing gum...

HA-ha-ha...!

A kid gets lost in a big store. She walks up to a security guard and says she can't find her *dad*. The guard asks, 'what's he like?' The kid says, '*Mom* says beer and women...'

Well, *that's*...

In *bowling*, what's a *perfect* score?

Um...I *think*...

The *bartender*...

*Providing*...

Yeah...

That's...*better*, honey...

*Welcome*, babe.

# Loves the Holidays...

*Hey, Red. How was work?*

*Hey,* Blondie. *Not* bad. Burning *more* midnight oil, I see.

*Another* article...

I *just* saw Boy Across-the-Walk knocking on his door... wonder what *that's* about?

Maybe The Ex just dropped him off?

At *this* hour? No; the kid's *shivering* on their porch in this *icy rain* and *nobody's* coming to the door...

Mom Across-The-Walk's *number* is on the refrigerator; *call* her...

Yeah...

***

Huh; no answer. Wonder *what's* going on?

Dunno, but get him *over* here until his *mother* comes home... dry him off and warm him up...

*I'll* get him *here*; *you* handle the *rest*; I need a *shower*.

Just don't come *down* half...

You think I'd wear a ratty robe and slippers in front of our seven-year-old neighbor?

He's seen you in *less* when you're *sunning* yourself...

*True*, but...I'll *even* wear a *bra* for the first time all week. I'll be back...

***

Blondie; how's...?

*Shh...* he's *forcing* himself to stay awake...

What's he *watching?*

A Windy City station that pay TV puts on after *they* sign off...best way *I* knew to warm him up was...

Soup and your *quilt...*

That and getting him out of his wet clothes.

*Where's* his...does he have *underwear* on?

His clothes are in the dryer. I left his underwear on for *your* benefit, Red...

Thanks *so* much...*I* may have to force myself awake, too, waiting for *Mom* Across-the-Walk to come home...*if* she comes home tonight...she *doesn't*, always...

I'll wait *with* you...

***

*There* she is, Blondie...hey, *babe...wake...*

*Huh?*

Mom Across-the-Walk's *just* coming in...let's wake The Boy up...

*Time* is it?

*Quarter* to *two...*

Let *him* sleep. Get *her* over *here* so we can find out if we *need* to be concerned...

*Better* idea...

***

The Ex was supposed to *keep* him overnight but *brought him back*...want a *shot?*

Sure; warm *us* up...he didn't wait for Mom Across-The-Walk to open the *door*, either. The Ex probably had a *hot date.*

Some people play *dangerous* games with their kids. We need to watch *out* for The Boy.

Yeah...*you* went through a divorce.

But I knew *what* was going on and *why*...besides, both Step-Mom and I were *glad* to see the *north* end of Step One's *south*-bound *ass*...

I don't mean to pry.

Yet, you *do*, but I've come to *welcome* your *intrusions*. You've made me wonder why I've been *so* damn solitudinous...

Soli—*what?*

Solitudinous...*hell* of a word, *ain't* it...the state or habit of being characterized by solitude. I've *preferred* being alone until *not* very long ago...

Just hanging *out* with you, I learn things, even at two in the morning. Before I moved here, I wondered if you use a *dictionary* for toilet paper...

Ha. Ha...

So, why *have* you been so soli-*what-you-said*, and what's *changed?*

It's just felt...*safer*. Sometimes I think about that *semi-date* I was on with Co-Worker. She acts like it just *didn't happen* when we're at work. I *try* to do the same. I sometimes ask myself why I *didn't* just get hammered *with* her and try to *talk* her into the sack.

Because you didn't really *want* to?

But *part* of me *did*. *Part* of me thinks I've been actively using my *eremitic* personality for birth control...

*That's* funny...but...*what* kind of personality...?

Hi-*larious*...eremitic; reclusive; stand-offish; hermit-like...

Oh...*well*...

But *part* of me *wants* to get *lucky* with someone who cares for *me* as much as I care for *her* just to see if I *enjoy* it.

How often *have* you...?

Heat and friction: *less* than a dozen but *more* than a *half-dozen*. With someone I really *cared* for: a *lot* less than a half-dozen...

*Less* than...?

I sometimes go out in the weeds in the summer so *something* would *suck* on my *neck*...

HA!

My doctor asked if I engage in regular physical activity. I asked if sex counted and he said yes. I said, 'then, no.'

HEHE...but now...another *shot?*

Yeah, why not...to be *honest*, there's been a couple nights and *mornings* I've been tempted to go into *your* room...

What's *stopped* you?

I value our friendship too much to take *that* risk.

What *risk*...after *we've*...?

My doing *that* without your *permission would* change *us*, and *maybe not* for the better. *No* amount of mere *desire* is worth losing a friend and I don't *have* enough of 'em to *spare*...

*Most* nights or mornings, babe, I *wouldn't* stop you...

*Some* you *would*...?

*Not* many...but I *wouldn't* get *mad*...

Then I'd just be one *more*, honey...

*No*, babe. *You're* different...

Different...*how?*

Since I've lived here, I *never* locked my door.

Why *not?*

Because I've trusted *you* from the beginning. Can't say *that* about *any* of the *other* guys I've lived with.

Why?

You're *not* from the 'hood; you were *respectful* to me New Year's when *I* was something of a *bitch*; you have a *houseful* of *books* and no smut *anywhere* that *I've* seen...

That's...*good*, I *guess*...*some* nights I want to cuddle, then I remember...

*Next* time, knock *softly*...

*You've* made me *want* to be more *sociable*.

*I* did?

*You* did.

Blondie...*babe?*

Huh...*honey?*

C'mon over *here*, babe...

Come over *here*...

OK...we're *not* going to *do* anything...just *hold hands*...

This feels like a first date...

First date *after* sharing a bed?

*That* was...not to mention...

*Those joy* times, yeah...

*This* is nice...quietly sharing...

*Space* together...I get the feeling you got something *else* on your mind...so...*spill*...

Red...*honey*, can *we*...

Just *ask*, babe...

*Cuddle? Tonight?*

***

*Hey*...

*Hi*...what *are* you...?

Just...coming *around*...and...

*Spooning*...you *are* warm...and *wearing*...*what*...?

*Later*...

*Mm*...what's...*that's* our *neighbors*...at a *quarter* to *three* in the morning...and *loudly*...

I *hear* 'em...she must have a *fever*.

What makes you say *that?*

Women get a slight fever when they *ovulate*. They want a *baby*, so...

Ah...well, *they* didn't take long...

Yep. *He* was ready...

Sounds like *she* was, too...

Are our pornographic neighbors giving you *ideas?*

*You?*

I'll *check you* for my*self*...huh...I can *feel*...yeah, *you're* coming around...*want* to...?

*Please* don't, Red...

Why *not...?*

'Night, honey...

'K...'night...

***

Blondie...*hey*, babe!

*Huh?*

*Morning*, babe...

*Morning*...hi, Kitty...

*Where's*...purring and taking a *bath* on the end of the bed.

She's *hungry*...

*Probably*. I think that's the *soundest* sleep I've had in a *long* time...

The *second* time I've *ever* woken up with a woman in my bed...

That's *genuinely* sad, babe.

Why?

Waking up with a lover is the *very best* thing to do...*babe*, can we *please* take *this languorous intimacy I'm* feeling to its logical conclusion? *I* can...

I *like* you, Red...but I *don't*...

I like *you*, Blondie...a *lot*...can't *that* be *enough?*

Red, *you* haven't bunked out since you *moved* here, and I haven't *seen* any guys on sleepovers *here*, either...

There haven't *been* any sleepovers...but I *can* be *very* convincing...I *won't* say I *never will* give more for *real*, but... *love* and *lover* are *not* the same, babe...

For *me*, they *need* to be...at least, *something closer* than...

*I* can be...*Kitty's* gonna see if it's warmer *under* the covers ...coming up *your* side, taking the *long* pillow route...and...

*PFFFT!!*

*HA!*

*Ho* and *ha*, it *is* to *laugh*...flick your *tail* in my *face* while you're *deciding*, cat, and *I'll*...

C'mon, Kitty, get under there...*that's* a good girl...what *are* you *staring at* so *innocently now...?*

Your...what *is* that?

Teddy *top*...

Is...*very short*...and *no*...

*The pants* get all twisted up in *bed*...*don't* forget where my *face* is, cowboy... now...*gaze*...*up*...can *we*...*please*... *babe*...?

You *know* what *I need*...

Yeah...but...*sometimes*...*grownups*...

Yeah...I *know*...but some grownups get it *wrong*, and I don't want that to be *us*...I don't want to ruin us *just because we can* and *you're*...

But...*just* some *more complete joy*...

Look, neither of us wants to ruin whatever we *got*. We haven't *talked* about love, but it *feels* like we're dancing around the edge of it. Maybe that's where we're headed...I don't *know*...

*Love* and *lover* don't *have* to be synonymous...

I've avoided *using* the word because I *don't* want to scare you *off*...

*But*...

Love *should be more than* just *sticking it* in a warm and moist place, or *having* it *stuck*, because it *feels* good...*I've gotta have more than a burst of passion, honey*...I don't *know* where love starts...but...*huh?*

You *done* now...?

Yeah...

*Nursing* is where *real* loving starts, babe. *That's* why guys are so hung up on breasts and *you* keep *glancing* at *mine*...

*Yours...ah...are* kinda *falling out*...

In *polite* company they're called *breasts*...I'll make 'em *easier* to *ogle...see?*

Ah...Red, as *much* as I'd...you're *not* offering to *nurse* me *just* so...?

If I thought it would *help* you, I *would*, but no woman can give a grown man an understanding of *loving* by shoving a boob in his puss, as tempting as *that* is right now...

*I* was never nursed...

I *gathered*... if a guy doesn't understand *loving* as an infant, getting him to *feel* it *later*...I don't *know* how...

I can foresee...something...sometime...can you *wait?*

I *can*...even if...*now I really*...

Even if I'm *not* your type, I *seem* to have done OK with *you*...

*Any* guy who's *not* a caveman has not *been* my type.

So I'm *not* a troglodyte.

A *what?*

Caveman; a cave-dweller.

*Why* do I *like* you so much? Why do I find just *talking* and... in bed to be...I dunno...pleasant, yet...not as *arousing* as... despite *your*...

If I recall, *talking* in bed can be followed *quickly* by...

Yeah...if it *wasn't* for the *cat* taking her *bath* between us right now, *I'd*...

*You can remove her...*

*Want* me to...?

*Only* if...

No...there's more than *her* between us...being in bed while you are *not* trying to jump my bones...even with *that* in your *pants*...

Your lack of modesty is *endearing*, I admit...and *this*...is unique in my experience...

Babe, *I can't* do *this* too often; go *this* far without...go, Kitty... need to get *closer* to Daddy...

*Real* close...you *have* to...relieve *your* stress...you *know* what I *need*...to...yet...as *much* as *you*...

*You're ready* for this...*look* at my *face*, babe...just...be *still*...

O...K...*then*...

*Have* to...just...*hook* my *leg*...and *press*...

Mm...*oo*...that's...*AH!*

*YEAH!*

***

You *OK*, babe...?

*Fine...hoh...fine*...honey...

If *you* were *any other guy* in the *world*, we'd have *done it* several times already...

If you were any other *gal* in the world...hell, *I* don't know...

But *better* than Mother Thumb...?

*Much*...but... *what* about *your*...*stress*...?

Mine's...*fine*...

***

*Breakfast* before I go for groceries?

Um...sure...honey, *we* need to...

Yeah. Something is *definitely* off with my *seduction* skills... couldn't get *into* your pants and I was nearly *naked* in bed...

It's *not* that; your *skills* are fine. It's...ow...

You've got *something*...you're in *pain?*

Toothache... *just one* of *several* cavities I can't *afford* to *fill...*

Oh...*since...?*

I woke up. Just been getting *worse*...before it gets *too* bad, Red; I need to tell you that when I wake up with it like *this* I know it'll get worse as soon as my heart starts pumping more...

So, you *didn't* want *sex* because it would make your *toothache* worse?

Yeah...

Babe, that's *too lame* an excuse from a *gal*, but from a *guy*, it's *gotta* be true. You gonna *be* OK? We *did...*

Yeah...but it didn't *take* much...um...

I never *need* much...*I've* gotta get to the store and get ready for *work...*

*Sunday?*

Boss has some *family* thing today...

***

*Hey!* How's your *toothache?*

*Better.* Took some of my painkillers I had left over, so at least it's not as distracting...does a *job* on my attention span, but...

I'd offer you a *shot* of something, but...

Better *not.* The stuff I took is pretty heavy-duty...*you're* home early...

Yeah...pretty *dead*, even for a Sunday, so I closed early... babe, I *know* a dentist who...

Honey, it's *OK*...this ain't *that* bad that I can't *function*. Besides, compared to kidney stones, *this* ain't nothin'...and I *didn't* find money anywhere to *pay* for it...

You *sure?*

Yeah.

Let me get a shower and I'll be back down.

***

Hey...

Hey...what's *on?*

Last-minute *political* ads every *ten minutes* on the network stations; something *freakish* on pay TV; a *limey* show on public broadcasting; some *stupid* things on the independents...

And you *settled* for...?

Public broadcasting. Fewer ads...

Ah...what's *Kitty*...?

She *dashes* up from the basement, *jumps* up on the sofa, *stares* at me wide-eyed, *licks* herself a few times, then dashes *off* again...*there* she goes *upstairs*...

Why does she *do* that? Not the *first* time...

They *call* it a 'mad minute.' *Hunting* instinct, maybe.

Huh...this show is about veterinarians...?

Yeah. *It's* not *bad*; funny sometimes...ah...your brain's on overload again?

That *OK?*

*That's* OK...

***

Red...*Red*, honey...

*Huh...?*

175

We fell asleep...TV's signed off; it's nearly *one* in the morning...

Uh...how's your tooth?

*Pain-free* for the moment...

You get *up* in another...

Three *hours*, but I *need some*...

Want company?

Um...

Maybe *I* killed your toothache...

Worth a *shot, but*...

No *head* in *lap* in *bed*...

*And* your *nightshirt*...

***

*Ugh!*

Just my *alarm*...

Mm...toothache?

Um...nope.

I *cured* you.

If *only*...I'm gonna get going...

*Have a good day*, babe...

You too, honey...

***

Hey, Blondie. *What's* the...

Hey; *looks* like we'll have a new commander-in-chief. President Peanut gave it up to The Gipper before *dark*. Did you *get* to vote?

Yeah. Same precinct as I voted in *last* time.

Hope The Gipper's scarier than President Peanut. Amateur couldn't keep the embassy safe.

Yeah. When it *snows*, what's *our* responsibility?

Why? You see flakes?

Just wondering.

We should clear our sidewalk and whatever we need to get to the garage and out of the driveway.

Good to know. *Here!*

*Woah*...a check for *a hundred bucks?*

Boss *loved* your frame sample. And *here's* my *rent.*

*Bounty* from *heaven*...does he want *more frames?*

*Three* more by the end of this month. *Here's* the dimensions...

*What...?*

*Just* like the sample, Boss says. Now, how long does it *take* to make *one* of those frames?

Raw stock to finished assembly labor's maybe *two* hours and three for stain and finish.

Material cost?

Um...*this* frame stock's $3 a foot. The *matt's* $4 a sheet and I can get *two* this size out of a sheet; add the glue, stain, and *finish...thirty* bucks.

So, *thirty* bucks and *five* hours and you've got a *hundred* in your pocket. Woodburn a name and you can fetch *three times* that. Feel *better* now?

You've got a better head for business than *I* do. *Wow...*

Looks like your hobby's gonna pay off. Hey-*hey*, what is *this*, tears of joy?

*Relief...wow...so...relieved...*like *catching* a *life preserver...*

And *you* have *another* toothache...

*Yeah...*

S'OK, babe...shh...*relax*...shh...did you *eat?*

Not that *hungry...*

You need to keep your strength up. How about some scrambled eggs?

Yeah; OK.

***

Thanks for the *late* dinner, Red...

Welcome...*I'll* just...

Hope we don't fall *asleep* like this again. Freshly scrubbed woman's head in my lap *could*...

It's not that *late* and *I'm* not that *tired*. What are we watching?

A whodunit that I'm not sure I'm *following* after taking another *pill*...

*And* eating a *small* meal...oh, I *like* that actress...

Yeah, she's good...

Your stomach's growling...

Still *hungry*...

Banana?

OK...*thanks*...you OK watching this sideways like that?

Yeah...how's the toothache?

Controllable...with your *head* in my *lap*...controllable...

Maybe I should rent myself out as a painkiller...

*Then* you could cover your *rent* at the *beginning* of the month...

For *that* snide remark, I should *sit up*...

Manage my *toothache* again and I might *forget* your *rent's* a *month* behind...

I've *got* it...still *want* it?

What do *you* think...?

***

Hey! Mom wants you to come to Thanksgiving dinner.

In days of yore, an unmarried person inviting a member of the opposite sex to a holiday meal with the family was significant, like they were an *item* or something.

You're *not* the first guy I ever invited...

Maybe I should be insulted...

You *want* to come or not?

Since I have no other invitations, sure. *What* shall I *bring*?

Your appetite. *Don't* bring wine or anything else.

Good. I don't know enough about wine to *buy* it.

OK, so three o'clock Thursday at my *parent's* house...

Red, I *think* we can go *together*...

Oh, yeah. Never *did* that...huh...*what*...?

Just thinking about last *Thanksgiving*...

*What* was...?

Ever spend Thanksgiving in a *hospital*, hooked up to an *IV* with a *catheter* and a *bag*...alone?

Nope; *you* won't *this* year, either, babe; not if *I* can help it...

***

Thanks for inviting me, Red...despite *another*...

Thanks for *coming* despite *another* toothache. You did well in the card game afterwards, even *after* your pill. Won *Dad* over.

It's just rummy.

It's Dad's favorite game. I was never very good at it. *You* cleaned up.

Just chips. Whenever there's *real* money on the table, I always lose.

You play often?

Just socially.

Did your family tie on the feed bag at Thanksgiving?

Usually. Step-Mom *didn't* in '68 when she divorced Step One; we went out to the club. Step Two and Step-Sis *joined* us at the club in '69. In '70 I was inside; '71 was him and *both* his kids and his grandkids...

You should reach out to your stepmother...

Yeah; I'll call her *now*...

***

*That* was a pleasant chat.

Didn't mean to put you on the spot, but she *wanted* to talk to *you*.

That's OK; *she* wanted...*you* were sitting there listening; why do I *have* to...?

You *don't.* I didn't know Step Two had *another* grandkid now...

How well do you *know* Step-Bro?

Hardly at all. *Nice* talking to Step-Sis...

What's *she* do?

Med school...there's a Christmas movie on if you're interested...

OK...want something to drink?

Um...water?

***

Just because it takes place *at* Christmastime does *not* make it a Christmas *movie*, Blondie...

Maybe not, but it *was* a *brilliant* performance by some out*standing* actors...

That *woman*; the lead *actress*...

She does good work. The *only* woman to win Best Actress three times...

Huh...this is our *fifth* date, Blondie...

Yeah? That makes *us*...?

In *dating* terms...going steady.

OK...*then*...?

*Then...most* couples who have reached the *age* of consent...

Red, I value our *friendship* too much to ruin it with *sex* simply because we've reached some im*aginary milestone*...

*Not* imaginary; it's in *all* the *magazines*...

The *women's* magazines?

The *teen* mags, but it's mostly girls reading *them*...want *company* tonight, babe? I *promise* I *won't* lust after you in bed...

De*spite* our...?

No...

No official *fifth-date* ceremonies...

See you *up* there, babe...in my *nightshirt*...

***

*This* is nice...

It *is*. Gimmie your *hand*, now...'night. *Happy* Thanksgiving; hope your toothache goes away...

Thanks; *you* too. 'Night.

***

Morning.

*Morn*ing...*bright* morning...

How's the toothache...?

In a*bey*ance, once again, thanks to what*ever* it is *you*...

Ab...*bay*...*yeah*...gimmie *both* your hands, babe...*look* at me...my *eyes*...what could be a *better* time to make love to someone for the *first* time than on the morning after Thanksgiving?

I...dun*no*, what *could* be?

The instant *after* we say we *love* each other. Can *you* do *that* now?

*I'm* not...*sure*...I get the feeling *you* can't, either...

Are we trying to *tell* each other something?

*What?*

We're *waiting* for each other?

Now *that*...

Uh-*huh*...I've gotta *work* this afternoon; might be *late*...

Black Friday a big day for neighborhood tap rooms?

So Boss tells me. But *first*...

What...you're *very close* again...

Mind...?

We gonna *come close* again...?

*You* still have your *pants* on...and...

OK; you *don't*...c'mere...

*Oh! On top! Woah*...gotta... *DON'T stop*...now...ahh!

*AH!*

***

You *OK?*

I'm...*great*...you?

*Never*...better...

That was *some* heat and friction, babe...

It *was*...

So...*what's* the *difference*...? We *both*...what's...?

If I take my pants *off*...it's *real*; it's *commitment*; it's...

Lovemaking...

It's *that*...

And not *quite* as *messy* in your *pants*...

*No*, but...don't *trivialize*...

But those *pants* of yours...the fabric's a little *coarse* on *my softer* parts...

Sorry...

No; *don't* be. I'm just *trying* to say...

I have *flannels*...

Now *that*...but our *feelings* are the same...

Can you *honestly* say 'love' yet?

I'm not...sure...

As much as I care for you *I'm* not sure either. But, *just now,* I *had* to...

*Something* took over...it was very *gentle* for something you couldn't *control*...*I've*...

I *know*...let's...

Yeah...*think* about...

What's *next*...

***

Hey...*a Christmas tree?*

*Hi,* Blondie...plastic. I *keep* it at...

Huh...you've got *ornaments* and the whole...?

Yeah...garlands; lights; even plastic icicles...

Kitty is *very* interested...

That's why I've put it on the *platform* you made for my *plant*...

Where'd you put your *plant?*

On top of the water heater; Kitty can't jump *that* high... found *your* ornaments...I could hardly *miss* a box labeled *Christmas*...

That white clothespin reindeer; my *mother* made that when *she* was a *kid*...

Oh...who's in the picture on the *snowflake*...?

Me and my dad...I was *eight months* old...

And the *brown* clothespin reindeer...?

Step-Mom and I made *that* when I was six. Still remember how *proud* she was when I got the *eyes* glued on right...I didn't *do* anything *last* Christmas...

*This* Christmas, you *will*, babe...found *that*, too...

Step-Sis shot *that* into the box as a *joke* when I was moving out...

Mistletoe?

Yeah...

*I'm* not laughing...c'mon...

Your *wish* is *my*...mmm...

***

Hey. See the news, Blondie? It's *tragic.*

Hi, Red; *yeah.* There will never *be* a Fab Four reunion, now.

Sad. The guy that shot him *resented* his *lifestyle?*

That's what they *say.* Makes more sense than the *government* did it.

*What?*

Some kid in the grocery store said that this morning. The news is just *full* of *that* today. *Forget* everything *else* that's going wrong all *over.* All that's *important* is that a Lad from Liverpool got killed by a loony in the Big Apple.

That's *harsh,* Blondie.

*That's* the real world, Red. What have you *got* there?

Crocheting yarn and a smaller hook. Going to hook some *tops* for Sister's kids for Christmas...

Um...if I *might*...

What?

*I* believe your *nephew* might prefer a *vest* or *sweater* to a *top.*

Huh...you *might* be *right.* Need a *pattern* for...*I'll* figure it out...what's *that* you're *scribbling* on?

*This* is a markup for my new *resume.* I got a call from a headhunter, says there's a *market* for tech writers...

Oh...you, ah, un*happy* with Big Boss?

I'm unhappy with the *money* he pays me that doesn't let my

*head* get above water; he says he can't do any better *now*. Selling frames *helps*, but ultimately it's nothing more than *pocket change* compared to what I *owe...*

I need a shower...

***

So what prompted this sudden *urge* to get a new job?

I got *another* call...as I walked in the *door* yesterday; an unfamiliar voice from the finance company—that's *two* calls in *three days*. They're *getting belligerent...*you're still working on that *skirt* for your *niece?*

Um, *yeah...show* me your...*wow!* You had a *4.0 GPA* in high school?

Yeah...call me a *nerd...*

*I* barely graduated with a 2.0 the *state* required...

How are you doing *now?*

Now *you* have to call *me* a *nerd...*you did the *same* in *college?*

Kept me *busy...*

Yeah...Blondie, I want to *say* something that *you...*

I'm not *about* to ask your *family* for a *loan...*

I *want* to say that *we'll* work all this *finance* stuff out...

As much as I appreciate...why *we? One* thing to *say* it when I'm *blubbering...*

*And* under my sweater. Because, babe, I *want* to. There *may* be *something* in the not-too-distant future that could change *both* our lives...something *big...*

You gonna win a *lottery* someplace? Inherit a *fortune* from a rich uncle who named *you* as his sole beneficiary?

Just...*trust* me on this...*OK?*

I *trust* you...OK...*still* gonna *update* my resume...see what *might* be out there...

***

Hey, Blondie...*what* are you...*looking* at...from the *kitchen*...?

Do you *know* our Kitty-Corner neighbors?

The guy's a teacher at my school. Don't know his wife that well; she's not *from* the neighborhood. Never *met* the kids; they *avoided* me when I was out in the sun...why?

Heard a ruckus back there as I was coming home. Didn't *sound* good...

What *kind* of ruckus?

Stuff *breaking*...ended *very* suddenly...

That was...*how* many hours ago...?

*Too* many...no lights over there *now*...

There's a *light* upstairs, behind a curtain. *Your* room might have a better view, babe...

Yeah; let's *have* a *look*...

***

Not a *curtain*, Red; like the window's *covered* over...

Mom Across-the-Walk's home...I'm gonna *talk* to her...

I'll go *with* you, Red...

***

Hear that *crying* through the *wall* of *her* bedroom, Red...?

*The Boy* can hear it, too...kid's *terrified*...

I didn't know The *Ex* was in the sheriff's department. She's afraid something'll *happen* if she *calls*? *Bullshit*...*she's* been abused, too...

*Signs* are there...

How about *your* friend the deputy, Red?

Yeah...*I'll* call *now*...

***

So *many* deputies and *city cops*...

Standard for domestic calls...most *dangerous* kind...

You know this *how?* Your *personal* deputy sheriff...?

Yeah...didn't really *know* him in school, but I ran into him after he joined the department...

Date much?

Some. Didn't *go* anywhere, but we...

How many guy friends have you got that you didn't *do it* with?

More than a *few*, babe...you've *met* most of 'em...

You need a *shower* yet...?

Do I stink *that* bad?

*No*, but...

After the cops all *leave...you* should go to bed.

With all those *lights* in the driveway...? One's coming to the door...

***

*Damn;* I *should* have *known*...

*How*, Red?

I *should* have seen the bruising on her *and* the kids. And *he's* a *teacher?*

Not for *long*; not after *this*.

Maybe not...*oh*...

Red, *you...Red?* Hey, *Red? You...? Red*, honey, c'mon... shh... come *on*; let's get you to *bed*...just...*let it out*, honey ...*let... it...out...*

***

*Shit*, I *hate* when I do *that*.

Just what was *that*, Red? Looked *personal*...

It *was*; it *is...I* need to *soak* in the *tub*...

***

*Sure* you want the curtain *open?*

Nothing on *me* that *you* haven't *seen*...let's *wait* till the tub fills up *and* I put my *hair* up...

*That* looks like a *lot* of *work*...

*Some* days more than *others*...this is just a big *braid and wrap*...I need to *wash* it...hand me that big *claw* clippie on the toilet top, *will* ya?

Here...

Water feels *good*...*join* me in here...?

Tub's *way* too small for two...

You're not *that* much bigger than me...

An *inch* taller, but *you're* a tall woman...

And *tired*...*watching* the *water* rise...

Like watching *paint* dry...

Or *grass* grow...

Or coffee to perk...

***

Or *water* to boil...

Or *grades*...

Or *checks*...

Or the right *guy*...

Or the right *girl*...

***

*And*...as the water *reaches* your *chest*...talk...

Gimmie your *hand*...

Stop *stalling*...

*Shh*...

Don't *shush* me or *I'll* just get ready to go to *work*...

*Don't*...please...

Let's *hear* it...

Just...a...*minute*...babe...

***

OK, *I'm*....

My best friend in high school got married a year after we graduated. I stood up for her; she was pregnant at the altar. *Everyone* knew it. At least, we *thought* everyone knew...

OK...the *guy* didn't...

The shitheel *said* he didn't...

And he freaked when she *reminded* him...

*Worse* than that. He denied ever *having sex* before their wedding night.

Ah. So...

So he beat her up. *I* took her to the hospital; he'd busted an eye socket. Shitheel came all apologetic, said he didn't know *why* he went off like that. She *loved* him, so she for*gave* him.

Funny *meaning* of *love*...

Yeah...I *like* this...

Uh-*huh*...that *wasn't* the end of it...

Not hardly. While Friend was in the hospital, Shitheel came by me, said if I ever *hid* her like *that* again he'd come after *me*. Next thing anybody *knows*, our *dog* was poisoned. *Dad* filed an order of protection.

Shit. Did you *know* this guy *before*...?

I *thought* we did...babe; we've been *up all night*...adjourn and reconvene in your *bed* in *half an hour*?

Yeah...sure...

***

Nightshirt...?

*And* teddy pants...and *you're* in...*flannels*...where *was* I?

Um...someone poisoned your dog while Friend was in the hospital...

Yeah...so, everything *seemed* OK with them until Friend went into labor. Then Shitheel locked her in a closet...

Like *Kitty-Corner Neighbor* did...?

Yeah. But *she* only had a *busted jaw*...

*That's* why *you*...

Yeah. Friend cried for help for *hours* until the neighbors came home, called the cops and they busted the door down. They found her in the closet and the cord had strangled the baby. The doctors couldn't save Friend without a hysterectomy...

Shit...

Shitheel strolled into the police station *three days later*—found the cop's card at the apartment—said he was on a *business trip* and didn't understand why she wouldn't answer the *phone*. Since no one else was *in* the apartment all this time, they couldn't *prove* he *didn't* call.

Oh, my *God*...

Yeah. But he went to the hospital and Friend *screamed* at him for locking her in the closet. Shitheel said he didn't know the closet *could* lock. On top of *that*, he says that Friend had been *depressed*, didn't *want* the baby. Nobody could *prove* anything else, so...

Nothing happened...

*Nothing.* Friend didn't *want* to go back to him, so *we* got an apartment together, over where *you* were when *you* first moved here...

A step above a trailer park...*I'm* falling asleep, babe...

Me, too...

*****

Coffee? Mom Across-the-Walk's off to work...

Thanks...yeah; right about *now. You're* late for work, babe...

I can plead a migraine, honey; neither of us *slept* more than two hours before my *alarm* went off...*you* OK?

I'll be *fine*, babe...I'm gonna call in sick today...wanna hear the rest...?

Sure...

After a couple of months, Shitheel knocks on our door and says he wants to *talk*. They go back and forth through the door and she finally let him in just to get it *over* with.

*Big* mistake...

You *know* it. Next thing *I* know, Shitheel's walking Friend to the balcony with a *gun* to her head. I said I'd call a cop if he didn't leave and *he* said *I'd* be *next* if I *did*. I called anyway, got a frypan out of the kitchen but by the time I could get *back*, he's got her standing on the railing—we were on the third floor—hollering about how she killed *his* baby...

Suddenly it was *his*..?

Yeah. Said she *made* them take her *girl-parts* because she wanted to *deny* Shitheel *his* children. He screams, '*either jump or take a bullet.*' I threw the frypan at him; got him in the shoulder. He turned around and was pointing at *me* before a cop busted the door down and *winged* him...

*Wow*...

Yeah...

Honey, I gotta ask: you gonna have your *rent* next month?

*Yeah*, you *miser*. I feel like a *stew* tonight.

Sounds *great*, honey...

If you plead migraines...do you ever *get* them?

*Oh*, yeah...like a spike in my right *eye* and my whole *right side* goes numb.

Didn't know guys *got* migraines...

*This* guy does. Doctor thinks mine are *allergy*-related, but he can't *find* any allergies in the standard tests. Might be some *foods*...

*My* cooking or *yours?*

Haven't *had* a real one since...*huh*...since I had *barbecue* at Big Boss's last *event*...

Something to *think* about. Take anything *for* it?

I've got some heavy-duty painkillers just in case...know what? Maybe *I'll* take a sick day, *too*...

I gotta *warn* ya: I'm gonna *wash* my *hair* today...

So *I* should...?

Just...*fair warning*...

I can *duck* when you *whip* it...

I can *whip it good*...

***

Got enough *towels* there, Red?

Don't want to get the sofa wet...*damn mess*...*love* it when it's clean, but *managing* it is a *pain* in the...*duck*...!

Flail away...does doing that *work*...? Makes my *head* hurt *watching*...

*Better* than...*now* these *knots*...

They're not *that* bad...

*Grab* a *brush* and *help* me de*tangle* it, *wiseguy*...not *that* bad *my*...

'K...*here's* one...just...like *that*...

One day I *will* get it *all cut off*...like *yours*...

You'd *look* funny...there's...*another* one...*just*...*see* how *easy?*

Just keep *at* it...

*Another* knot...like...*that*...

*How* is it *you* can pull them out *faster* than *I* can?

I can *see* them better? Beginner's luck? How should *I* know?

*Kitty*, baby, *don't* play with Mommy's things...*red* hair on a *black* cat...

She *does* like your scrunchies.

I *know*; keep finding them in the basement after she bats them down there...*headband* down there the other...

*Beautiful*, like burnished *copper*...

I *work* on it enough...enjoy the color *now* because it'll be *brown* in ten years or so...

Hope I still *know* you in ten years...

*Me...too...*UGH...*that's...the...last...then* it goes white; *not* gray...*now* all I need to do...placenta...I'll go put *it* in...*time* is it now?

Two-forty five...

It's got to *sit* for an hour...so...*three*-forty five, then rinse it out...dinner at five?

Sure. So, after all *that*, how's Friend *these* days?

She had a breakdown a year or so later, never *fully* recovered; in and out of institutions. I *think* she's living on the streets somewhere...your *phone*...

*Machine*...what about *Shitheel?*

Somebody shot him in the head *four times* last year... what's...who's *that?*

The archdiocese inviting *faithful* couples for *fellowship*... huh? Any idea *who* shot him?

*Yep*...want I should pick up your phone and take him *up* on it?

That *might* be fun, but let's *not* waste his time...well, Friend got some *justice*...here's another of *your* movies...

Placenta...I'll be *back*...

***

How many movies *have* we watched here today, Blondie?

I lost track...*four* or *six?*

Can't *say*...*slept* through *half* of 'em. Had breakfast and dinner *all* in the living room...

*Yeah*...and *you* worked on your *crocheting*...

Yeah; got *most* of it *done* at the expense of the *chapter* I was *supposed* to *read* today...and now I've got a *reason* to *shave* my legs in the winter...

Yeah?

*You.*

How often *do* you...?

*Rarely; mine* aren't *that* bad...*you* like 'em, though, *don't* ya?

You *know* I do...

And you've been *ogling* 'em all *day*...

Yeah...can *I* ask a...

*What's* stopped you *before*...?

As an almost-engineer, I'd like to *know*...that *top* you've got on...I can see *through* most of it, but *not*...

The *important* parts...wish you had a pair of those x-ray glasses...?

Those things don't *work*...

How do *you* know those glasses *don't* work?

A *friend* snagged some; they create an optical illusion.

A *friend* named *Blondie*...as your *tenant*, I have to ask *when* are you gonna turn up the thermostat? You've *gotta* see the *goosebumps* on the *legs* you've been *drooling over* all day...

I can't *see*...

Well, *look*, babe. Look *closer*...

Ah...OK; *I* see 'em. *Cold* snap today, but gas ain't *cheap*... gonna try a kerosene heater somebody at *work* is *dumping*

...you *working* tomorrow?

Gotta make the *rent,* you *skinflint.*

Then *I'm* for bed, honey. 'Night.

'Night...

***

Hey, Blondie. What's *that?*

Kerosene heater. I *told* you I was gonna *get* it...

*Oh,* yeah. How's it work?

Turn the knob to *there;* press *this* till it lights...like *that;* trim the flame...like *this.*

*Wow. Yeah;* that's *warm.*

The kerosene can's out in the garage.

Set it in front of the fake fireplace and the TV.

That's closer to *my* end than *yours*...

Maybe I'll spend more time on *your* end. Kerosene cheaper than gas?

Gasoline is nearly a buck twenty a gallon now; kerosene is not *quite* ninety cents; the natural gas bill was fifty bucks *last month* and will only go *up.* Let's see how much kerosene this thing consumes in a night. Got a new *action* movie on...

Popcorn?

***

I'm gonna knock off, Red. The kerosene gauge...says it's... over *three-quarters* full.

Huh. It was on for *five hours?* Sure made it warmer in *here*...

It *did.* Colder in the *rest* of the place because the thermostat's just over *there.*

Yeah. I'm nice and *warm* now. Why did you shut it off?

*Can't* leave an open flame all night.

I can *feel* the cold coming back...

Science defines cold in terms of heat, not the other way around. What you feel is the heat being dissipated, not the cold returning.

What*ever* it is, I'm getting *cold.* 'Night.

'Night. Working *late* tomorrow?

Probably *not. See* ya.

***

Hey, Red.

*Hi*, Blondie. *Our* stool's empty. Beer?

Sure, thanks. Kinda *dead* tonight.

Yeah...*and...?*

Reason I came *by*, Red. I've been given an extra vacation week—all my *hard work.* I'm gonna take the opportunity to go to Motown.

Oh! When are you leaving?

*That's* why I came by: tomorrow morning early. I *also* got a bonus, so I can *start* to catch up on the bills this month; maybe *slow down* the phone calls. You can take care of Kitty?

Sure. You *heard* from The Guy again?

No.

Makes *me* think you ain't *gonna* hear from him...

*I'm* thinking the same *thing...*

Boss wants two *more* frames; here's the dimensions. How fast can you make them?

First week of the year.

Good. I *won't* be late tonight. I'll close up by ten...I've gotta *go*; customer over there wants...

I should go, too. Late supper? I won't be *here* New Year's, so we can have *our* New Year's raw beef and onions to*night...*

*Sure.*

***

Aren't you *cold*, wearing nothing but that ratty *robe* and *teddy pants?*

Thick onion slices and ground sirloin on marbled rye. Beautiful...do *I* make *you* uncomfortable...

*Less* than before I figured you *weren't* doing it for shock value...

You figured me *out...?*

*That* part...just one of your charming quirks...

I have *charming quirks?*

A few.

Want to *see* if I'm a *natural* copper...?

Saw *that* fire *before*, remember?

Yes, and you *are that* worthy, babe...

I'm *honored*. Besides, I've *always known...*your freckles... your hazel eyes...you're a *natural* ginger all right...

Natural *copper. Gingers* are a shade or two *lighter* and have *more* brown *...you're* a blonde; your skin's *so* fair and your eyes are *so* blue...

You saw *that*, too...there's a package under the tree for *you...*

*Yeah? Lemme* see...*what's...*a *robe!* A *big fluffy robe!*

Thought *yours* was due for replacement...*wrapping paper's* all *yours*, Kitty...

*Finally*, after *years* of *freezing* and *flashing* in this *moth-eaten thing, one* of my roomies *finally* got the hint! I was just about to add bleach next time I washed it so it'd fall *apart* in some spec*tac*ular fashion that I could put on *you...*

Well, I circumvented *that...*

*What* you *said...I* have a present for *you...now* under the *tree...*

Well, I...what...a *camera*. Wow! I never *had* one...*flash* cubes...wow...let's *finish* our *supper...*

Let's...

***

Now we *must* say goodnight. I've got a *day's* drive ahead of me, and I *gotta* go before *dawn* to beat Windy City rush hour...

And *now...cowboy:* our annual *holiday tongue-wrestling* under your mistletoe...

Our *annual...?*

Gotta start *some* time...

*Anything for a little lady...OK...mmm!*

***

*So...O...K...that's...*

*Before* we get carried away...or...

*Yeah...*Merry Christmas and Happy New Year, Red...

Same to *you,* Blondie...*thanks* for the robe and see you *next year...*

*Next* year, honey...*thanks* for the *camera...*

***

*Merry Christmas! Hello!*

Merry *Christmas,* Red...It's...

*Blondie!* Hey! I was just watching Christmas cartoons before I went by the house for the annual festivities...

Yeah, well, *Step-Sis* is home from college; she talked me into *calling* this morning...

Glad she *did.* She there *now?*

She *is.* Want to *talk* to her?

*Yeah...*

OK; *here* she is....

***

What was *that* about? She told *me* to *get lost*...

Just *girl* stuff...

Uh-huh...have a *great* Christmas, honey...

You, *too*, babe...

***

*Hey*, Blondie! How was your *trip*?

Good, Red; *great*, even. How was *your* Christmas?

*Fabulous*...everybody was asking where *you* were.

Everybody?

Even Idiot Brother and Loser. So, *how's* the family?

They're *great*! Step-Mom let me call her *Mom without* getting annoyed. Got to see Step Two's whole familial *menagerie*. Went to a *New Year's party* with Step-Sis. It was *great!*

She *do* what I...?

What *did* you...?

I *asked* her to *pretend she's me* and to give *you* a *big* hug and a *kiss*...and by your *blush*...she *did*...

*That* was weird. I mean, she's not my *real* sister, but...

She got *involved*?

She *did*...not *quite* as involved as...

*Me*?

No; I mean *yeah*; I *mean*...she's almost as *nice* a kisser as *you* are...

Huh; I'm a *nice* kisser...?

You *know* what I...

Yeah...get your *ashes hauled* New Year's?

Ah, *no*...

Kiss *lots* of *strange women, anyway*?

Like they were *lining up* for it...most were pretty *drunk*, of course...how about you? Kiss lots of strange *guys*?

Well, let's put it *this* way: *no* guys escaped the bar *un*-kissed New Year's. *I* even laid one on *Door-Guy*; *Sister* smacked Beard...

Yeah? Did *you*...what's the female equivalent of getting your *ashes* hauled?

I *dunno*, but *I* didn't *sleep* in any *wet spots*, either...

Oh...sorry...I *know* you...

*Don't* worry about it, babe...

Step-Sis gave me...*this* for *you*...

What's...for *me*?

All the rage around med school, *she* says...

A *lounge-kini*; *heard* of 'em, never *saw* one. Huh...*roomy* skorts and a *tie-on* tube top...can see *freckles* through this material...like being *naked without* being *naked*...

I *think* that's the *idea*...Step-Mom gave me *this* for you...

A *red silk sarong!* It's anything you *want* it to be: dress, shawl, drape, wrap. Must be *ten feet long*...instructions, too...huh. I'll *have* to drop them *both* a line... *thanks*, babe.

Welcome, honey. What *else* did you get for Christmas?

A scarf; some *cool* stockings, a *briefcase* for my *school* books. What did *you* get?

Step-Mom and Step Two gave me money enough to knock my *credit card* down so I can *use* it...and Auntie gave me *this*; my parent's wedding picture...I'd never *seen* it before.

Never *seen* it?

My father was *very* bitter about her death, Auntie said; blamed *me*. He gave her *all* his pictures with her in them after she died.

Huh.

Step-Mom *half*-told me she married him to protect me *from* him.

Huh. Think it's true?

I think it *could* be.

You should hang it with the rest...

Uh-huh. Saw The Girl, too.

Does she know who *you* are?

Her aunt won't *let* her forget. How did Sister's kids like all the stuff you made for 'em? You spent enough *time* on them...

My nieces were *more* than thrilled...you were right about Nephew; the vest was *well*-received...that *reminds* me; *Cousine* sent me *these* pictures.

*Us*, at the *wedding*...we didn't *pose* for these...*you* look *gorgeous* in that dress...

Better than *now?*

*Just* as gorgeous as *now*, but more *elegant* in basic black...

*Nice* save...

*Thank* you...*we* look...um...

Like a *genuine* couple...I read *more* of your books. Some of 'em are confusing.

They are indeed...

I'm hanging *this* picture...here...with the rest of our family...

*Our...?*

Uh-*huh*...babe, *this* is from *our* family...

*Beautiful* card...with a *dentist's* business card...*paid* in... honey, I *can't* accept *this*...

*Yes*, you *can*, babe...get your *teeth* fixed. He's Dad's *cousin*; *waiting* to hear from you. Mom and Dad will *cover* it...babe, I *missed* you...

I missed *you*, but I *can't*...

Blondie, if you're going to hang around *my family*, you're going to *have* to learn that they are *not* shy about showing their gratitude. What you've done for *me*, for Idiot Brother, for Sister, her kids *and* her Loser...*this* is a *token* of our thanks for being there for a bunch of people who were complete *strangers* before *July*...

Not *complete* strangers; *we* met New Year's...

*Now* you're splitting hairs to avoid *talking* about it...knock it off...

Yeah, but...

Yeah, but *nothing*, cowboy. Look, you gotta get over this insistence about not accepting help...this is *not* pity, it's heartfelt thanks. Don't be such an ingrate. Get *over* yourself and get *used* to our largesse. You're *stuck* with us.

OK...

You saw a *need*; you knew you could *help*, and you did, expecting *nothing* in return. *This* is no different.

OK...OK; *thanks*, honey. I'll *call*...so...

So *c'mere*...*mmm*...how's the teeth *now*?

O...*K*...

I'm going to *model* this lounge-kini...

Um...

We can watch a *late movie* in *your* room...no *alarm* in the morning...

Ah...

*Live* a little; *hold* a *hand*; maybe something *softer*...

O...*K*...you running a fever?

You'll *see* when we *get* there...*and* after I put my *hair* up so you *can't* roll *over* on it...

***

So what kind of friends *are* we, babe...?

You mean outside of that dumb acronym? *Wait* a minute: hold it *right* there...*before* you get in bed...

What?

*I* want a *good look* at that *lounge-kini...*

*You* want a good look at *me in* it....

Yeah...

You *like...?*

*Beautiful...twirl* once...

You're mistaking *me* for a *model*; it's too *cold* for that...*I'm* getting *in...*

But what *kind...?*

I mentioned that acro-*what*ever to Sister, and she looked at me like I'd lost my mind.

Maybe you *have.* We're the kind of friends of the opposite sex who watch an R-rated movie in a warm waterbed who do *not* have sex...

Yeah. What do you call *that* kind?

Why does *our* kind of *friendship* even have to *have* its own name?

There *has* to be a name...

*Technically* chaste *near*-lovers, maybe...

Oh, GOD! I've *taken* a *vow* of *chastity?* I'm a *nun?*

As in *getting none,* or the Flasher Nun?

Or *both...*

We'll get *that* actress to play you in the movie on pay TV after midnight...

I'm *twice* her size...

*And* she's a brunette...let's *watch...*

***

This is a *fun* movie, but *dumb,* Blondie...

Yeah, it *is* kinda stupid...

*That* woman *always* gets goofy parts...

Yeah...

There goes a *guy* into the *pool*...

*First* guy in the drink. *Next* there'll be a girl whose top will get *just* wet enough to see *through*...

You were *right*...

And a guy falls *on* the girl...

That *is* funny...

Yeah...what's *two things* you should *never* do in bed?

What?

*Point* and *laugh*...

Now *that's*...or say 'about my *lab results*...'

Yeah, *that* too...you *had* to have *known* girls in high school... couldn't have been *just* college...

No *time* in high school...

Why no *time?*

I spent two years—including summers—catching up with my class.

You certainly did *that* with a 4.0 average...

I graduated *with* them, but they treated me like a leper...

Because of what you did to Bully?

*I* think they were afraid of me because of that; *Step-Sis* thought as much...

WOAH! Almost *full frontal* in *that* shot!

Nearly; *not* quite. It *would* be full frontal if they showed this *after* midnight...

True. Sounds like *Step-Sis* was...

I hung out with her. She helped me with my Spanish and introduced me to *her* friends who were...

*Not* afraid of you?

Yeah; there weren't *many*, and they didn't *last*...I helped her with calculus and made sure *her* dates were OK.

Like *any* good brother would...

*Same-age* brothers are hard to *explain*...

Take your *word* for it. So, *what* girl came *after* your first...?

Well, *she* set me up for...

Turn this *off*; I'm *tired* of it. Kill the *lights*, too...*next* girlfriend after the *first*...

Met my *next* in drafting. Her *favorite* thing to do was *sleep*.

*Sleep*, as in...?

Eyes *closed*, lying-*down* sleep. She'd had mono as a child; had no memories of *anything* before she was nine. Never got past second base with *her* and only *once*.

She couldn't stay awake longer?

*Something* like that. We dated for most of a semester; she ended it around Christmas; said I was *too*...*something*.

*She* couldn't figure it out?

Nope.

What about Yearbook?

She wasn't *completely* standoffish, just...*I* dunno. We'd *known* each other since grade school; she was one of the *few* who didn't think I was *crazy* for bashing Bully...winter *before* I graduated college, she was *seeing* the guy who got her pregnant, then he *split*. *I* was around when *he* took off, when she *delivered*, when she got *sick*...

So...gratitude there?

More like *familiarity*. We hung out for a *long* time before *she*...

A girl buddy?

Yeah, kinda. Kissing her was weird, like a *sister*, kinda.

That *would* have been weird... *did* you...*once*, at least?

A *couple* times before she couldn't, yeah. It was...*seemed* desperate, but so was *I*...*sleeping* with her...by then we knew that *her* kind of leukemia...they could barely *treat* it; could only slow it down...

Wow...

I *tried* to find work in Motown as I got ready to graduate, but *she* said...she *said* I had to go where the *money* was and Motown was *dying, too*...and she was *right*. I wanted her to come with me, but she was *too* sick and someone *had* to care for her daughter...

*Sorry*, babe...

*Then* I moved over *here* to The Slum and there was a woman who moved in two doors down the same day. We were both new to town; didn't *know* anyone. We *hung out* for a while, then...

Then...*more*...

Yeah. Two Doors Down was *divorced* in the *worst* way. We got together on weekends, spent Christmas together in '75...then New Year's '76 she said she'd found a guy who would take *care* of her...moved *out* the next *day*.

Shit...

We were more physical than anything *else* and I started thinking about...

Heat and friction...

Yeah. Tell me about your boyfriends *after* your cousin.

My cousin was my first *sex*; my first *boyfriend with benefits* was my Boy-Across-The-Street...we played hoops in his driveway until all hours...Mom *didn't* find us in his back yard *glider*...I was *his* first...

How many virgins have you deflowered?

Just him and my cousin.

*He* was...?

*Yep*...

OK, who came next?

Junior year, there was a quarterback and a wrestler, but no *sex*; *senior* year, there was *another* football player and a basketball center *with some* fooling around. *After* graduation...lost *track*...*but*...since I moved in *here*, I haven't been *able* to...*you* know...I've *tried*, but... somehow I *can't*...

Why *not*...?

Why do you *think*...?

*Me*...?

You...

*Why* did you pick *me* New Year's...? Red...? Why *me*...?

I'd been *with* Beard for about *three months*—off and on, but *mostly* on. Since *Christmas* we'd been...*he* wanted *me* to commit; sign a *lease* on a place, the whole bit. I looked at him and thought, '*this* would be a *disaster*.' I said '*no*;' he said, '*think* about it; let's go party.'

And so you went because *partying sounded* like a good idea...

I *didn't* drink much that night; didn't feel *safe*. He kept asking 'you *thought* about it,' like it was some kind of *assignment*...

It was an ultimatum, then...

*That*, too...we drove around to a *couple* of parties and finally ended up at Our Bar. As soon as we *got* there, Beard grabbed Bleach-Blonde and started to *fool around* with her like *I* wasn't *there*. After a few minutes of them *tongue-wrestling*, he looked at *me* like, 'see what you're missing?' *That* was when I saw *you*...

From across the room...

From *across* the *room* and I *thought*, 'do I want to stay with this *bearded louse* or try something *else?*'

And *I* was...*else?*

You were the *only* guy in that bar who Beard didn't *know*. *That* made you the *one guy* who Beard couldn't retaliate against, and he *has* a temper. *That* made you *safe*.

Great; I'm *safe*...

It helped that you were as *cute* as all get-out, *attractively* shy at *first*...

I never *got* that...

What?

*What's* so attractive about reticence?

Reti...*what?*

Shyness.

Ever heard the expression opposites attract?

Not sure I *buy* that...

Buy it or *not*, you *didn't* retreat when I started bumping you off the stool, and you *didn't* back up when I started talking that *bullshit* about redheads...

That was *good...?*

*Yeah*...the *instant* I started talking to *you* I *knew*...*shit*, I *knew* there was a better kinda guy than the guys I *had* been looking at *all along*...

The neighborhood was no longer your model...

My *life* was no longer my model. I'd signed up for business classes already; they started the next Monday. But *you*...

I needed *more* than...

*You wouldn't give me your damn number!* You were *so* cute and *so* polite and *so damned...everything this 'hood isn't*...

Because I *turned* you *down*, you...

*You turned my world upside down* when you said *no*...

Sorry...

I *had* to get re-oriented, so I went back into the bar after the pizza joint, got a ride from Door-Guy, woke up with *him* and...everything was back to where it *had been*...except nothing *looked* or *felt* right. My heart wasn't *in* catting around anymore. I hung onto Door-Guy until June...

Then...

We just *stopped* and I got *out*. I dated every guy *but* him and Beard after that...even *Cousin*, as you *know*...

But *that wasn't* a date...

*That* was...he's the one *other* guy who's opinion of other guys I have *any* faith in...and I asked *him* about *you*...

And *he* said...?

*He* said you were a thoroughly decent guy...

If you can't *seal the deal* since you moved *in* here, *why*...?

Why do I still live *here*...?

*Or* why do you still go *out*...?

Babe...I'm...making *sure*...and *waiting* for *you* to...I *know* you were halfway sold New Year's...

*And* after the *question on the stairs*...

*And* I keep thinking I *could* with the *right*...why *didn't* you take me up on it...?

New Year's...I wasn't as *broke* as I am *now*, but I didn't have any *way* to...

*Entertain* me?

That, *and*...if I'd taken you *up* on it and I *weakened* and we ended up...

*Here*...

Yeah. Given my *physical* issues at the time, I didn't know if I *could*...

*Perform?*

Yeah. I've had more dates since I met *you* than...

At least *three* of 'em were because *I* set *you* up...

*Chesty* don't count; well, maybe *half* a date...

Neither does Labor Day: *one* guy and *two* girls is a *party*, not a *date*...I think the more dates you *have*, the more confidence you have in *yourself*, and the more dates you *get*, and the *more* you are...*able* to...get...

Um...honey...you're creeping over here...*very* close...

Uh-huh...I *asked* you *before*...now...just...don't *think, babe*... just...*feel*...

*That's* my *drawstring*, honey...

I *know*...just a *tug and*...pull *mine*...there...now, gimmie *your* hand...*gently*...*don't grab* or *poke*; just *caress*... there...mmm...

Red...*honey*...I...

Babe, just *let this happen*...*this* will be *more* than heat and friction; *so much* more...it's from my *heart*...and I *know* it's from *yours*...relax, now...just...*weaken*...ah...like...*that*...

***

*That* was *more* than *heat* and *friction*, babe...

That was...*gratitude; relief; release; affection*...*whew!*

*Better* than Mother Thumb...?

*Orders* of *magnitude* better...never *had*...*that*...before...

You never *had a hand*...?

*Not* from someone *else*...can't *kiss* myself when *I* indulge... nor have I *given*...

Pretty good for a *first* time...

Let me *ask*: what do *you* get out of doing *that* to *me*...?

*I* get the pleasure of knowing you *enjoyed* it...like *you* did *me*...

Somehow, my sense of reciprocity feels out of balance since you *didn't*...

Recip...*what?*

The sense that *you* didn't get *nearly* as much out of it as *I* did...I felt *that* down to the marrow of my bones; you, *not*...

Babe, there is *something* you should *know*...in *relationships* like...

*This*...

Yeah...not *everything's* in *perfect* balance *all the time*...I felt *enough*...I never *need* much...

Never been *in* a...honey, that *had* to have been for *more* than just for my *relief*...

Mine, *too*, babe. Trust me; we'll balance *our* scales in *time*.

210

I *trust* you...our *fourth*...um...

*Don't* count...you OK...?

I'm fine...*you*...?

*Fine*, babe...know what the *worst* thing to talk about *after* sex is?

No; *what*...?

The *clap*...

*PHH...HA!*

'Night...

'Night.

# Wants...

*Hey!*

*Hey!* Did you *call* the dentist like you said you would *this...?*

I *did*, yes.

*And...don't* keep me in *suspense...*

*And* they *asked* if I was in *pain...*

And *you* said...?

I said there was always *some*...so I go there in an *hour...*

*Very* late appointment? It's nearly *four...*

Yeah...

Didn't know dentists *worked* this late...

*I* didn't either, but *they* said he was there to relieve *pain* and he saw *me* as an emergency.

Want me to go *with?*

*Naw...*

*Sure...?*

*No...?*

I'll get my *boots...*

Never thought I'd look *forward* to a *root canal...*

*****

Want some *ice*, babe?

Yeah...want to *sit down...*

You'd *better*; you look a *little* wobbly. What *else* did he say?

There's one *other* potential root canal and five *fillings* I need, but *this* root canal was urgent. I *still* might *lose* the *tooth*...

You were in there a *long* time...*shoo*, Kitty; Daddy's not *up* for you right now...

*Four hours. Cleaned* 'em and started the root canal. Got *another* appointment next week to *finish* it and get ready for the inlay. Then *another* for the *other* cavities and evaluate the *other* potential root canal...

You *gotta* get Big Boss to offer a dental plan...

*This* will *cost* your *family* a...

*Babe: don't*...it's a gift.

And I'm grateful, and I don't want to *seem* like an ingrate, but...

You're *not.* Hungry?

Famished. Eggs and toast?

Coming *right* up.

Aren't you *working*...?

I'll be *late*; they *can't* fire me...

***

*Hi, babe*...dentist again today?

Yeah. Finished the root canal; took the casting for the inlay.

How's it *feel?*

Like someone tried to *pry* my *jaw* apart. *One* thing, though...

What's that?

*No* toothaches since last week...hurts *more* where they numbed me up...at least I can afford *their* painkillers...

*That's* something.

*That's* a LOT. *You're* home at an *odd* time...

Yeah...we met with some vendors, some *other* people... Boss said he'd pay me for the night and closed up.

You don't look *happy* about it.

Just...can *I* sit by you?

Sure...*hold* my...no *shower* tonight?

I'm not *that* dirty... didn't really *work*...do I *stink*?

Like a *spring rain*...

*Blondie*...

No; you're *fine*...what was this *meeting* about?

*Stuff*...the *future* of the *bar*...

It's *got* a future, though, *right*...?

*That's* what we're meeting *about*...what's on *TV*?

A new private eye show. *Fairly* well done...too *cerebral* to last long...*hey*; you *OK*?

I *will* be. Can I borrow your *shoulder*?

Yeah; sure...

***

Blondie?

Red...

Has the furnace stopped all day?

I can't say I've *heard* it shut off since I got home this afternoon...and it hasn't stopped *snowing*...

I *can't* warm up and I've got *three blankets* on my bed...

*Uh*-huh...

*I'm* close to pulling that kerosene heater into my room...

*Can't* sleep with it *lit*...

I *know* but I'm *cold*...*your* bed's *warmer*...

Uh-*huh*...

***

OH! Your *feet* are *freezing*, Red...but *nice* long johns.

I *told* you I was cold...Kitty, *warm* my feet...*good* girl.

215

Good thing tomorrow's *Sunday*...

*This* place isn't well insulated...

*Talk* about *non-sequiturs*...

Non-*what?*

Never *mind*. Let's get some *sleep.* 'Night, Red.

'Night, Blondie.

***

Morning...

Morning...*you* are *radiating* heat...

Explains why I'm *cold* all the time...and you shucked your pants...

*Too* warm...seriously, babe; you should *glow*...I'm scooting over *there*...

Fine...it's *still* cold outside *and* in here...

*How* cold?

Let me check that thermometer...holy *Christ*, it's *twenty-five below* out there...and I can't *see* the *road* for the *snow*...

Get *back* in this *bed* and *warm me up!*

Right *now...you* can warm *me* up...

Scoot *closer...take* my *hand*...

OK...*what...?*

Just *warm up* by me...

OK...no...?

Too *cold* for *funny business*...

***

*Mm*...hi...waking up the sleeping guy with a kiss?

*Hi*, babe; yeah. We fell asleep again...wanted to tell you that I'm *done* settling...

*Huh?* Settling *what...?*

I'm *done* going out with *shitty* goons with bad haircuts just because we've been *neighbors* since we were in diapers, and...

Slow *down*, honey...feel like I just walked into the middle of a conversation and should start taking *notes*...

I'm done with *sex* with guys I've known most of my *life* who only want *one thing* from me, and I keep *giving* it because I always *have*...

Red, *hey*...you *took* your *shirt* off...

*Don't* interrupt. I *won't settle* for my *old* type of guy *anymore*. I want a *different* kinda guy; the kind with a brain who's able to use his *head* for something besides a battering ram or a hat rack...

*Jeez*...I ain't had *coffee* yet and...you *said* it was too *cold* for...

I'm just *snuggling*...*now* I have a *new type* of guy...

*What...?*

Someone who's kind, generous, and with a brain *better* than *mine*. With career prospects *and* higher aspirations than working on an assembly line or in a fast-food joint... someone *like you*...

*Like ME?* Does 'snuggling' mean *grope* my *chest under* my *shirt...?*

*Like* you...it *does* when it's *this cold* and I want to *warm* my *hands* up...

Red, that's a *helluva* announcement to make *out* of the... *warm* your *hands*...

Yeah, but I've *made* it...*and* warmed my hands, but *I've* gotta go!

You *upstairs*, me *downstairs*. I'll start coffee. *Then* we talk... and *put something on*...

***

We *need* to...

*Discuss* my *announcement*...

Discuss your *decision...when* did...?

Hard to *say*, exactly; been thinking about it for a *while*, *while* I was serial dating since I moved in *here*...

So it's something you've *been* thinking about...?

*More* or *less* since *we met*...

*New* Year's?

*Yeah*. I *never* dated outside the 'hood...*except* for *you*. Even college is with people who've lived around here all *their* lives. They all know *me*, or my *family*, or my family's *business*.

I've added variety...

More than *that*. Your insistence on some kind of meaningful, lasting affection *before* sex is *rare* in *my* world... and *reasonable*...and *so* refreshing...*now* it's what *I* want...

That doesn't *change* my...

Wouldn't *want* it to, babe. *Good God*; don't you *dare* change *anything* about *you*.

I'm not sure *what* to...

*Don't say anything*. There's nothing for you to *fix*; nothing you can say that would make it go away or sound any *different*. We're sitting here in a conversation pit *shivering* our *asses* off in our long johns while the kerosene heater warms the room, and I've *simply* declared, *out loud*, the realization that I've reached a *turning point* in my life. That's *all*...

You're *starting* to sound like *me*, honey.

God for*bid*, babe.

Does *this* mean...?

It *means*, my *dear* and *dreamy* blonde landlord/housemate /buddy/friend/*nearly*-lover/hand warmer, that I'm *looking* for a guy with *your* qualities...maybe even *you*.

Maybe even *me*? I *care* for you a *great deal*, Red...

*I* care for *you*, Blondie...

What's your *announcement* do for the *appearance* of our *commercial transaction* that keeps you from looking like a rent-slut?

We'll still *have* to date *others, won't* we?

To make it look good...since you *haven't* been, ah...

*Putting out* on dates?

*Yeah*...has the *gossip* changed?

Not that I've *heard*...but those guys *don't* compare notes. I'll have to find one of *you out there*...

Yeah...un*less* we...

*Wanna?* Why *stop* with *hand?* What's the difference between *that* and...?

With *you*, it's...*hard* to *describe*...you *want* to go *beyond*... *don't* you?

Yeah...? So *you* never did anything between third base and...?

Not...*no.* Can *you* say that you're giving *more* than *just* friction...for *real*...?

I...*maybe*...

Can't use *maybe*, honey; not for *that.* We need to tell each other *everything.* I *need* it to be *real*...

Let's get *breakfast* going...

***

*Christ*, there has to be *fifteen* inches of snow out there...

Our little furnace can't keep up...

I don't know that it's shut off in *days*...

Gas bill from Hell...I'll *help* with it...

May *come* to that just to keep it *coming*...it's Sunday, so the usual routine; laundry, bills, bathrooms, articles, *cat* box... and *no phone calls*...

*Homework; nails; hair*...

Wash it *again?*

It's *time*...I'll start our laundry...

*Our?* You *mean*...?

You think your *stuff* is going to *put out* to *mine* in the spin cycle?

*No,* but...

Then, *our* laundry today and maybe *every* day. Save *water* and *time* that way. Want to finish embroidering that *skirt*...

Gonna *finish* it before she *outgrows* it...?

*Shut up* and wipe that *silly grin* off your *prepossessing face*... to the *cat box* with you... I'm *finishing* it *today*...or *tomorrow*...

At least your *vocabulary's* growing...

*Go,* naysayer...!

***

*Hey!* Our new neighbor's got a *snowblower!*

Makes *our* lives a *little* easier...

I'll start to dig *our* sidewalk out, clear around *your* car if I can *get* there...

I've *got* to wash my hair, so I'll change *loads* and go out and move snow *first*...

I'll *let* ya...get our car *batteries* into the basement before I *relieve* you...

Then I'll *finish* this *chapter*...

***

The *news* says it won't warm up until mid-week, Blondie.

Great. How are we doing on laundry?

Done. I pulled chicken out of the freezer.

Great...*hm*...no potatoes in the cupboard; a *mouthful* of rice...how about mac and cheese for a change?

Sure; OK. Grate the *cheese*; boil the *pasta*...anything *good* on pay TV?

There's a *really* long Red revolution movie in a couple of hours...have I seen *that*? *You* ever see it, Red? It's pretty old...

Um...*maybe*. We can always watch something *else*...*and* it's *snowing* again.

My *aching* back...*that's* a...*flower* you're embroidering...?

Yeah...the *leaves* are too *big*...

They're OK...

Glad *you* approve; just hope my *niece* will... a kerosene heater, two blankets, and a quilt apiece *should* keep us warm...

And *Kitty*...

Let's not forget *her*...

*** 

I dunno if I ever *saw* this movie, Blondie...

When it was in theaters, I *probably* did...not sure how *popular* it was...is the chicken about done?

Another hour.

I should start the mac and cheese in another half-hour...*this* movie will be *half-over* by then.

Maybe I'll be *done* with the *skirt* by then...get on the *bralette*...I *envy* girls her age...

Which *one?*

The skirt's for Twelve-Year-Old; the bralette's for her eight-year-old sister. Twelve-Year-Old's at that age where bras are *optional*, but *exciting* if you *need* one...

Why *envy?*

I first wore a *real* bra when I was eleven. By fourteen I was *tired* of being squeezed, used alternatives like camisoles and thicker tank tops when Mom didn't *catch* me.

An important consideration...

Yeah. By high school, I could get away with peasant blouses and heavy sweaters; the gym teacher couldn't *tell* I was *au naturel* most of the time...*now* I only wear one when I *have* to, or to create a *look*...

Huh. So...what *does* a training bra *train?*

It gets girls used to being squeezed into uncomfortable clothes. Guys don't *have* those issues, you *beasts*...where did *that* come from? I've been *out* of one since 6th Grade...

Just *came* to me...

*You* have a *funny* brain. Some *guy invented* the bra...

No; a New York socialite did about seventy years ago, trying to get the *support* of a corset without the *restrictions* of one. I could look up her *name*...

No, I *believe* you....

We had an instructor of engineering who said that the stress calculations for a well-designed bra are more complex and inter-related than for a suspension bridge...

What did the *girls* in the class say to *that*?

One of 'em said, 'just *show* me a *well-designed bra.' Another one* said '*yeah*; in a *D-cup*.'

*That's* funny...

*Another* said, '*I'm* going to *design* one that will give me *cleavage*.' It was all we could do *not* to bust out laughing. We finally *did*...

I'll *bet*...*why* am I talking about *bras* with *you*?

*You* brought it *up*...you wore that *bandeau* last *summer*...a bandana bra once or twice...

You *noticed*?

Yeah...

*That's* why you're my *new* type: you don't always *talk* about what you notice. Need something to drink. You?

Sure; water's fine. What's *that* under your robe?

Winter body suit...*heavier* and *this* one's *warm*...

***

*Here*...*what* did I miss?

Snow; horses; a *machine gun* on the back of a car, and a *train*...they'll get back to the love story soon enough... dinner out here?

Sure...

***

Red...?

Hm...?

You gonna *sleep* down here?

You *woke me up* to ask me *that*...?

Being *polite*...

You turned the *heater* off...

*Had to* before *I* fell asleep...*Red*...?

Hm...?

Wanna *mess around*...?

*WHAT?*

*Thought* that'd *wake* you up...*I'm* going up to bed...

Can I *join* you and...?

*No* messing around...

*Just*...

I'm ex*hausted*, Red...

And *I'm* half asleep...

***

*Twenty* below this morning...*heat* wave...

Yep...the batteries test good after being on a charger all night...I could stick *yours* back in...

I don't *need* to get to work until tomorrow...*you* do?

Not sure. Couldn't *raise* anyone *at* the office. The TV is saying that the busses aren't running. In the *past*, that told me *we're* not working, either, but it usually means *snow*, not *cold*. I'm calling Big Boss...

***

From what I *heard*, no work today?

Nope; *not* today...so it's just *you* and *me*...*again*...think we'll survive?

Unless we run out of food and Kitty eats us, we will...I can think of *worse* things...

Me, too. You can *finish* your embroidery...

Yeah, and for *that* remark, *you* can make *breakfast...babe.*

*And,* I need to *start* on my *taxes* and *vacuum* today... *honey.*

Ooh, yeah; *about* that...I *forgot* to *tell* you the vacuum cleaner's busted...

*How? When?*

I hit a hair elastic the other day and suddenly it didn't *suck* anymore...

Probably broke the belt...I'll show you how to replace it... didn't *have* this problem before there were *hair elastics* on the *floor...*

*Huh! Nobody* can control those things...

*Kitty* seems to do well enough...c'mon; I'll *show* ya...

OK, you *slave-driver...your* phone...what's...who's *that...?*

Never *heard* of...what's *that* outfit...never called be*fore...*

*Shh...what's* he *saying?*

He *says* he can have the *gas* shut off...to*day...*

*Can* he?

No...don't *think* so, anyway...*can't* go to the gas company and *take...*he knows I'm *probably* here because of the weather...

Tells you he *might* be a *local* outfit...*can't* use the gas company to collect on other debts...*can* he?

Don't *think* so...weird...the usual threats and promises... '*pick up* or we will disconnect the gas in an *hour'...*

*But...*he *can't...can* he?

No...I *don't* think...*no,* you *asshole,* I'm *not* going to...he's gone...

Blondie...?

It's *OK,* Red...he's bluffing...

Then why are you all *white? Babe?* C'mon; *sit...*

We'll know *soon enough* if he's bluffing...

In the *meant*ime...just...re*lax*, babe...we'll wait *together*... get breakfast...

*And* fix the vacuum...*and* do my...

*I'll* do that... go work in your den; it's where you're *happiest...*

Where I'm most *distracted*...except with *you...*

At *this* point...*I'll* get breakfast going...*you* work on *something* that has *nothing* to do with *money...*

***

Pretty sunset over the fields...

*Heat's* still on...*seven hours* later...bluffing...

Yeah... wonder what *would* have happened if you'd picked up?

*My* guess...ask for a credit card number. *What* kind of people do they get to *make* those kinds of calls? If it wasn't for *you*, I *might* have...

Me...?

I was *acting* more courageous than I *am...*

But you *didn't*, babe; *that* was brave...

I *would* have just to *shut* him *up*, on the *off-chance*...I'm *so* tired of this *desperation*...like a cold *chain* wrapped around me. Every *dunning letter*, every *nasty phone call*, the chain gets *tighter; colder. GOD* it wears me *out...*

Any *chance* for a tax refund?

A couple *grand*...won't come *close* to paying anything *off* except the credit card, but it *might* bring me up *even*...but *that's* a ways off... *months...*

*Maybe* you could use that money more...*defensively...*

Like...?

Talking to a lawyer about...

*Bankruptcy...*

Yeah...it *is* where you *are*, babe.

*Yes*; it *is...*

Undeniably...*stand* up; *c'mon...c'mere...*now just *hold me...*

I'm *so...damn...tired...*

I *know*...just *hold onto* me, babe...*we'll* get through *this...*I'll *distract* you tonight...

*Please...*

***

Two straight days of uninterrupted companionship, confined to our little townhouse, ends this morning, honey. Life goes on...

Yes; our *halcyon* days together, babe ...

Good grief: *halcyon? Where* did you get *that?* You even used it *correctly*. It's *perfect*...I'm impressed, but *not* surprised.

Living with *you* is an education. So is sleeping with a guy *without* real sex. And I've greatly enjoyed our time together.

So have *I*, honey. But *we...*

*That's* not *exactly* sex...I *saw* what you were *thinking* this *morning...*

That's not me *thinking*; more like *reacting...*

To *me?*

No; to *biology*, they tell me. Sign of a healthy heart...

You're *healthy*, all right. By the way, I *finished* that *skirt...*

*Finally...*

I'm *opening* tonight, *smartass...*

Everyone likes a *little* smart in the *ass...*

Gonna *call...?*

See what I can find...ask Big Boss if he knows a lawyer who'll take *credit cards*...inaugural night, so probably *not* much on TV...

See you this evening.

***

*Blondie! Blondie! Wake up!*

Wha...what? It's...*one* in the *morning*, Red...thought you be *earlier*...fell asleep down...the *hostages* are on their *way* back...*why* the big *grin* like...?

*Before* I go into *that*...*here's* my back rent...

OK; *great*...*now*...

I *said* Boss wanted to get out of the saloon-only business, right?

Yeah...

I *said* there were big changes coming to my work, *right?*

*Right*...

Boss *is selling*...

Oh. That's...*good? Red?*

C'mon, you *slug*. I brought a split of *top-shelf champagne!* We need to *celebrate* after I get a shower...

Ah...sure; OK...

***

*Hey*, Red! Never *saw* you so *cheery!*

Let's *crack* that *split* open!

Too bad we don't have *proper* flutes...

*Pour* it...Dad's been talking about investing *outside* the family business for a *while*...

OK; he *mentioned* that...

Well, that pizza joint where we ate last New Year's went up for *sale* for a *song*...

OK...

And they *own* the property where that *easement* would go... to connect to the *side* road, so when the *main* road closes, it'd still have *traffic*...

And...?

Boss and Dad formed a joint business, a *division* of our family business. *I'm* going to be the general manager...

Of...the *bar*...?

Of the bar and the pizza place *combined*. We're gonna convert the *pizza place* into a *hall*, build a long driveway to the side road, then renovate the bar into a restaurant/tavern after *that's* done...

*Wow.*

Tonight we sealed the deal: the pizza joint, the easement, *and* the bar are *ours!* Signed all the paperwork for the partnership, the licenses and all that; signed over the checks...

Congratulations, Red! *Big* plans...

They...are...*terrifying.* I'm a just-*barely* high-school graduate with a half-dozen college courses under her belt who's about to *run* a three-million-dollar-a-year business...

*That* big?

That's what *Boss* and *Dad* and *I* are projecting...

That's *something,* honey...

That's *scary* as *hell*...

*You* can do it, honey. You're *smart* enough; I've always *said* that.

I'm a *co-owner* of the new venture, with access to a *much* bigger budget and a *manager's* salary...I can now *afford* to live on my *own*...

OK...

But I don't *want* to live anywhere else...Blondie?

Yeah...?

*Here's* to you...

Here's to *you* and your *new venture*...

Here's to *us*...

To...*mmm*, better than that hooch we had at Sister's birthday.

Yeah.

O...K...

And I *will* buy *our groceries* from now *on*...

*O...K!*

*Drink* up...

OK...

*C'mon*...

That's some *grin*, there, honey...like a *cat in a tree*...

*Kill* the *lights*, babe...

Um...

*Shut up* and *kiss* me...c'mon; *upstairs*...

'K...are *you* trying to...?

I'm *going* to give *you much more* than heat and friction, babe...I *promise*...from the *bottom* of my *heart*...and *we're ready* for *more* than a *hand*...

***

*Mad* at me, babe?

How could I be *mad* at you, honey? I *just* had the *best* sex of my *life*...

You probably say that to *all* the women you've...

Just the *first* and *you*.

*Mm*... for a guy who *says* he hasn't *done it* much, *you're* pretty *good* at it...

Luck, imagination, *and* watching how *you* respond to what *I* do...

*I've* found a guy who doesn't *twist* my *boobs* like they're door knobs...*you're* quite *passive* in comparison with *other* guys...

*You're* quite *relaxing*...

*That's* refreshing...

Have you been thinking about *this* for six months?

We've been *dancing around this* since...how about *you?*

Every time I *glimpse* you with your robe open, honey...

You *should* have gotten used to *that* by now...

I will never *quite* get used to your *fabulous* bod...

You're the *first* guy who ever said *my* bod was *fabulous.* Well, the first since junior high, anyway, and it wasn't *much* then. It isn't *that* great now...

*I* think it is...

I'll have you know this *wasn't* an impulse, babe...

You *planned* to seduce me?

Uh-*huh...look* at me, babe...

OK...

No; *really* look at my *face*, Blondie...

How's *this..?*

*This* can't change *us*, Blondie...we *can't* let it change *us*...

Meaning...?

*You'll* still get embarrassed when I stroll around in an open robe. *I'll* still find your embarrassment sweet and endearing...

Maintain the *innocence* we...?

We *have* to stay friends...

Sure...*once* more, honey?

You're *kidding?*

Do I *look* like I'm *kidding*...

*Uh...that's* a definite...n-n-no...

***

What are you thinking *now?*

For once...*nothing*...just...*relief*...what are *you* thinking?

This is the end of my longest drought without *real* sex since *high school*...and with the *second*-best friend I've *ever* had...

*Second*-best?

Sister's my best...

*Good*...but there *was*...

Yeah...hard to count *that* as *sex*...babe, we *have* to stay friends, even if we're *more*...

Friends and lovers sounds like a made-for-TV movie where there's one of each for *everyone*...*that* what you're...?

Of *course* not. You *know* what I mean...*this* can't change us...I never felt *this* good about sex...

Does *that* make *this*...?

Making *love*...

Honey, I *don't* know what comes next or what I'm *supposed* to say, but I *enjoy having* you here a *lot* more than I *ever* liked being alone. *That's* the *best* I can do...

That's *fine*, babe. *Just* fine...know what *else* you *shouldn't* talk about after sex?

No; what?

*Exes* and *crappy* sex...

True...'night, honey.

*'Night,* babe.

***

Red...*how*...?

*Make* a *lap*, cowboy...you've got an inch and at *least* twenty *ounces* on me, so *I* get to sit in *your* lap on the sofa when it *suits* me...

Yes, ma'am...

Don't ma'am *me, mister*...last night was beautiful...

A *lot* more than heat and friction...I don't *know* if I love you, but I believe I *could*. Does *that* make sense?

From *you*, sure. I believe I *could* love *you*. But...what I feel when I think of *you* is...safety.

Safety...not sure if *that's*...

Not every woman *likes* bad boys, but *don't* interrupt me. Our lovemaking was great; loved *every minute.*

Uh...*huh*...I hear a *but* coming on...

*But*...does *this* mean we're *sex* partners? Lovers? Friends/housemates with *privileges*? Still dating...*others?*

Well, I can't *stop* you...you've been *serial dating* for a *long* time...I guess if you still *want* to...

I'm not...*sure...*

Of *what*? Me?

I look at my parent's marriage—stable, happy as far as I can tell. Then I look at Sister's—a *disaster* for the past decade...

So, fifty-fifty...

And Friend's *tragedy*, and so *few* of the kids I grew up with are *happy* or even still *married...*

The marriage/long-term partner numbers aren't adding up for you...

No.

So you still want to play the field...

I don't *know.*

So this was a *one*-time...

*Two*-time...

OK, a *never-again* thing? It *was* just so's we'd *know?*

*NO*...babe, don't get me wrong, because I *care* for you more than I've ever cared for any *other* guy. But long-term...I just don't...

OK...how *about*...no grand plans, *no* timelines...if it *feels* right, we *do* it; if it *doesn't*, we *don't...*

A *gentle* push-off when *you* have an erection is as acceptable as *me* pleading a headache...

I *hope* so...

Seriously, if *either* of us says *no*, then it's *no*...frankly, *that* sounds better than sex-every-night...gets *tedious*...*this* may be weird, but I *enjoy sleeping* with you...even if we *don't*...

*I* enjoy sleeping with *you*, but *you* don't like my alarm going off at the *ass-crack* of dawn when you *close* at night...

True; *good* reason to *keep* my room...

Good as any. *We* need groceries today.

*After* breakfast...*my* closet's overflowing and you have an *enormous* walk-in...can *I*...?

*I* don't fill *both* sides, anyway. You can have a couple of *dresser drawers*, too. Just consolidate what little's there...

Makes it more convenient to get *dressed* there...

I aim to please...

And you do *that so* well...now...I need more coffee and I need to eat something. You?

*I* gotta get started...

You off to *work*? On a *Saturday*...?

Yeah; lunch meeting with *another* new client. Gotta *do* what ya gotta *do*...

***

*Hey*, Red. How's *work* today?

*Hey*. Busy filling out paperwork, finalizing new contracts, dealing with lawyers, lining up new vendors...what's *up*?

Ah, the *firm's* having its holiday party on Saturday...

*After* the holidays?

Yeah; couldn't find an affordable venue for a hundred-odd people, so *now* we're doing it in our *warehouse*. I want *you* to come as my...

Date?

Can you *make* it? Are you *interested*?

I *am* interested and I *can* make it because the *first* thing *I* did was hire *two* more bartenders this month, then budget one more *next* month.

Great; I'll tell 'em I'm *not* stag this time.

How many hearts you gonna break when you tell 'em that?

Don't *know*; don't *care* as long as one of 'em *ain't* mine. Dinner's a stew; you started bread?

I started *rolls*...ya know, we should define *us*; our *relationship*, *my* dearest housemate, *before* we go *public*... so there's...

So there's no *surprises*, *dearest* housemate...?

To*night*; after...

After *what?*

*After* I...

Yeah; *I've* gotta think about it, too...

***

Blondie, I want to *know*...hi, Kitty...under the covers; OK... what *you* make of *us*...where *are* we? What *am* I?

The *best* kind of friend *anyone* could have...you're *biting me? Take* a *hike*, Kitty...*out* of the bed! OK, *there's* fine. *Take* a *bath* if *that's*...yeah...

Yeah. So, what am *I* to *you?*

You're my friend, my sounding board, my *fashion critic...*

Only once or twice...

Only those we *talked* about it. *Now* I've got you in my *head* every time I *think* about getting dressed...but don't *we* want *more?*

In *bed?*

More...*everything?*

*I'm* afraid of what would happen when you finally realize that you could do better than *this* town and leave...*or* when you find *the* guy you *really* want...

Think *either will* happen?

I *hope* not, but I want what's *best* for you, and I want you to be happy because I *care* for you...

What if *this* is the town, and *you are* the *guy* I *really* want...?

I would be...de*lighted*. Even with*out*...

Maybe *especially* without. It isn't important in *your* life; maybe it *doesn't need to* be in *mine*...

*Sort-of-mostly* chaste lovers? Kissing *always*, but sex *not* very often?

Maybe...kissing *you* is *tempting*...

Kissing *you* keeps me *awake* nights...we've never *smooched* in public...

Um...*no*...does having had *actual sex* make *this much* difference?

Well, it *is*, as *they* say, the *next-to-last step* in a relationship; the *ultimate mystery* between two people...

*And* who have been seeing each other *naked* for *months*...*and* have had clothes-*on* and *hand*...

Yeah, *that's not*...

So maybe *for us* it *does—has—*made a difference...

Yeah; for *us*. Does kissing *many* guys *tempt* you...? It *would* keep a *guy* out of the *army*...

*Heh-heh*...kissing *most* guys is kinda mechanical...but when I'm around *you*, I'm not lonely anymore...

At least I do *that* much. Eventually, sex wouldn't be so...*so*...

That *might* be true, but it might *also* be sad. Sex is *important* for couples, isn't it?

So I understand...where *are* we in defining our relationship?

I *think*...um...

*Yeah, maybe*, by a buzzword that'll be forgotten tomorrow...

Yeah...Red, *does* the 'hood make you out to be a *rent-slut*?

From what *Sister* says, the 'hood thinks you're like every *other* guy I've roomed with who I *paid rent* to, so...who *knows*?

What *does* Sister think of...?

Us? She keeps asking 'how's it going,' as in, 'have you *slept* with him yet?' Since I've been *chaste* for *months*...

*Technically* chaste...

Yeah; she's finding the *waiting* hard...nonetheless, *she* thinks the *sun* shines out of your *ass* for giving *Loser* what-for...

Good to know I've got *one* fan...

More than *that*. *Mom* thinks we're *hiding* what we're *doing*, but she *likes* you...

Somehow *she* got the idea I know something about *business*...

Don't know where *that* came from. *Dad...hard* to say what he thinks of *us*, but *he* likes you, too...

Thinks I'm a genius with wood...

Uh-huh. Idiot Brother thinks you're a standup guy, *not* much more.

Doesn't *like* mirrors held in front of him...

*Not* much, but he knows you told him the *truth*. All in all, I *don't* think we'd surprise my family, but a *rent-slut* won't enter *their* thinking. As for the 'hood, they think *any* relationship between two people is like how my instructor says *statistics* are like *skimpy swimsuits*...

How's *that*?

What they *reveal* is *suggestive*, but what they *conceal* is *essential*...

Now *that*...and as *soon* as we...um...

I think you mean '*come out* as a couple;' What would we *reveal...Kitty*, if you're going to *huck up* a *hairball, get OFF the...just* in time...

We'll clean it up when we're *done* here...

Now where *was* I?

Statistics, *skimpy swim*suits, and coming *out*...

Yeah...to the *world*, do we *want* to *look* like...act in *public* like we do in *private*...without the *sucky*-face and the *groping*...

Of *course*...

Even though we're *not*...

*Committed*...?

No, babe, *we're not*...even after as much affection as I've given you and you've given me...no...not...yet...but what *difference does* that make?

The difference between *rent-slut* and *girlfriend*...

What *kind* of commitment would change *that*...?

I can only think of *one*...

*I* can think of *two*...

What?

Marriage *or* putting *my name* on the *lease*...

It *is* coming up at the end of February, but how would *that*...?

First Monday of the month, look in the business classifieds, in the back. There's a listing of new leases, commercial *and* residential. We put *my* name on *our* lease and state law says they *have* to publish that information...

Huh; never knew *that*...never *looked*...

*That* means we'd *really* be public *and* I'd be *legally responsible* for the *rent*...so, lease *yes* or lease *no*?

Lease...*yes*. I'll call Landlord, tell him *we* want to add you when he comes by...one *more* thing: what's our *end game*? Where do *we* want to end up?

Together, or individually...?

Either...

I don't *know*...let's...c'mon, babe...*act* like a couple *right here* and *now*...

*Let's* clean up that *hairball* first...

You *really* know how to *sweet-talk* a girl, babe...

***

*That* was a *fun* party, Blondie; *thanks* for *asking* me.

Thanks for *coming*, Red. Big Boss sure liked *you*...

Did you *know* about his relationship with the actress in that dopey desert-island sitcom?

I always thought the picture of *that* ginger in his office was just a fan autograph. Never *knew* she was his *niece*... niece-*in-law*, technically; he's the brother of her husband.

Long-winded connection. You *really* wrote *all* those books?

*Most* of 'em I recast and expanded from material the customers already *had*. I've got a knack for jump-starting dead projects. Big Boss markets my services with *that*.

Ah. Your *workmates* now know *we're* an *item*.

Yep. Co-Worker dagger-eyed you all night.

She'll get over it. Let's watch TV in *your* room...

***

This movie's *completely* without plot...

Like this kind *needs* a plot...just scantily clad people around a pool doing what comes naturally *while* scantily clad around a pool or *getting* scantily clad...

Take that thong *off*, girl. I don't know *how* they *wear* those things...

*Step*-Sis wore one around the *house* once. Step-Mom had some *choice words* about it...it was *odd*...

*What* was?

Step-Mom was...not *mad* like *Step Two* might have been, but...not *Mom*-like but...

Woman-to-woman...

*Yeah*...Step-Mom said something like, 'I don't care, but Blondie doesn't *need* to *see* your...'

Ah-*hah*...what did *Step-Sis* say?

She looked at *me*, and *I* said, 'I can *see* it without looking.' She looked *surprised*; looked at Step-Mom and asked, 'do *you...?*' Step-Mom said, 'I *wouldn't* without something *over* it.' Step-Sis looked at me, said, '*you're* wearing underwear; *give* me your *shorts.*' I said, 'if you *want* to *get into* my *pants...*' And we *all* cracked up while *I...*

*That's* funny...did *she* put 'em *on?*

We were *laughing* so *hard* she couldn't *finish...*you wanna keep *watching* this *plotless* thing or should we just decide it has *made* its *point* and...

Just remember to call *Landlord...*

*I'll* remember...

***

What are *you* doing up *this* late?

I brought dinner home...Valentine's Day is *tomorrow.*

What did you *bring?*

Prime rib. I'll *make* baked potatoes and beans.

It's *today* since it's nearly one in the morning. Where'd the *beef* come from?

Client did a photoshoot this afternoon. It was a prop for their food service equipment...

Let me get a *shower* and get into something more *appropriate* for this occasion. Get the spuds and beans started...

***

Red...*what's* ...*woah!*

I *made* this last week...took about *two hours* to crochet...

I wish I had a *dollar* handy to put into *those* bottoms...even *with* those leotards under it...

*Cost* you more than *that*...how about the *top?*

Um...would be *very revealing* if it weren't for the leotards... *why* are you wearing...*that...?*

Because you're *treating* me to a *romantic* dinner and it's too *cold* to wear it without something underneath ...

*Romantic?* What makes it romantic?

It's *Valentine's* Day; you *surprised* me. *That's* romantic enough...

Valentine's Day was *made* by a single guy who wanted every *other* single guy to feel as *bad* as he did. *That* or a greeting card company...

You're a cynical and habitual bachelor, but I'm *stuck* on you. *Dad* said don't ignore the one you're *sure of* and *flirt* with somebody else. When you come *back* to the *first* one, he *may* be gone...good *beef*. Beer?

*Great* beef; sure, beer. Maybe I was alone because I never forwarded a chain letter...

Now *that* could be...

Isn't that...*costume*...cold?

It would *be* colder if not for the leotards. See what we *do* for you *guys?*

You *don't* suffer that outfit for *me*, Red.

Yes, I do it for *you*. The imagery of women all *over* depends upon your imagery of *me*...

I *work* with admen. The imagemakers can make the *awful* look *desirable*, the merely *good* look *exquisite*. You do *that* suffering for *yourself*.

Egad! You have single-handedly exposed the deepest secrets of the sisterhood! I shall *have* to report this to the Queen Mother!

I should fear for my life, then?

Naw. *I'm* too lazy...

Red, I *might* be up for another *job*...

*Where?*

A heavy machinery outfit that the *headhunter* found, forming a *new* technical writing *department*. They've *got* the *work*, they said; it'd be a captive shop...

Captive shop?

*One* client; *one* style. A *lot* less variety but steadier work...

Ah. Where?

Their headquarters are across the state. Might *make* the move if Big Boss can't or *won't* match what they *might* offer...

Do you *want* to leave?

I need the *money*...

I *know...when?*

I haven't even *interviewed* with them yet, so let's not *think* about it.

I was *hoping*...with my new *venture*...would you *go?*

I *need* the *money* because I *still* owe too much...I'll also need a new *car* sooner than later...if the *money's* right... would you *want* to come *with* me...?

My life is *here*...I've lived in this neighborhood all my life. My parents are three streets over and nine down. Sister lives not far from *them*. I'm an hour from nearly everyone I've ever *known*. Now my business—my financial *future*—is going to be the hub of the neighborhood and is *less* than a mile away.

I *know* all that...*would* you...?

I'd *have* to *think* about it...let's just *eat*...

***

Happy *birthday*, honey!

*Thanks*, babe...some *party*, hey?

Yeah. Having it at *your* work was *Sister's* idea...

*Sounds* like hers. *All* the guys...the whole *neighborhood's* here...

Live in one place long enough and you know *every*body.

Yeah...it's *time*, babe: *kiss* me like you *mean* it...now *hold* me...

*Honey;* they're *staring* at us...

*That's* the *idea,* babe...OK; *that'll do. Now* we're *out...*

There are a *dozen* guys in here want to *brain* me right now...

*They're* too drunk...*just look* at Mom *grin...*

If I might be *impolite,* how *many* of these guys have *you...?*

*Some* of 'em *more* than once...jealous?

No; I don't *think...*so...

*Don't* be, babe; these *chowder*headed *knuckle*draggers are *all* out of the running...*I've* gotta sling some booze. Be back in a few.

***

You were *right* about the guys. *Half* of 'em want to beat you up, but the *rest....*

Shook my hand like I'm an old buddy. Wasn't expecting *that...*

I *sorta*-did. *Most* of 'em are good guys, but *some*—those that *I...*

Yeah. Don't want the competition...

Especially *not* from an outsider.

Guys are territorial...

*Some* guys are. *You* aren't...

I am, sort of. Your *father* had some *words* with me a few minutes ago.

I *saw* that. Anything *I...?*

*All* personal; *all* to do with *you...I* told him I only wanted *you* for your *body...*

And he believed *that?*

*Absolutely...*

C'mon; *what* did you *tell* him?

I said I *like* and *respect* you as a *friend, confidante,* and now...

Now a POSSLQ...Mom, too?

Your mother only wanted me to know that she'd *eviscerate* me if I *hurt* you in any way...

*E—what?*

Eviscerate; *gut...*

That's *Mom*, all right...I've been meaning to ask: when's *your* birthday?

I don't pay *any* attention to it...

Why *not?*

Because it's *not* a big deal for me...

But, it's a celebration of *life*, of *living...*

It's an excuse for a party...

So? *Why* don't you *celebrate...?*

Buddy got blinded on my fourteenth birthday...

*Oh*...babe; *I've* gotta go and *you've* got work tomorrow. See you at *home...*

*See* ya, honey.

***

*Hey...*

*Hey!* What's the *grin* for?

*Dad* saw the *paper...*

The...*oh!* What did he *say...?*

Well, he said it would *please* Mom that I finally made a legal commitment to *something*, even if it's just a lease on a place...

That grin says more than *that...*

*Sister* saw it; spread the word at her salon...

Now the rest of the *neighborhood* knows...

Yep; we're *legal...*and *public...*

***

Hey!

Hey, Blondie. Midnight oil again?

*Another* article. *There's* your latest batch of frames. What ya got there? *Big* bundle of paper...

Architectural concepts for the new hall. *I* get to pick one; *Boss* picks one; *Dad* picks one. We *compromise* on the *final*.

OK...

They're just *concepts*, not drawn to *size* or anything. I want *your* help...

What do *I* know about...?

*Help* me? *Please?*

OK, fine; you put it *that* way. Will this place be for *public* or *private* events?

*Both, but,* we can't *get* more than a hundred parking spots on that lot, according to the architects *and* the city...

With *wide shoulders* on that back driveway, you *could* get *another* hundred...

That's...huh; didn't think of *that*...

OK...let's *see*...different hands drew all these...

*That's* because they're from different *firms*...

OK; let's *roll* 'em out on my drawing board...hmm...no...no...*maybe*; put a sticky note on *that* one...*uh*-uh...um, *maybe*...hell no...huh, *maybe*... no...no...no...*maybe*...no; wait...ah, *maybe*...and...*no*...

I *said* thirteen was an unlucky number...

And there's four *maybes*. Which did *you* pick?

*My* favorite was your *hell, no*...

Let's look at it...huh...*my* problem is that it's too *big*. I mean, the *scale's* huge for *that* lot...

But it's *not* drawn for the location, just...think of the overall *effect*...

Well...*eh...no...sorry...*

I *see* what you mean...it's just too...

*Busy* for *that* lot...

Yeah. In *that* case...*this* one...

*That* was one of my *maybes*...huh...yeah, *I* could see it...

Me, too...want to go into the saloon business *with* me...?

Ah, no...

I sense *hesitation...*

*I* sense that you're trying to work your feminine *wiles* on me with your hands on my neck like...*that...*

*Wiles* are *tricks,* babe...*this* is *hardly* trickery...why *not...?*

I was *in* that general line of work before I started making picture frames. *Broke* my *back* bussing tables. With all the corruption in the restaurant trade, I didn't want to *stay* there.

The *corruption* is *manageable...*

I dunno about *that.* Where *I* worked, you got your linen, your glasses, your booze, and your tableware from the *right* suppliers, or you didn't *have* a restaurant *or* a bar. I get the impression that it's the same deal around *here.*

Yeah, but, like I *say,* it's *manageable...*

How *much* do you *know* about...?

Because of the *family's* business I'm being pulled *into,* I know *enough.* The police chief downtown keeps saying there's no organized crime here...

He's either an *idiot* or he's taking *payoffs...*

Maybe *both...*

And with Idiot Brother in the system, it might be all the *easier* for them to leverage your compliance...

*If* he goes into the system...

It's *when* for him, honey. *This* time or *next...*

Maybe you're *right,* babe...but...I *need* you...

*Hypothetically,* what would I *do* for you, anyway?

*Hypothetically,* you'd help me with all that crap I don't know *anything* about...will you *help* me...*babe* ...just *relax*...?

Mm...sure....OK...*honey*...

For how *long...shh...?*

*What* are you...?

Just...*stick around?* For *me*...?

I'm not sure I can *do* what you're *asking...honey*...

I'm asking very...*very...sweetly...babe*...for just a *little* commitment...if I give *you* one...

What...*kind...how...long....?*

Keep *us* together for, let's say, a *year...my* name's on the lease, too, now...

Don't know if I *can...honey*...

For *me....?*

With your *hands*...on my...*neck...like...that...mmm*... not... *fair...honey*...

All's *fair, babe*; all's *fair...a-hem*: Blondie, I want to pay you a retainer.

For *what?*

*Mostly* business advice, but *also* for picture frame manufacture.

What does *Boss* have to say about *that?*

It's not *his* money.

Who's *is* it?

The venture's...

So it's *yours*...how *much?*

Twice my *rent* to be *available*...we'll *also* pay you by the *frame.*

*Under* or *over* the table?

*Has* to be *over.*

*Tell* me this *isn't* charity, honey...

It *isn't*, babe. I'll *only* pay you your monthly retainer *if* you meet the frame demand on a *timely* basis and provide advice *when* I need it.

Groceries?

*Not* part of this negotiation.

You know, *despite* what I seem to owe the *universe*, I still *make more* than *you* do...and you're *working* your *feminine charms* on my *neck* again...*mmm*...aren't you...?

Negotiating strategy...*relax*, babe...*shh*...just say *OK*...or I'll just...*stop*...

*Don't* do that...I'm *thinking*...you negotiate with *everybody* like *this*?

*Just* the *guys*...Kitty's after...what's *that*...?

*Another* toy of opportunity...

Little hair clippie...say *yes*, babe...

*What* do I get if I *do*, honey?

*Two months' salary* in *ad-*

Yes.

Good...

Did I tell you I have an *interview* next week...

Oh...no, you *didn't*...

*Change* anything?

I *started* intending to make the offer, so no. I *want* to wish you *luck*...

But you *don't*...

But I *do*...

*Kind* of...

*Kind* of, babe ...

***

Hey.

Hey...

What's *up*, babe? Interview not go well?

Interview went *fine*, but...*listen*...

The Guy...*what?* He's going to *what?*

Start legal proceedings to *confiscate my rent*...if this guy's *legit, I'm* a monkey's uncle...

But...that's *Sister's* shop he's talking about...

Yeah...she's got *zilch* to do with...

Did you ever call a *lawyer*...

Couldn't *find* one who would take credit cards...gotta wait for my tax refund.

I happen to know one or *two*...

*No more charity*, Red...

No; *self-defense*...*we* want to help you...you *have* a decent, steady income. You *didn't* get into this mess by spending like a drunken sailor...talk to *our* lawyer, the one who's been doing *our*...

*I* can't even afford his *fees*...

We can *help* with *that*. I *have* resources, babe. Not infinite, and I'm *not* able to just write a check and make it all go away, but I *know people* who *know people*...

Honey, I...

*Forget* your pride, babe. Think, instead, of *me*. Of my family—*our* family...

Every time the phone rings, my heart sinks a little more, and there's no amount of *love* that'll *change* that. *Every* piece of mail; *every* knock on the door...it's like I've committed some crime that wasn't my *fault*...

I *know*...

Honey, as *much* as I *love* you, you *don't*...you *can't know*...

I can *love* you and then we'll pick ourselves up and...

I don't want to *anchor* you where I'd become a...

*Problem* for a new business, yeah...

*Not* that...

But there *is* that...don't *concern* yourself...you've got *enough*...

I just don't want *you* to...I'm just getting *used* to the idea that somebody loves me back, and *not* because we're related by marriage...

I've heard *I love you* so many times from *so* many guys, I'm not sure anymore what love is *supposed* to feel like...but it *feels* different with you...

You said we learn it at the breast?

That's how children *learn to love*, not how *love feels*. *That* we have to figure out on our own.

Let's...

*Join me* in the *shower*...

***

Feel better, babe?

Feel *clean* after *two* showers today.

You didn't get *that* much soap...did we say 'love you' this evening?

I believe we did...

I thought so...I *do*, you know...

I do too...love feels...*good*...

Feels...*great*...

How did you know...?

Because I can hardly *wait* to *see* you again every time we part...you?

I've started to see a future *beyond* just another day at *work*...

I want you to stay here...

Will if I *can*...honey, is it a good idea to discuss *this* in bed after...*that?*

When else *would* we, babe?

How about after a fine meal?

The finest meal I've *ever* had was that pizza after Door-Guy *dumped* on me...

*My* finest was last Valentines' Day...

I was *cold*...

*You* changed costumes...

You're the *first* guy I've ever had *this* conversation with...

Which conversation?

Leave or stay...

You're the *second* gal I've had *this* conversation with...

And?

I *still* love you, but I don't *know* if it's enough to *save* me... or *us*...

*Babe*...

I'm *right here*...

***

*That*...was...

You were *right*, honey; it's *so* much better right *after*...

*What* did I *tell* you?

I *know*; I *know*...*you* were *right*...

Should have said it *before*...

*Might* have been *untrue* before...

Might not have *meant* it before...but I *felt* it...

You mean it *now*...?

I *do*...do *you*...?

I *do*...are declarations of love while naked in bed as valid as those made under other conditions...?

Like...*what*...?

Oh, like...in front of a *firing squad*, say, or just before jumping into a *volcano*...

Babe, you are the *weirdest* lover I've *ever* had...

How many guys have you *told*...?

Two...

Me and who else...?

OK, *three*...

Who...?

You, Dad and Idiot Brother....

*Lovers?*

*No*, silly; guys I've told that I *loved* them...

*Oh*, OK. You've been *proposed* to, but you *never*...?

*Nope. They* just wanted to tie me down...do *you* want to tie me down...?

*I* want you to be happy...

W*ay not* to answer...

You already *know* this...it's nothing I haven't *said* before. But *no*, I *don't* wanna tie you down. I just...

*You* want to *know* that a girl will *always* be at *home* for you...

*Sounds* like you're trying to talk yourself *out* of...

I'm *not*. It's *just*...with *my* history with guys...call it a bad habit, but even after my grand declaration last month, *part* of me wants to *hedge*...

But...

But...*you*...

# Helps...

*Blondie? Where are you, babe...Kitty, what are you crying about...you look wet...dirty-wet black cat...is he down... why's the saw...BLONDIE! OMYGOD! NONONONO!... HELLO! I NEED AN AMBULANCE...*

***

*Ugh, my head...*where...where *am* I? What...? Hey, Red.
*Hey*, yourself. Let 'em know you're *awake...*
My *head* hurts something *awful...*what *happened?*
I'll let *them* tell you...
Just *push* that *button* there...*that's* the one...

***

*Hey*, Red.
Hey...
I *hit* my *head...*
Last *night...*
Yeah, against the *wall* or the *floor...*don't *know* which...
The *wall* has blood and hair on it...but there's blood everywhere...
*Ugh.* Got a mild concussion, cracked ribs, *twelve* stitches in my scalp, they say...

Uh-*huh*...how do you feel *now?*

Sore as *hell* almost *every*where. The saw kicked that plywood back into my *chest* and shoved me *back*...serves me *right* for *ripping* on a radial arm...*you* found me?

Uh-*huh*. I called 911, and the paramedics came; *they* called the cops...

*Cops?*

Everybody had to be satisfied that *I* didn't do this to you...cops *said* they'd be around for a statement once you woke up...any *idea* how long you were *out?*

I remember looking at the clock at about seven, and I worked for *about* another hour...what time did you *find* me?

About nine-thirty. The saw was still running when I got home; the cops pulled the plug. I called Step-Mom; she told the *hospital* I was your *fiancée,* said *I* could decide *for* you if it came to *that*...

Congratulations, honey.

Same to you, babe...Big Boss says take what time you need...

You called *them*...?

Yeah. Co-Worker was here this morning, brought *those* flowers. Sister was here this morning, brought *those* flowers and some stuff for *me, and* my *car*...

Some *stuff* and your *car?*

Yeah; I came in the ambulance with you...*borrowed* your *shower*...

You've *been* here...?

Since last night. Dad gave Idiot Brother and Loser some money to clean up the basement...

Nice. C'mere once...

I'm *here*...

You *saved* my *life*...

Nothing *that* dramatic...they said it was *messy* but not *dangerous*...

Then *why* are they *keeping* me...?

*Ask them...* now that you're *awake* and *sassy, I* need to get to work. I'll come back tomorrow *before* work.

*Before* you...

*Huh?*

Just *c'mere...bend* over; c'mon...*mmm...*

Slow *down,* cowboy...

As *sweet* as before...

As sweet as *always...See* ya, Blondie.

*See* ya, Red. And, ah, honey...?

*Yeah,* babe. *Me,* too...

***

*Hey...*

Hi...*mmm...*

You look *glum...*

The *finance people* were just here...

Yeah?

*Yeah, asking* about my *guarantor...your dad...*

Oh?

Red, *don't* try that *innocent act* with *me...*

Blondie, I honestly don't know *what* you're talking about... what were they *saying?*

Just that I could *sign* the guarantor agreement as soon as the doctors cleared me to *do* so...c'mere...

I'm *here...*

*Gimmie* your *hand...*look me straight in the eye...OK: *you* didn't know *anything* about *this...*you didn't *ask* your dad...?

No...but...

*BUT...*

But...they stopped *your fiancée* as she was leaving yesterday... asked *your fiancée* about payment, asked if *our finances* were still *separate. She* said we hadn't gotten *that* far yet; the engagement was *very recent....but...Dad* was about *six feet away* at the *time...*

Yeah, he was here right after you left; we *talked* about... oh...*ho-boy...that* part that didn't make *sense; now* it does... what was *your* conversation with the *hospital* like...?

It was...*quick* and...well, I *had* to say, since *Step-Mom* told 'em, that we were *new* that I...hadn't even told my *family* yet...

Saved yourself *that* one...

Yeah...I had to dash and Dad just said *he'd*...don't know if he told *Mom* or...oh, *shit*, I'll find *out* soon enough 'cause I've got to get to *work* in fifteen minutes...*what* did he say to *you?*

It was...there was something he *didn't* say, but *nothing* about *that...now* what, Red?

You're asking *me*, Blondie?

I'm *asking* my *sudden*-fiancée...ho-boy...*do* we...after deciding *against* commitment...?

Let's *talk* about...*this*...ho-*shit*...commitment we *didn't* make...

Hope the nurse doesn't walk in...*should* we *just say* we *are*...?

The *hospital* thinks...*Dad* thinks...for *safety*, do you *want* to...?

Don't want to *think* about what the *hospital* would *do* if we *say* we're *not*...

*Then* we'll say...we'd *just talked* about it in the past few *days*...

And Step-Mom heard *me* talk about it on my *weekly phone call*...

And then she *leaned forward* a bit...

But we weren't *ready* to *say* anything...*right*...

*That'll* work, Blondie.

It *better* work, Red, putting it all on *Step-Mom. You'd* better get going.

Yeah. See you tomorrow, babe.

*Tomorrow*, honey.

***

Hey! Feeling better? *Pucker...*

Hi! *Yeah...mmm...*how'd it *go* last night?

Just the usual...

Your family *didn't...?*

Nope.

*Step-Mom* called this morning. For expedience, *she* told the hospital we *were* engaged because she's tied up in some complicated case and just *can't* get away; kept her from jumping on an airplane or spending a day *driving.*

Explains *that...*

Yeah. I told *her* about the guarantor requirement just as the finance people came back: the doctors said I *could* sign...so...

You signed?

I *did.* It's *one* thing to *say* that over the phone in an emergency; *another* to say it's *real.* As an attorney, Step-Mom had, ah, *objections* to such a *seamy* deception...

Yeah...we *are* a *seamy* pair, ain't we? And...?

Of *course* she went for it. She said she'd call your dad *and* the hospital to make the required financial arrangements...

*Required* arrangements...?

They want *money* before they let me *out* of here...

How's *that* gonna work? Strap you to the bed...put a guard on the door?

Heh, *good* one...I dunno. I remember thinking that night was how making *this* frame might pay for *this* month and maybe keep *one* voice off the answering machine *this* Sunday...

*We'll figure* it *out,* babe...

*Not* soon enough...

***

*Hey*, Blondie. You *look* better. How do you *feel?*

*Hey*, Red. I'm *feeling* better. How was *work?*

Fine; getting busy on the *books*, now.

Get to your *mid-terms* on time?

Yeah. Talked to Dad last night...

How did *that* go...?

I, ah, tried out the *engagement discussion* explanation...he understood...

That's good...he tell your mom?

Said he'd hold off...when are you going back to work?

*Monday.* Our families gave the hospital enough money to let me *loose*, but now that I've got another *catastrophic* medical bill, I've *got* to be making money...a *waking nightmare* with an intermission on Sunday while I write checks with the *account numbers* distorted...

I answered your phone a couple days ago; some woman I *thought* was Step-Mom, but it *wasn't*....The *Guy* using a bait voice...I just said you were *ill* and would get back to him...he asked who *I* was and I said I was renting a room... then *he* said 'oh you're that *redhead* he's been *screwing*. Are *you* the one on the *lease?* We need to discuss *your* family's liability...' and I hung up...

*Your* family's liability...?

Yeah...he called back a few minutes later, said 'we will go after every *dime* in *your* name and in your *family's* name if you do not pick up the phone *imm*ediately...'

*That's* what that message was...*shit*, Red...you *sure* you want to be stuck with *this*...*what* are you grinning at?

I called Dad...he just said '*ignore* them, my dear. He's just bluffing.'

*Probably*...but if he knows *who* you *are*...

He knows *shit* other than a *name*...babe, we're in this together. All *you* have to do is *get well*...your phone... who's *that?*

A *new* voice...*not* familiar...*law firm*...somebody's *suing*...?

No...*not* suing...?

*No*...I'm picking *that* up...

***

Step Two's *college roommate* is an *attorney*...?

Two counties over...appointment next Monday...fees *paid* by *Step Two*...I barely *know* him...

Wow...

*Yeah*, wow...light at the end of the tunnel that *isn't* another train...

That *finance* lady gave me...a mimeographed...yeah; *this*...

From their *legal department*...huh...*beware of fraudulent collectors*...sage advice...honey, that deputy friend of yours... you still on good terms?

Yeah...*yeah*...I'll *call* him...

***

Odd...I'm still a little fuzzy...did *that* conversation make any sense?

What I *heard* was that that woman he transferred my call to is with the sheriff's *frauds department*?

Yeah. Apparently, The Guy's been running a scam for a while. The hospital has been complaining about *some* of their customers being bilked by him...

Is it *that* easy?

Honey, it's like offering a mouse a way out of a trap: they scurry for it and *everything* after is easy. Most people would sell their *souls* to get out from behind *that* eight-ball...

I believe *that's* a mixed metaphor.

I believe *you've* become a *grammarian*.

I'm taking *English comp* next semester so I can *keep up* with you.

***

Hey, babe; how's work?

OK. Step-Mom called, wants to come over *here* the week after next, see how I *am...*

*Oh...*

C'mon, *sit* with me. She *may* tell Step Two that we *are* engaged to simplify *her* life...

What would *he* care?

*He's* pretty straight-laced; I don't know that he slept with Step-Mom before they *were* married. *He's* not as...*open...* as Step-Mom...

Probably why *she* had those words with Step-Sis...

Yeah...Red...*honey*...Step-Mom gave me *this* at Christmas... will *you...?*

Blondie, *GET UP off your knee...!*

It's the ring my *father* gave her; it will *help* to *confirm everything* we've said for the sake of appearances...

A *ring...*

Did any of your *other* suitors ever go *this far?*

*Oh, HELL* no!...*beautiful* ring, babe...c'mon; *get* up; you *look* like you're in a *movie...*

*Not* until I get an *answer...will* you *wear* it, Red...? If nothing *else...*

*This* is...you just come up with this *harebrained* idea *today...?*

I *thought* about it when Step-Mom *gave* it to me...I *thought* about it a couple times *since.* Now Step-Mom and *you* have made us *quasi*-official...blabbermouth...

She made us *pseudo*-engaged for *convenience* and so did *I*, *damnit...see* if it...well, it *fits...*a *little* tight...

*Will* you *wear* it, then? If we *don't* work out...

Yeah...OK...it *is* beautiful...

You've made me the happiest guy on Earth.

Good thing I didn't *have* to make any of *those* decisions while you were knocked out...

The *legal* implications might have been catastrophic.

Not just *that*. I don't know that I *could* have...

I believe, my *dearest* housemate, that, come down *to* it, you *could* have...

*Dearest* housemate, *I* need to wash the saloon off me. I'll be *back*...

*I'm* going to *bed*...

See you *there*.

*** 

Feel *better?*

*Cleaner.* Babe, do *we*, as a hypo*thet*ically engaged couple, *want* kids? I *don't* think the subject's ever come up.

Well, it has *now*.

*We* would have beautiful babies if we ever *got* that far. But I need to warn you: I *may* not be *able* to have kids.

Not even *hypothetical* ones?

*Those* I *could* have...those cysts they removed *could* grow back.

Well...do you *want...?*

Part of me does; the other part looks at Sister's brood and thinks *I want that kind of hassle?*

Huh...*this* is a first.

*What* is?

Talking about having kids...

Never?

Nope.

Bizarre that a good-looking, smart, nice guy like you hasn't been snapped up by a *dozen* different girls...do *you* want kids?

Most girls *never* showed *that* much interest in me...Red, for the *first* time in my *life*, I think...yes; I think I *do*...maybe two or three? Hypo*the*tically, of *course*...

*Three. No* more.

*Hypothetically* speaking...three kids...but *not now.*

*Hypothetically*, of course...but *not now.*

And *tomorrow* we start...

*Acting* like *engaged* POSSLQs...*and* I'll have *tons of* homework to catch up on because I have to work *all day tomorrow* to get ready for St. Patty's Day.

*And* we have to move more of *your* stuff into *my* room and make *yours* look a little *less* lived in.

*And* we have to clean our *love-nest* from *top* to *bottom* because your *mother's* going to see...

*Step-Mom*...

Same *diff* as far as *I'm* concerned. *Dreading* it, too, because *no amount* of time can erase the memory of a good cat, and *no amount* of masking tape can ever *totally* remove its *fur* from the *fur*niture.

*Deep*, Red. It strikes me that we've never *had* a *serious* fight or even a *disagreement.*

*Except* when we rearranged the *living* room...

And when *I* changed the subject from *making out* to *cat shit*...

*And* after I *broke* the vacuum cleaner...

*And* when you saw me trimming my toenails in the living room...

*And* when you *sat* on my *favorite* big hair clippie with that *bony butt* of *yours*...

*And* when *you* stepped on that *frame* I'd spent a *week* woodburning with those *bloody big red boots* of *yours*...

Have we *agreed? Hypothetically?*

Yeah. But *now*, sleep. 'Night.

'Night...

*Shit*...oh, *GOD!* I didn't *think* of *that*...my *family*...

What...?

I need to *explain* the *ring*...shit-shit-SHIT-shitty-*shit!*

Explanations *are* required *in preference* to *shocking* the *family* with *significant* jewelry before making *formal* announcements...there's *china patterns* to choose, after all.

Are *you* making *fun* of me?

Maybe, *just* a little...just...you're over-thinking this... getting panicky. Re*lax*, calm *down*...*deep* breath. It'll be *fine*, *you'll* see.

*Tomorrow night* at the *bar. Be* there...

*I'll* play *my* part...

***

*That* was easier than you *thought* it would be, Red...your *mom* was...

She *expected* it...she heard the nurses at the hospital talking about me as *your* family...she added it up.

Ah. Sister thought it was *funny.*

*She* thought it was a *joke*...until she saw the *ring*...it *ain't* a cheap one, either.

Red...*tell* me we're *not* a joke...

We're *not* a joke, Blondie, but I never *got* this far...*not* even close...but, *babe*, I'm *glad* it's *you.*

Me, too, honey; me too.

***

*Hey*, babe...

Hey...

You're...*quiet*...what's...you saw that lawyer?

Yeah.

263

So...what...?

He gave me all this paperwork to fill out...everything I owe everybody, *including* the *credit card* I've been relying on... once I *file, it's done*, too.

Can't *save* it; keep it *separate?*

Apparently not, even though I have a *little* credit on it.

I know you've been using it for...

Material for the frames. And it gets a little *worse*, kinda... any settlement also eats up my *tax refund...all* of it. But, there's things *short* of bankruptcy that I *might* be able to... since I have a good-paying job...

What about my rent and groceries?

Kept that out; nothing formal about it and you're on the lease. I need to fill all this out and get it *back* to them ASAP because...*listen...*

The *Guy* again...he's *what?* The *BAR?!?!?!*

Says he *can* grab it for *my* debts.

Pull that answer tape out...*Dad* needs to...

No; *your deputy* and that *frauds investigator* needs to...

***

*Erin go Bragh*, Red! *Kiss* me, I'm *Irish!*

As Irish as *I* am, but *c'mere...*

*Mm*, sweet. Hope you didn't go *this* far with any of the *other* revelers in here, drunkenly proclaiming Celtic heritage...

*Only* one or *two. Have* a corned beef sandwich on the house. Talk to Step-Mom today?

Yeah. She'll be flying in next Thursday; leaving Sunday. She's *bringing* Step Two *and* Step-Sis.

Great! Let me sling a few drinks. Go on and *eat*, babe...

***

Good crowd, Red...

*Yeah*; we're flush for the *month* now.

*Fabulous.* I told Step-Mom that *with* Step-Sis *we* can't put 'em up. And we spent *all* that *time cleaning* and *moving*...

Still *needed* to do it for my hypothetical *in-laws-to-be*, babe. I *have* to close on Thursday, but I'm going to *open* the rest of the time they're *here*...

I thought you *had* new bartenders...?

Either Boss or I *have* to be here until they're *all* bonded. I *can* control my schedule, though.

I have a *client meeting* Friday morning that I *can't* miss, so they'll be on their own for a bit. They could come *here*, once.

*Friday.* We're trying a catered all-you-can-eat fish fry. We're using that fish fry place *you* like so much. Mom and Dad are coming, they said.

Yeah? OK. Remember Step-Sis is *our* age, so nothing *special* for...

My hypothetical sister-in-law-to-be and your dance instructor/prom date/first *gal* in your *pants*? I'll put on the *dog* for *her*...

Don't go *too* overboard on the first gal bit; I don't know if Step Two ever *heard that*...so...*that's* what you guys are planning?

Yeah. The architects are working on specifics now, say they should have it ready for bids and permits by next month... they'll be surveying the easement...*your* easement...next week for the county to approve...demo to start in a few weeks...leave an empty shell...

*Exciting*, Red...

*Scary*, Blondie...

As scary as meeting Step-Mom?

*Her* I don't *have* to see all the time; *that's* my *future*.

***

Hey, babe; what brings *you* in here?

*Hey*, honey...took all the paperwork to the lawyer; signed the forms. He says he'll *try* to *save* the credit card; there *might* be a way to save me short of bankruptcy.

*OK*, then. Beer?

Sure.

*Yet*...you're...

I get the feeling I'm on this *road*; a road that doesn't end, like a hamster wheel that goes nowhere. Filing all that paperwork with the court in the next few days *should* stop the phone calls and the dunning letters, but...

*But*...

My *credit* will be destroyed; I took *seven years* to build it up, and I *destroyed* it in as many *months*...

It *wasn't* your *fault*, babe...

It *kinda* was. I *could* have stayed in The Slum; *not* bought all that furniture *and* the washer and dryer...

And *we* would *never* have *met*...

But I *wouldn't* be *broke*...but I *still* would have gotten sick a *second* time; my *car* would have broken down, *anyway*...

*And* we would *never* have *met*...

Who's to say? I might have ventured over here on the *right* night...

And I *might* have tried to pick you up if the *Beard* situation was the same...

And I *might* have asked the same *question* about your bra and panties...

And I *still* wouldn't have been *wearing*...hey, *back off pal, private conversation here, OK?*

*No ogling the fiancée*, pal...

if it wasn't for *customers,* we could say what*ever* we *wanted* in *here*...

*Yeah...*

And *no gawking* at the *braless barmaid,* ya...I *oughta...*

*Easy* Red, don't *flash* the *customers...*

You're *right; not* without a *cabaret license...*

Might not make much *money* in the middle of the week, but...

We sure have *fun* trying...

***

I *like* your family, Blondie.

Me, too...I'll *take* your jacket...

*I* got the mail...junk and bills...you want to be *Occupant* today?

Pass...Step-Mom likes *you.* Can't *tell* about Step Two; I don't *know* him that well. Step-Sis...

She's *lots* of fun...

She *is*...what were you two *nattering* about at the *other* end of the bar?

Just the usual *girl talk* about getting into your *pants* and a few *other* stories...

Really? She'd *never tell* about the *incident* on the *patio...*

What's *this,* now?

*Never* you *mind...*

I'll have to *ask* her about that. So, never *bonded* with Step Two?

Some; *not* much. I worked in one of his stores on weekends for pocket money. *He's* into bowling; *I* wasn't, but I went *with* him sometimes. *Now I owe* him...

He said you *don't...*

I *feel* like I do...

Did you know that Step-Mom's Step Two's *third* wife?

He's *her* third *husband,* so...

Eh, yeah.

I'm glad our folks hit it off...

Me, too. Mom was being *more* than polite. She's happy to see me *affianced* to someone she *approves* of.

She *approves* of me?

*Definitely*; she asks how you *are* all the time. *Dad* even *enquires* about your *career*.

Huh. He doesn't expect *me* to take a place in *your* family business, does he?

Not *that* way...they're branching out to leave *us* with something *more* than...

None of you kids went into their business?

It never appealed to *us*.

Except *now*...

Except *now*...yeah. *I'll* be into it up to my *neck*.

Glad Sister dumped Loser and brought the kids.

They're separated; she kicked him out and filed...

*When?*

*Last* Friday.

You date a *facade*, marry the *truth* and divorce your *mistake*.

*Words* of *wisdom*...*I'm* glad that the weather was good enough we could eat outside. Didn't expect *that* many people.

Five bucks for all-you-can-eat beer-batter fish and chips, yeah. You make money?

We *did*. So...your family's coming *here* tomorrow morning, going to dinner by Mom and Dad in the afternoon, and I'm meeting you *there* after work...?

Right. I'll show 'em the sights around town, take 'em down by the lake, all the usual...

Uh-huh...what's with the *look*...?

It's just...just *happy*.

*That* happy?

*Happy* to be with *you, honey.* Are you *that* happy?

Let's not go overboard, babe...

Just a *little* overboard, honey?

I'll throw you a *lifeline...*

***

Thanks for being so *nice* to my family...I'll take your jacket...

Blondie, for *you, anything...here...*I think they really *enjoyed* their visit.

I think Step-Mom wanted to see for herself what her only *close-to* child's best friend in the whole world is *really* like.

I think you're *right...*I *asked* Step-Sis about the *incident* on the *patio...*

And she *said...?*

*What* incident on *what* patio...or was it *which* incident... anyway she *clammed up* right quick-like...

That's *Step-Sis*; loyal to her buddy...

But she *said* it *was* hilarious...something about *her friend's hat* in *your...?*

Friend's hat...oh, *that...*heh-heh...I asked her to stand up for me when the time *came* for us to...

*I* wanna hear about the incident on the *patio* and the friend's *hat* in *your...*

*Never...*

Why do I get the feeling that...*incident* on the *patio* my *ass...* pull the *other* one...I'm gonna sit on the porch, watch the sunset over the fields...

And *smell* the *fertilizer* like you *just* did...I'll *join* you...

***

*Beautiful* sunsets this time of year...

Yeah...Red, do you *like* making love with *me...?*

I never knew sex could be *quite as satisfying* as it is with *you,* babe.

Even after *all* the...?

*Because* of *all* the...but I *want* children someday.

But not *now*...

I'm *on* the *pill*...

It's not 100% effective...

No, but those *cysts* might be...*work* tomorrow...

On a *Monday?*

*Boss* has got something else with *his* family; his *mother's* not well.

*****

Hey! Any *news?*

Hey, Red. Maybe there's something *to* The Curse after all.

What *curse?* Is he *dead?*

Not *yet*; *hurt* pretty bad. Every president elected every twenty years since 1860 has died in office. We elected the Gipper in '80.

I wouldn't know about *that*; I couldn't even tell you who was president before...um...The King of Camelot? Not even sure when *he*...

1960, Red. It was Ike before him.

Ike *who?*

Never mind. You working late?

Early. Got a *date* tonight...

Really? Should I be *jealous?*

Less a *date* than *dinner* with a *guy* who once asked me to marry him because his younger sister was getting hitched... we were *naked* and had *just*...

I *get* it...how many guys have *asked* you?

Um...counting *you*, five...*one* was *in* high school; one was *this* guy; one was just a loser on a bar stool who could barely pay his tab every week, let alone support a family. The last was Beard; *kinda*.

Huh...technically, I didn't *ask*...

Yeah...he's one of those who shook your hand.

How's *that* gonna go over?

It's just dinner. Babe, are *we* long-term?

You mean, *serious?* You *wear* my *ring*, honey...

What if it *wasn't* just for show...my dad really *likes* you.

Yeah...I'd rather spend my life with *you* than *alone*...

But *I* don't *know*...

I'll be *here*, regardless of your dates, honey.

And I'll spend my *nights* here, babe.

***

Hi.

*Hey.* How was your date? *Time* is it...?

Either *early* or *late* and I'm *just* out of the shower...Behind-Neighbor has a fever again...so do *I*...not *that* kind, but...

*Mm...sweet* kiss, honey...

So's *yours*, babe...more than I got from my *date*...

And you're *not* stopping *there*...

*Uh*-uh...

***

You *OK?*

I'm *great;* you?

*Great*...don't you feel a *little* funny doing *me* right after going out with *another* guy?

He said *he* had a girl he was *banging* tonight.

He *said* that...?

*Yep.* He congratulated me on our engagement...half my class was married within a *year* of graduation and *more* than half of *them* divorced or separated within *three* years.

Only *half* of 'em are *still* married, and some of *them're* near the rocks.

As much as I'd like to *continue* this conversation, I've got to get up for *work* in two hours...

I'd like to *thank* you, babe, for being my buddy...*and*... for...

*This* is what *buddies* are *for*...

*Making love* in the middle of the night?

That *and serious* conversations, Red; *serious* conversations... two *hours* to...*hell* with it; *c'mere*...

I'm right *here*...

***

Hey...what?

*The Guy* left *this* in the door; found it when I got home...

What's...*final notice*...of *what*?

Says he's going to take everything in this *townhouse* in thirty days if I *don't* pay the *paltry* sum of *eight grand*.

*Twice* what they *first*...?

Yep...there's *this*, too...

*Looks* like a *summons*...

Writ of attachment. Says they own *everything* I *have*...says there'll be one on the *bar* tomorrow.

*How* can he do *that?*

Not *possible* without going to court, and the bar isn't any part of *my* debt. It *would* be scary *if*...look down *here*...

It's...a *photocopy*...

Not even an original. Little turd is trying to pull a *fast* one. Your dad was right, and I'm mighty *sick* of this *shit*...*I'm* calling that investigator...

*And* your lawyer... they *filed* that paperwork, didn't they?

Haven't had a *legit* call in two weeks, so yeah...*what's going on?*

And *how* do they know *so much about us?*

# Loves Spring...

*Hello; tech pubs...*

*Dad's* had a heart attack...
Oh *shit*, Red. Is *he...?*
In the hospital...
I'm *on* my *way...*
But it's *noon...*
Don't *argue*, Red!

***

*Hey*, Red...uh, *oh! OK, I'll* just...
Just *shut up* and *hold* me...
Sure...*shh*, now...what are they *saying?*
*I'm* saying *shut up* and *hold* me...
Here's *Sister...*
*Shut up* and *don't* let me go...

***

Thanks *so* much for coming...
*You* came for *me,* honey.
*I* came *with* you, babe.
What *are* they saying?

273

The next 24 hours will tell.

Then we *wait...*

*You* don't *have* to...

Like I'd *want* to be anywhere *else?* Need to call the office, *anyway...*

***

What did your office say?

The client is *not* happy that I couldn't make the meeting, but they under*stand* family emergencies. Want something to eat?

I *should.* I haven't *eaten* since this morning.

And it's dusk now. C'mon; cafeteria's down *this* way; c'mon...

***

I never *liked* hospitals, especially when someone I know is *in* one.

*This* one's pretty quiet.

*This* one's on the verge of being *closed.* The nurse said one wing's already deserted.

But it's handy for *us...*

Handy for you and Dad...*and* me...

*That's* what I *meant...*at least the cafeteria's still open.

***

For a hospital cafeteria, the *food* wasn't bad, Blondie.

I never saw burgers jond fries next to scrambled eggs and hash browns on a steam table.

Probably because they were closing up. There's Loser. Wonder *why;* he and Dad *never* got along. Mom's *not* doing well.

She *seems* pretty upbeat.

You don't know what to look for; she's devastated.

*Sister* seems more devastated than your mom.

She's *scared*...Dad's been keeping her and the kids afloat since Loser got himself *fired*.

Think your mom would cut her off?

I *don't* know...Sister's not as close to Mom as she is to Dad...

Different family dynamics. Sure glad *mine* was more straightforward.

*Yours* were just more screwed up.

Yeah, well, there *is* that...

***

They're moving him to County hospital?

They *say* he's stable enough to be moved for an *Angie*... *some*thing, whatever *that* is...what were you and Mom talking about?

Grief; loss...some *other* stuff...

*Like...?*

*Like*...Sister wants to get the kids *out* of here. Why don't I take them to *our* place, wait for the news?

But, I...

*You* need to be with your family. Isn't *that* an aunt and uncle?

*Dad's* younger brother. But *you're*...

It just makes sense, honey. See you at home later.

***

*Hey...*

Oh, *hi! How's...*

Resting comfortably, the doctor said. Auntie picked the kids up?

Yeah; about ten. They were half-asleep already.

So am *I*. Can I *hold* you for a while?

Sure...my *alarm* goes off in...three hours...*just* so you...

*I* know. 'Night.

'Night.

***

Hey...

*Hi*, Red. How's your *dad?*

Better than he *was*; got some *color* now.

*Good*. How's your mom holding up?

She's...babe, can we *talk* about something *else?*

Sure. *Two guys* are sitting at a bar. *One* guy says, 'did *you* know that lions have sex 10 or 15 times a night?' The *other* guy says, 'damn, *I* just *joined* that *gear* club...'

*He-he!* Hadn't *heard* that one...need to remember it next time they *meet* in the bar...*Twelve-Year-Old* told me one this afternoon: why is *poop* tapered at both ends?

Why?

So your *butt-cheeks* won't slam shut.

*HAH...Twelve-Year-Old?*

*Yeah...*

Well, yeah, *junior high...*

*Middle school* now...so, what are *you* doing?

Brushing up this *article...*

What *about...?*

How many lumberjacks it took to put a *tank* on a *beach* during the Big War...

OK, *what's* the *punchline?*

Oh, it's *not a joke*. I've worked out that it took *nine* lumberjacks working *forty* hours a week to harvest enough *wood...*

Is there *that* much *wood* in a *tank?*

No, but it *comprises* a *lot* of metal castings, and they made the casting molds of wood back then; they shipped all the parts between factories in wood crates *and* the ammunition; they made the landing craft that got the tanks on shore of wood; then there's the tank crew's *orders* printed on *pulp paper*...

Huh...yeah, I guess. I gotta admire how your mind *works*... *greatly* admire...works...

Not gonna do that much *more*...*work*...while *you're* doing... *that*...

You're *tense*...re*lax*, babe...*how's*...

The old *blind him with a shirt* trick. *Now* I can't *see* my *typewriter*...

Do you still *want* to...?

Not...*now*...

*I* want to go upstairs and re*lax* for a while...come *with* me...

Kinda *early* even for...

*C'mon*...I'll get in the shower...

***

*Hey*...

*Hmm*...?

Now *that* was...

Re*laxing*...*told* ya...

I somehow always thought that sex was...

*Fast* and *tense*? Yeah, *most* guys think so. But if you just... *slow down*, *watch* the sun go down, touch-don't-*grab*...just...

*Soothing*...

Except at the *end*...

Even *that* was...different...

It helps if it's *not* a *first* time...babe; when Buddy died, I *know* it's a sore subject, but...

Yeah...?

Where did you *put* your *hurt?*

*Part* of it went into beating Bully's *brains* out.

I'd *imagine*...

*Most* of it's like a *book* I've *poured over* for a *long time* that I finally put on a shelf. Once in a *while*, I run *into* it, *remember* the contents, *smile* or *cry* and *move on*. The *other* part's still telling me I'll never hear another of his *godawful* jokes...

They *that* bad?

*So* bad I still *remember* some of 'em...maybe in his honor.

Like what?

OK...um...what did the fish say when he swam into a wall?

I dunno, what?

Dam...

Yeah, *that's* pretty *bad*...

What do you call a *can opener* that doesn't *work?*

Um...

A *can't* opener...

OK; *that's* enough...

Once I start, it's hard to *stop*...

I guess...you *tired?*

Not really...you *OK?*

I'm *better* now...let's watch some TV...

*Here* or...

Here.

***

Hey, Red. Working on a *Sunday?*

A *little*; went to see *Dad*. You *busy?*

Just shuffling paper from one pile to another, trying to figure out how to wrangle around having *no* credit cards.

In *that* regard, *here's* for the last *three* frames...Boss wants... no, *we* want three *more* this week...

OK; *thanks*...I'll have the frames by Friday...how's your *dad?*

They're saying his heart is failing. He's *home*, and they put him on a transplant list, but he's got a rare blood type.

Sorry, Red...

Dad made his choices...

Sounds *cold* coming from you.

*Business* is doing *that*...Mom said I was to give you *this.*

OK, thanks...

What's...?

Um...*ah*; *Step-Mom* called your *mom* last night...

Why...?

*I* called *her*...

*Why...?*

I needed to talk to somebody who wasn't in the middle of all the *drama*. Your mom says she was glad to talk to someone who wasn't, *either*.

Ah. Something to do with *that*...

Yeah...*something*...

*Don't* tell me you're starting an *affair* with *my mother*...

Honey, your parents and I have an under*stand*ing; the *same* kind I have with Sister.

An...*under*stand*ing*...?

*Yes*, dear; an under*stand*ing as to my *int*entions towards your *family*...and *other* things.

*What* kind of *under*standing...?

Your family doesn't *know* me, honey. I had to make myself *clear* to them I *wasn't* after the family fortune...

You are the only guy I've *ever*...from outside the 'hood. Just *how*, pray *tell* me, did this *under*standing come about?

The *usual* way; introductions, followed by close questioning, cavity search, background and credit checks, rubber hoses and bright lights...

*C'mon...*

It's...just getting to *know* and *trust*. Not *that* complicated, just...*gotta* be *done*.

Never *had* to before...why *now*?

Like you said; I'm your first guy from out of the 'hood. That *and*...

And...*what*?

It's between *them* and *me*, and I *can't* disclose it to *you*.

*Why...*?

It has to do with your *family's* business and with *mine*...I can't go *any* further...*please* trust me on this.

Huh...guess I'll *have* to...you *know* the *first* two bartenders I hired?

*Dated* Legs; the *other* I didn't.

Glad you didn't *date* the *guy*.

Really *not* my type. What *about* them?

The *till's* light sometimes.

*How* light?

As much as twenty bucks a night.

*Risky* for that *little*...I know *she wouldn't* do it; can't *say* that about him.

Why?

He just seems *fishy*, that's all. Did you...?

No; he's one I *never* dated, but I've *known* both of them since *grade school*.

There's a *lot* of guys you didn't date in the 'hood?

*Enough*...now; about that under*standing*...

I *can't*, honey; I *won't*...that's between *them* and *me*.

***

Hey, Blondie!

Hey, Red! Getting some sun, I see. *That's* that outfit you wore Valentine's day...with*out* the leotards...

Yep; lets in *all* the sunshine I can *get*...

Lets in *all* the *everything*...it *doesn't hide*...much...

Not *supposed* to...

Hope *Boy* Across-The-Walk *didn't*...

*He* got a *good* look; so did Guy-Neighbor-Behind. *Mom* Across-The-Walk, *and* our Kitty-Corner neighbors all stopped by for a *chat* while I was on my *back*...

Very popular in *that*...

And *very* comfortable...do me up in back?

Sure...is Mom Across-the-Walk looking jealous 'cause I'm doing this?

She has a *boyfriend* now. I see him leave when I come home late. *Gal* Neighbor-Behind...hard to say...*you* have something to *say*...

I've got *another* interview...

Same outfit...?

Yeah...

When?

Saturday...

I *see*...

*Don't* cry, Red...

No...*I'm* going inside...your mail's there; I *didn't* feed Kitty yet. I'm *trying* to accept what's coming with *you* and *Dad*, and I need to...oh, *hi, cowboy...very* nice...

You're *warm*, little lady...

*You're risqué*, wrapping yourself around me with the *door* open.

Does my pseudo-fiancée in a *peek-a-boo* bikini who's under duress *really* think I'm being *risqué* by hugging her in a *semi-private* place...?

She *does*.

Does she *mind*?

She does *not*. *Shh*...just *hold* me.

Long as *you*...

*Shh*...*less* chat, *more* hug...*much* better...

***

Sun's setting later every day...

It *tends* to *do* that after late December...must have *something* to do with the calendars.

*Must* be...glad I *got* these chairs; makes sitting on our little *porch* a *damn* sight more comfortable...this wine's... *wine*...

Just old grape juice.

You romantic *devil*, you...take the *fun* out of everything...

Habit of mind...so, *two* or so tonight?

Yeah.

Do you think we're becoming domesticated to each other?

Heaven for*fend*...

For*fend*? Red, are *you*...?

Just *stifle* yourself and enjoy the *sunset*...

***

Oh, *hi*, honey...

*Hi*, babe...

Good *night*?

*Loads* of tips...

You still *get* tips even if you're management...?

As long as I'm slinging booze, my *cleavage* will get tips... customers don't *care* if I'm management...hell, half of 'em don't *know*...

Too bad...I *know* you...

I *like* the *money*...

*Anyway*, I've got another road trip next week; *new* client, maybe. Couple of *days*...

I will *miss* you...

*I* will miss *you*...and *you*...

*Shh*, babe. *This* won't *take* long...*shh*...

***

*Hi; just* finished putting *groceries* away. How...?

Hey...you *cut* your *hair*...

Yeah, but *how* was the *road trip?*

*We* got a *ton* more work out of it. Never *saw* an internal combustion engine *that* big before. One of 'em takes up a *flatcar!* So, your *hair*...

I got tired of *you* rolling over and *pulling* it every night.

There's *less* radical solutions for that than cutting it like that *princess*...

*Not* one I *like* as much. *Like* it?

Yeah, I *do*. It's *cute*...

It's not *too* short...?

No; it's just about right. Just a *guy's* opinion.

A *guy* who's opinion I respect. Dad was being nice when he said the same thing. Boss said it was *different*, but *he's* known me most of my *life*...

It's *just* right for fondling that downy hair on the nape of your neck.

I wanna find *out* about *that*...

Then...I'll...like *this*...

*Mm, yeah.* I *see* what you *mean*. It's *just* right. *C'mere*...let me...*mmm*...is *that* a roll of quarters in your pocket or are you glad to *see* me?

You *feel that* through *those?*

Old *baggy tights*, babe...

The longer we *stand* here, honey...

The longer we stand here, *what*...?

You mean you're *not* tempted…?

Tempted to *what*…?

*Empty* my *till?* That's *ten whole dollars* there…

Being in your arms feels safe *and* arousing even with *that*… of *yours*…

But not…?

Like the *little* thrill I get in the shower when I…

Holding *your* hips against *mine* is a *shower-level* thrill. Way to boost a guy's confidence…

You're holding a *gorgeous* copperhead on a *beautiful*, breezy, late April Friday afternoon just a *few seconds* from your bed…*that* should give you confidence…

*Honey*, are *you*…interested?

*How* about…a *before*-dinner…*teaser*?

*OOO!* Red, how'd you *do* that?

*Practice*. Just a *little* thrill I used to give at the end of an *OK* date.

*This* was an *OK date?*

This *is* a *fabulous* welcome-home *fondle*.

*Kiss* me …

*Mm…babe! Who* have *you* been *practicing* with?

Just *you, honey*; just *you*…you *closing* tonight?

Uh-huh. Want to do fish fry?

Sure.

*I'll* go change…

Can I *watch?*

*Hmm*…only if *you* change *with* me…

Wouldn't we *both* be…

Yeah, we *could* be…

And in between we *could*…

We *could*, and we've *got* the *time*.

***

*Hey*, Blondie; how was the dentist? Not talking 'cause it's still tender...and probably haven't *eaten*, right? Just nod... right. Tell you what, I'll *scramble* some *eggs* for ya and get a shower...

***

Hi, babe. *Eggs* OK? Good. *What's*...just *point* at the *guide*... OK...we *saw* this, *didn't* we? Wanna just *neck* for a while... no...then I'll just lay my head in your lap...

***

Red...?

Mm...?

You awake?

No; I'm *asleep*. The *voice* is your *imagination*...

Well...my *lip's* back and my *gum* doesn't hurt anymore.

*That's* good.

*I* need to go to bed.

Me, too.

About your *offer* before...still stand?

Which *one*?

About the necking...?

The guy who *named* it *necking* didn't know *anything* about anatomy...

Heh-*hee*...*or* necking...so...?

*In* bed our *out*?

*Which* was your *offer*...?

Does it *matter*?

***

*Another* road trip, Blondie?

Yeah. *This* potential client makes something called an uninterruptible power system.

What's *that?*

Like it says; something to do with batteries and generators. I'll be gone until Friday.

I'll *miss* you...

I'll miss *you*...kiss for the road?

Abso*lutely.*

***

Hello?

*Hey*, Red...

*Hi*, Blondie! Where *are* you? I was *just* headed out...

I wanted to catch you before you got away...

Well, you *did*...

Wanted to hear your *voice*...

You sound *tired*...

Been closeted with a self-serving *blowhard* of a marketing and advertising manager all day, telling me everything *he's* done for *his* company...

The *owner*...?

His *brother-in-law*...

*Ew*...sounds...tedious...

*Root canals* are *comfortable* compared to listening to *this* guy...he's a real *proctologist*...got his *head* up his...

Ooo...

Yeah; and *he's* my *primary* contact for *technical* matters... doesn't know which side of a schematic's on top, *or* that his sister's husband's *company* makes electronics...

*That* sounds...

Yeah, *don't* it, though...?

You *OK*, babe...?

Now I hear *you*...yeah, I *will* be. *You've* gotta get going...

Yeah...*love* you, babe...see ya *Friday!*

Love you *too*, honey...*Friday*, then.

***

Hey, Blondie! *C'mere*...

Been on the *road* for *three* hours; been needing *this* like you *wouldn't believe...you* feel *good*...

*You* feel *fabulous*...want a beer? *Our* stool's empty...

Sure; OK...

How was the road trip?

Good; borderline great, business-wise! We need another *writer* now. I can't keep *up* on my own. But, *technically*... *ugh*. I see they're *gutting* the pizza place?

Yeah. Went to city hall this week; got all the permits. The contractor started yesterday.

*I'm* gonna go get something to eat, un*wind* a bit, feed the cat, unpack, make this week's frames...

I'll be home by 9:30.

See you *there*...ah, Red...*you* OK...?

See you at *home*.

***

Hey.

*Hey*. There's a new chick-flick on in a few minutes.

Shower...

***

You *OK*, Red? You haven't said *more* than…

I had to *fire* the *guy*. I've known *him* since 4th Grade.

Ah. *Catch* him?

Legs *told* on him 'cause the till was light by nearly *fifty* bucks last night and she *damn* sure wasn't gonna take the blame…I never had to *fire* anyone before.

The *downside* of management. Hiring is easy…if they've got the skills, you give 'em a shot. If they don't work *out*, you let 'em go…

The books don't *prepare* you for *this*. This feels more *personal*, especially since I've known the guy and his family like *forever*.

I *get* that. But you *can't* beat yourself *up* over this. He took advantage and *betrayed* the *trust* of a friend who gave him a job…*you*. That *can't* slide.

Somebody once said you should never go into business with friends…they may have had *this* in mind. So, how's life as a consultant?

Not that much different from what it was *before*. This week's frame order's drying now…

I mean the *money*…

Oh, well, steady side income's welcome, *that's* for *damn* sure. Don't have to do much *for* it, either.

You have to keep *me* happy.

I find it remarkable that I don't have much trouble doing *that*.

You *sure?*

You want to find *out?*

*Mm*, I *would*, but…messy…

Ah. *Rain* check, then.

*Rain* check on *that*, but here's *more* to my happiness than *that*…

And *do* I keep you happy doing whatever else it is I *do?*

Unlike every *other* guy I've ever been with, you're here *nearly* every night; you clean up *after* yourself; you cook about every *other* meal; you mentor my personnel decisions... what's *not* to *like?*

OK...

Do *I* make *you* happy, Blondie?

You *do...*

How?

You stick *around;* you laugh at *some* of my jokes; you *don't* point and laugh in bed...

I'm serious...

So am I...it don't *take* much to make *me* happy.

Wish I...I wish *my* world was that *simple...*

It's only as complicated as *you make it,* honey.

***

Say, Red! How was class? Sold *another* article and the latest batch of frames is done.

Great! *Aced* my Econ *and* my Business Management 102 finals!

Hey, *fabulous!* Are you gonna continue for a *degree* or...?

I'm thinking I *might,* but in hospitality, not *just* business.

Ya know, I just *might* go back to school. Question is *where...*

You still thinking about that *other* job?

He hasn't *made* an offer, just a proposal.

What's the difference?

We talked about how I would fit into his management scheme. But his engineers and his marketing people all want control of any tech pubs *department* that would supposedly infringe on *their* customer contact.

*How* would *that...?*

If the users contact the *tech writer* about the *manual*...

Ah...

I had some ideas about how to deal with *that*; he said he'd *think* about it.

So, no *offers*...

No.

Sounds messy...

It *is*, but Across the State's in no *hurry*...

Ah...

Big Boss and I have been having *similar* discussions. For the *moment*, the two of us writers work for one of the account execs. Big Boss is thinking we *could* be a separate department...what're *you* thinking about...?

Idiot Brother's court date is next week.

You *going?*

*Everybody* is...

Yeah, well, *my first* court date's next *month*...

First?

The *first* one, I'm told, I just have to tell the judge that those papers are what I've *got*; what I *owe*...

There's *a question* about that?

Yeah; it's announced in the paper to make sure they have notified *all* my creditors. Like in the days when churches published *banns* before a couple got married...

*What's* a...?

It's an announcement so any *other* spouses could contest the marriage, *and* so anyone who knew that the happy couple was related by blood or were married *someplace else* that nobody *else* knew about could chime in...

That happen a *lot?*

Often *enough*, I guess...the *second* court date is for discharge... unless some creditors decide *they* object to what the *lawyers* work out...

So they could *still* say...?

Yep. Just like Idiot Brother's deal *could* be nullified by the judge, who could sentence him to *more time.*

*Neither* of us is out of the woods *yet...*

***

Mm?....oh, *hi*, Red. Good night?

Yeah. The new bartender *knows* what she's doing...

Good...you did *well* this semester; I *saw* your report cards...

I did *OK*...roll over and hold me.

OK...

I need *more...*

Back-rub?

*Try* it...mmm...ah...*that's* not my *back...*

I know *that* much anatomy...mind?

Not...*mm...*

*Feel* better?

You do it *well.* Makes me want *more...*

More *what*, Red?

More...*more.* Should *I* rub *your* back?

Trying to get me loose so you can have your *way* with me?

The way I feel right *now, maybe*; I *badly* need distraction... can I have *just* a *sweet* little kiss?

When you ask like *that*, absolutely...

*Mm*...yours are sweeter than *any* other I've *ever* had. Spoon for a little?

Sure. How's...?

Great...*sweet...love* your little *pecks* on my *neck...*

*Glad* you cut your hair.

Me, too...*shh...*

***

Hi.

Morning. Sleep OK?

Yeah. You?

With *you*, I feel as *safe* as if I were in my father's arms.

*That's* a little...

Yeah, it *is*...as safe as I could *possibly* imagine.

*That's* good to know...how long have you *felt* that way?

I'd *have* to say...since the *first* time I slept in this place...

I should be insulted or honored. Don't girls *like* bad boys?

Yeah, but not *all* of us feel *safe* with them...*look* at me...

'K...

I *love* you, Blondie...

I *know*. *I* love *you*, Red...

I *know*...

***

Hey, Red. How did court go?

*Not* good. I need to sit down. What'cha watching?

Evening news. Have *dinner*...?

Let's just *watch*.

***

He got a *year* in lockup and three years' probation.

That's *about* what *I* figured, but...

If he *hadn't* cooperated, he'd have gotten *ten* inside.

True that. Go out and lie in the sun. *That* always makes you feel better.

Not much sun left.

There's enough to improve your mood...

Only if *you* come with me...

Out back; I can find a tree.

OK. I'll get changed; you grab the chaises. I'll see you out there.

***

Mm. *Great* idea, Blondie.

Just looking out for my friend...ya know what *stumps* me? You *don't* get sunburned. I thought redheads burn whenever they *think* about going out in the sun...I know you oil yourself down *after*...

I don't stay *out* that long and I use *lots* of sunblock...*let's get married*, Blondie.

*Huh?*

Please *marry* me. I've already *got* the ring. Let's call an end to this *pseudo*-engagement and make it for *real*.

I...why *now*?

Know why I haven't dated the same guy twice since I *moved* here?

No...not...

I've been comparing them all to *you*...and they *all* come up short.

Why?

I couldn't trust *them* like I trust *you*. *Most* of 'em are still just boys trying to act like grown-ups. *Tired* of that; I need a *home*.

You need some *stability* after Idiot Brother...

Yeah.

Sure you *want* to be married to my financial disaster?

*We'll* figure it *out*, babe.

Ya know, I *read* somewhere that you *shouldn't* make marriage proposals when *naked*...

I'm *not...*

Close *enough*; *that* outfit leaves *nothing* to the imagination...

*Yeah*, but...I just *felt* it...

*Let* me just *say...*

*Maybe...?*

*Maybe*...let's get some *dinner...*

***

What are you thinking about, Red?

How do you know I'm *thinking?*

That *look...and* I can hear the gears grind...*what...?*

I've got a *look?*

Yep.

Huh. *Anyway*, it's *Dad*...how I'd love for him to know Mom won that argument over me *before* he...

You mean, you getting settled down...

Yeah.

Didn't the ring and the lease kinda address that?

Not as much as us saying '*I do*' somewhere. *That's* what I'm thinking about, babe...that *and...*

What *else...?*

*And, whatever* you and Mom are *hiding.*

Red, remember last winter, you couldn't talk about your business deal because of the financing?

Yeah...

Well, what your mother and I are 'hiding' is *confidential* for *similar* reasons...but *not* financial. You'll understand why later. For now, just *trust* us...

When did *you* start being a *big*-shot *business* guy?

Nothing *big-shot* about it. Like you, I kinda *fell* into it; in my case, drawn into it by *your father.*

How did *that*...?

*My* involvement in *your* enterprise interested your father in *more* ways than *one*. That's all I *can* say about it...

How long has *this* been going on?

Sister's birthday party...*what's* the long face for...?

If we say *I do*, we *have* to stay *here*...babe, *we* can *figure out* the rest...

Red, I *know* your family is well-off, but I *don't want charity*...

It's *not*...

It *feels* like it is...

Is *this*...charity...*cowboy*?

*How* do you...*do*...that? Your *hips* are am... a...ooo...

***

Your argument is *very* persuasive, Red...but...you'd *blackmail us*...

How firm do *you* think Across The State is?

I figure fifty-fifty.

*We're* a sure thing...

As *long* as I *stay here* and accept *your* largesse...

Of *course* not...don't *put* it that way...

But you *said*...?

I *know* what I *said*, Blondie, and I know you *have* to do what you *have* to do, but *we* need to think about *our* future *together*. If *I* leave here, I'd need to find a new *manager*... but then there's Dad and Mom, and Idiot Brother getting locked up in a few weeks...

We'd be just across the *state*, honey; *not* on *another planet*.

Right now's *not* a good time to be thinking about such life-changing...

Honey, if my creditors *don't* take what they can *get* from my tax refund, *my* life-changing *shit* will happen, too.

How life-changing?

This *bed*; the *pit*; the *washer and dryer*...gone...maybe *more* if the *hospital* wants more...*The Guy's* nowhere to be found...

But *he's* not for *real*...

We don't *think* he is, but...

Does Across The State *know* how broke you are...?

He'll run a credit check as a matter of routine, no doubt...

What do *you* think *he'll* think...?

Nothing *good*...

And even if you *get* a big pay raise, will it be *enough* to keep the wolves away...

No, but...*shit*, that's *my* phone...

Yeah...

*The Guy*...wants an answer on his last *offer*...like a *rock* in the *pit* of my *guts*, just *sitting* there...how tempting it is to just...

Where would *you* get eight grand?

*Grovel* to *your parents*; mine...

If we say '*I do*' it will be *my* rock in the pit of *my* guts, too... but he's *not real*...

Not sure I *can* ask you to...what if he *is*...?

That *investigator* said...

*She* could be *wrong*...we *shouldn't*...he's *gone*...

We *can*...*when* will *we* set a *date*...?

Let's do this *right*...

How...?

By *sitting down, fully clothed*...

Not as much *fun*, killjoy...

C'mon...

***

OK, cowboy; now that we're fully clothed and out of bed, *let's*...

We never talked about...I know you *go* to church about once a quarter...

Yeah; just to stay in practice.

You'd *want* a church ceremony?

Not necessarily. Do *you* have a preference?

Well, I *was* baptized, but the last time I was in a church was *Cousine's* wedding. Before *that*, Step-Mom's second wedding...no, *Grampa's* funeral...

You'd settle for a judge?

Would *you?*

Mom and Dad would want a church...

Isn't it up to *us*...?

It *should* be, huh? Soon as Mom finds out we're *setting* a *date*...

*Step-Mom* would be her first call...

*Second; her* older sister would be her *first*...

Want to be a June bride...?

*Sister* was one...a *month* away...maybe Dad couldn't handle the excitement. Better plan on small...

*Small* it shall be...

But *not* microscopic...Blondie?

Red?

Babe, do you *like me enough?*

Enough...what do you *mean?*

Love is *one* thing, but do you *like* me enough to put up with *my* bullshit and stay here to spend your life with *me* while *we* figure out your finances...?

Well, *your* bullshit includes loading the toilet paper roll upside down, not closing the shower curtain completely, and leaving your *hair* stuff all over. *Those* little quirks I've learned to tolerate. The rest I barely notice anymore, *except* your affinity for *bait* that I *still* find...

You *know* what I mean...*really*: do you *like* me enough...?

I *care* for you, honey; I want to spend as much time as I *can* with you because I also love you. But I've got *money* trouble that's *not yours* but would *affect* you, our life together...do you *like me enough...?*

Your inability to small-talk, your obsession with *money*, the *occasional* left-up toilet seat, yeah, I can live with *those*. Babe, I've *screwed* several guys; I've *slept with* a *few* guys...

*Neat* distinction...

Nearly *all* of 'em stop by the bar at least once a month, and *all* of 'em *know* each other...and *you*...

Good thing they're all friends...

But *you're* the one I've *made love* with...the *only* one...

But *why me?*

I *think* because you're not *from* here; you knew *none* of my friends before I introduced you; you didn't know *me* from high school or *before*...

The handsome stranger?

The *beautiful, interesting* stranger who was the first guy I ever *tried* to pick up *and* the first who said *no* when I propositioned him.

*That* made me an irresistible challenge. Do *you like me enough?*

I *do*. Do *you like me enough?*

I *do*. Honey, I have a confession: I have not been able to get you out of my head since we *met*...

Last New Year's?

Yep...

Babe...*I* haven't been able to get *you* out of my head since then, *either*...

*Like* at first sight?

*Is* there such a thing?

How would *I* know...Monday I go to *court*...

We'll hold off any other plans until *then*...

***

Hey, babe! *How* was...*uh*-oh.

Yeah; *uh*-oh. The *finance company* wants *their* stuff back and the hospital won't *settle* for...what they were *offered.*

So...repossession?

So the pit, the waterbed, the washer and dryer...gone within ninety days. They saved my *car,* and in the open market, everything I *own* is only worth *chump change,* so they *won't* take my typewriter or my tools. The court will garnish *nearly half my wages* until the hospital debt's *paid*...I'm not sure I could pay the *rent* here, let alone the utilities...pay TV...?

Oh, *shit*...babe, I...*I* can handle the *rent*...

You'd *have* to if we're gonna stay *here*...I'll be *chronically broke* for about *two years,* Lawyer says. And, we'll be *sitting* and sleeping on the *floor,* going to the *laundromat* once a week by mid-summer.

Nothing from Across The State...?

Not lately...

I can rustle up some furniture. There's the *little* bed in the spare room...

Yeah...

***

Hi, Blondie. *Mail's* there...

Thanks, Red. Yeah...*oh!* That magazine I sent a *big* article in to...they *like* that piece I sent them on the evolution of harvesters...

How *much* do they like it?

Let's see...*shit,* I *ripped* the...*check* for...*a month's rent!*

OMY*GOD,* babe! That's *great!*

And they want MORE!

Yeah? You *got* more?

Um...*outlines*, yeah...tractors, planters, sprayers...

Wow! You *could*...

I submitted this one in *September* and now it's *May*. Not a *steady* income, but...

But it's *something*, babe. *Something* more than *nothing*. Now, can your *creditors* come for...?

No; they don't *know* about it. It's a *side gig*...I could sign the check over to *them*, though...not *going* to, but...

Ah. Wanna celebrate?

How?

You *know* how...

OK: *what's* showing and *where*?

I dunno, but *you're* buying at that new multiplex...*eight* screens...

***

When is it *appropriate* to express gratitude for sex?

I don't know...how about gratitude for taking me out to a fine movie, followed by a splendid dinner and sparkling conversation?

*Thanks* for all *that*, Red...and the *fabulous* lovemaking *after*...

Welcome, Blondie. Makes it *sound* less like I'm a hooker, even if I don't *feel* like one. *Thanks*, Blondie, for all of *that*, too...

Welcome, Red...about setting a *date*...?

I talked to Mom and Dad and Sister. *They* say they'll attend anything we want to pull together...

*But*...

Mom and Sister are disappointed that we want *small*. Dad says it's fine, wants to dance with the bride...

He can do *that* anywhere...

*He* wants to do it in front of his whole *family*. I under*stand*, but he's so *frail*, and it means *so* much to him...when?

Need to find a venue first...

***

Some Memorial Day party, Red.

We went all out this year. The new complex's plans are getting a once-over like never before...

*They* seem to be a popular attraction. Who's the band?

Somebody Boss knows, did this gig cheap...they're not *that* bad...

Nope. Idiot Brother seems mighty upbeat for somebody who's gonna spend the next nine months at *least* in jail...

Yeah. They found Moron, finally. Idiot Brother's agreed to testify against him; delaying execution of sentence for at *least* another *two months*...

Does Moron have friends?

Connections, according to Idiot Brother, but no *dangerous* friends. Too low-level...

I got a call from Across The State; he's still *thinking*...I asked if he'd pay for moving expenses for *two* people. He said he'd *think* about that...

*Think* he'll...?

A *tactic*, Red. If he goes for it, at least I know he won't break *us*...

When would you *know*?

He said *soon*...

# Asks Questions...

*Hey. Got more groceries?*

*Hi!* No; *this* is it. Did Across The State get back to you?

Last night. You *working* tonight?

*Boss* is managing tonight...*don't* dodge the question: Across The State *said...?*

He's not *sure.* Almost sounds like he's got somebody *else* in mind if I can't move myself; *that* might be a maneuver, too.

Or he wasn't happy with your credit report.

Or that. I finally told *Big Boss* what was going on...

Yeah? How did *that* go?

He understood, but isn't *ready* to give me a *raise...*

*Sorry,* babe...

It's OK. I want to go lie down. *Join* me?

Few minutes...

***

We must have dozed off...

*Feel* better?

Some. I just feel so damned *powerless...*what *time* is it?

It's not quite dark...

Dusk. *Beautiful* this time of year...*you're* beautiful *any* time of year...

You're only *saying* that because I let you cry on my chest.

I'm saying that because you *are*, Red. Thanks for *being there* for me...

I've cried on *your* shoulder often enough...c'mere. Set your head down here...

Your *gut's* gurgling...

I'm getting hungry...

***

Blondie?

Huh?

I want to *help* you, and *not* just with the dishes...*this* one's greasy yet...

OK...help me with *what*...?

Your *finances*...

So you can *keep* us *here?*

*One* reason. Another is that I *love* you...

You're not *that* much better off *than*...

I'm *better off* than...*never* mind...

Until we are married, my *debt* is *mine*...after, *you're saddled* with it, too...

*That's* why I'm not changing my name, but *that* does *not* prevent me from *helping* you...

We'll *see.*

***

Hey.

*Hi.* How was work?

Uneventful. June *has* no holidays...

June and August don't, no...

So we're holding an *event* for *Juneteenth Day* next Friday, whatever *that* is.

*Something* to do with freeing the slaves in the Lone Star State. Started a big celebration. *Some* parts of the country throw parties...

Since *we* get a black person in the bar about once a month, *I* don't get it...

It's an excuse for a party. *Don't* resist, Red; resistance to marketing is futile. That *movie* you wanted to see is on in a couple of hours...

Shower...

*** 

Disappointing.

Yeah. *Big* buildup for *not* much.

*Lots* of shoot-'em-up, *not* much plot.

Yeah. You *working* tomorrow?

I'm closing.

Any more on the planning side?

There's a wedding chapel we can have the weekend after next. Everyone's free and Boss will throw us a reception at his lakeside restaurant.

OK...I'll call Step-Mom, my *aunt*...

We can get the blood tests Monday...*yeah*...

*Yeah*...Big Boss's son-in-law's a photographer. I'll ask him if he'll shoot *that* for *dinner* and we'll send *copies* to everyone...

We can ask that friend of Boss's if he'll play a set or even just one *song*...

That's *enough*.

*** 

*Wow*...

Yeah...

I didn't think Dad would want more than *one* dance...

He *did*, though. Danced with *every* girl in the place...

Even Twelve-Year-Old and Step-Sis.

And Three-Year-Old...

Her *too*. Mom wasn't sure he was going to be *well* enough... *Step Two* can cut a rug, too...

Never *saw* him dance before...didn't expect Step-Mom to get all teary...

Her *only child* got hitched. What do you *expect?*

I suppose...but *Step-Sis...*

Yeah...blubbering like a *real* sister...I'm just glad so *much* of *my* family showed up on such short notice.

Not like they have to come across the country; just across the lake...*now* we start thinking in terms of *us*...and I *will* answer to the consequences *with* you...

***

*Who...?*

That was The Guy. Now he says *five* grand would clear it all...there was a rented truck in the driveway, a couple of big guys standing in front of it. The Guy said 'we've come for your *check* or your *stuff.*' Well, I hauled out that camera you gave me last Christmas and started taking pictures of *them and* the truck. They *high*-tailed it...*couldn't* get away *fast* enough.

Tells you *something...*

It tells me *everything...*I'll turn the film over to the investigator...

***

So what did they say?

They would develop the film and see what they *can...*

Are there any *other* pictures on it?

A couple...hope I get the rest *back...*

How many did you snap of The Guy?

I *think* three...

***

Not a bad crowd for an obscure event, Red...

Most of 'em would be here on Friday night, anyway. Food brings families.

At least it's *business*...

It *is*. That poster was *inspired*, Blondie. Thanks for getting it made.

*Anything* for a pal. *All* the events till New Year's on *one* ticket. An *annual* ticket...

*Sold* a great deal more than we'd *thought* we would. Certainly more than Boss *thought*...

*That's* great. Big Boss wants me on the road again next week.

New business?

*Sort* of. An old customer of his wants to revive an older product line; they want *me* to figure out what it'll take to bring the documentation up to date while the marketing guys schmooze over an ad campaign...

I see. So...

*Monday* I fly out...

***

Hello?

*Hi*, Red. How's *things* around *there?*

*Hey*, babe...Dad's slipping; in the hospital last night...

Sorry....something else?

The Guy—I *think*—called again. Said he was giving a *last warning* before they came to take everything in the townhouse that can *move...then* they'd come for the *bar*...

Yeah?

Yeah. I hung up and called Deputy, told him. He said the investigator would run the call down...

*Good* for *you*, honey. Maybe *that'll* beat him down...

Hope so...*I felt that rock in the pit of my chest...*

My private circle of hell's not so private anymore...sorry, honey...

We're in it together, babe, better or worse...

*This* is the *worse*...

***

*Tech* pubs...

It's *Dad*, Blondie; *Mom* just called...he...he...he's *gone*...

Oh, I'm *so* sorry, honey. Want *me* to...?

Just come to *their* house after work, babe...

Sure.

***

*Thanks* for coming, babe.

Just doing what *any* husband is supposed to do. Where's your mom?

Kitchen.

I'll pay my respects...

Grab something to eat; there's plenty everywhere.

***

Your mom's pretty stoic.

More *relieved*...he was slipping away before our *eyes*...

You staying *here* tonight?

To*night* anyway...we don't want to leave Mom alone...

Have you made arrangements?

They already *had*...viewing Saturday; funeral Sunday... just...*hold* me a while *before* you go, babe. *Just*...

OK...

*Shh*...

***

Hey, Red. There's your mail.

Thanks...let me get a *shower*...

***

You're beautiful in that *sarong*...

It *covers*...

Even when you just *drape* it over your shoulders...

And *you're* in my tiny *shorts*, you slovenly *slug*...make *room*, Kitty; I'm gonna put my *head* in Daddy's *lap*...

Yeah, sure...wanna watch a movie, *honey*...?

*Shh...this* is nice...Kitty, *just...stop* crying and *go...there's* a *better* Kitty...

Honey, I...*Kitty*...ah, *shit*...

*Another* hairball *just* when...what *timing*, cat...it'll *keep*...

Ah, *yes*; there's nothing *quite* like a cat bringing up a hairball to en*hance* TV watching, meals and seductions... what's *this*...?

We've *seen* it...it's *fine. I* just want to be *still*...pull the quilt over; the air conditioning just kicked on.

Yeah; Landlord had a coolant charge put in...better?

Much...*shh*, now...

What *is* it you find so interesting about me...?

I *said*...

I *asked* a *question*...

OK: there's a great deal of depth to you, Blondie. I enjoy exploring that. I've fallen in *love* with that depth...what do you *love* about me?

That you could actually care about *me*, about what I *thought*, how I *feel*.

You've only known *one other* woman in your life *that* well and you *still* call her Step-Mom.

I called her Mom once *before* last Christmas; she looked at me funny and asked that I *not* do it again...

I never *heard* of that...

I know. Most women would find it flattering or endearing. I *think* because she couldn't *have* kids...

How would *you* know? She *tell* you?

She never had a period all the time I was living there. I noticed that there were never any feminine hygiene product traces in a wastebasket before Step-Sis moved in. I know because I emptied them every afternoon...

Did you *ask* her about it?

It seemed like the wrong kind of question to ask the only *mother* I ever *knew.*

You didn't think your guardian's reproductive possibilities were any of your *business?*

You listen to yourself?

Sometimes. Let's just *watch*...

***

Hi...mmm...we *slept* down here?

*Morning,* glory. You're *beautiful* in the morning.

*Ugh,* you need your eyes examined. My hair's a mess; I can *feel* a crease in my *face* from the cushion; I need a long bath...I'm so *scuzzy*... sarong's...*between* the... ugh... *pull* the quilt over...

Here...

What's on TV?

Does it *matter?*

Not *really.* You *hungry?*

I'm *starving.*

We didn't get *any* dinner last night.

I'm gonna *clean up* Kitty's...*right* in front of the bathroom... cat, you're gonna *drive* me to *drink*...

*First,* he asks about *food, then* cat puke...

She wanted to make sure we *saw* her latest gastric rearrangement...like when she put one on the kitchen table *and* one on my *desk*...what's in the *fridge?*

I'll make *coffee* and *look*...OK, *rice* and English muffins... and *a* hard-boiled egg...and *milk*...leftover meatloaf and mashed potatoes...should put some *clothes* on and... *hello!* Behind-Neighbors both *just* got an eyeful of *me*...

Want your *sarong?*

A little late *now*...but here's Boy Across-the-Walk off to school...*he* didn't *look*...

We'll hear about it tonight when Guy-Behind bangs Gal-Behind tonight...

Such a *crude* term...

But in *their* case...that's...

Appropriate...and *quick. Wow!*

*Hell,* they didn't even make it to the *bedroom...must* be in the living room...

Nope...stairwell by *their* bathroom...

Just the other side of this *very* thin *wall...she's* getting into it, that's for *damn* sure...

*Oh, yeah...*

*Inspiring*...are *you* getting...?

*Oh, yeah*...I can see *your* inspiration from over *here,* cowboy...*c'mon*...

***

This is the last of the groceries...

Good. Your mom looks tired.

She was probably up all night with Dad's family. There's something on the machine...

I'll listen...oh; Step-Mom...they're *coming over?*

Huh; *nice* of them. *I* need to go to the funeral home...

Want me to go with you?

Um, no; this is only for the *details*, babe. Come by the house tonight.

***

Quite a crowd, Red...

Yeah. He was well-liked, well-respected...

Your mom's holding up pretty well...

Yeah. There's *your parents*...

I'll go say *howdy* when they're done with *your* mom. Step-Mom's a thoroughly decent woman; *he's* OK, too. I *love* her, even if...

You're as close as she's ever come to having a son, babe; give her *that* much.

I suppose...Sister's kinda broken up.

Yeah...there's Idiot Brother...

On leave?

Forty-eight hour pass...uh-*huh*; *first* one he meets is Loser. *Not* Mom, *not* Sister or *me*...

Give him a break, honey. Loser *is* the closest to the door.

There's Auntie and Unk. *I* need to...

Do what you've *gotta*...and *I'll* do what I *gotta*...

***

*Hey.*

*Hi.* I need to get out of this...*corset* of a dress...un*zip* me... *there.* Thanks for taking the kids *outta* there, babe...

A semi-drunken wake isn't the place for pre-teen children. I figured *they* needed a break...

Sister picked 'em up?

Loser did; maybe an hour ago.

Babe: Monday morning, we meet with Dad's lawyer about the estate.

OK...

Will *you* be free?

Will *I*...oh, *yeah*; I *guess* I...*sure*.

Get used to being *part* of the family, Blondie.

***

Only ever saw anything like *that* in the movies, Red.

Never knew there was *that* much in the business...come on upstairs...the house and land and the business are *all* Mom's; now *I* work for *her*...

Thought you were a *co-owner*...?

I *am, but* the *family* business is the majority shareowner; *they're* putting up the capital for the renovation...I have to pay it *back*...

Ah...

And the rest of Dad's estate is *three-fourths*-Mom's. Sister, Idiot Brother and I divvy up the *other quarter* in trusts we get at thirty; Sister's already *there*.

Any idea how much is *in* those?

A *lot*.

Enough for you to finish school *full*-time and work *part time* with a *hired* full-time manager? I *know* it's what you *want*. That curious mind of yours needs training...

The only way to make money in the hospitality racket is to *own* the joint...*but*...

*But* you don't *know* if you want to be slinging drinks and flashing cleavage for the rest of your working life, even if you *have* the *title* of *manager/co-owner*...

*How* do you read my *mind* when *I* barely know it? *How* did you *know* I'm on the fence about the bar?

When you asked me to evaluate your *attire* so *many* moons

313

ago...*and* watching as you've come to realize how smart you really *are*...

Wasn't *that* long ago...how *smart* I...?

*Don't* interrupt while I'm trying to soliloquize...

*Don't* tell me *what*...you're trying to *what?*

Think out loud. Anyway, I sensed that you doing *that* was *not* something you...those classes have been telling you that you're *way* too smart to be slinging booze for the rest of your life; deciding how much of *you* you're going to *show*...

Asking a guy I barely know to stare at my chest is *not* at the *top* of *my* list.

Yet, you gave me the opportunity to *study* that *gorgeous* structure right down to that little *mole* on your *left*...

I *know* where *that is,* babe. I *still* don't know *why* I asked *you* to do *that.*

It was *my* pleasure nonetheless,

*Doubtless.* Being *asked* to stare at a woman's bust *must* be near the *top* of *every* guy's list.

I may be a *leg* man, but I appreciate a...a...

*Big balcony...?*

*Very* eloquent.

*Thank* you.

I smelled resentment then, but not of *me*; of your perceived *need* to ask a relative stranger to tell you what you already *knew.* I *also* sensed that you felt *stuck*...

You *are* a mind reader...

Sometimes. You were taking classes when you moved in; you were more interested, I *thought*, in my *books* than in *me.*

*At* first.

Uh-huh. Then, your condition and Door-Guy's response to the *possibility* that you were *expecting*; then...

And *your* reactions. *Those surprised* me. *And* being *single*, twenty-five and *still* being called *cute* without *trying* by a guy I was living-not-sleeping with who I found interesting *but* who I didn't have to push *off* every night got to be *comfortable. Then* I started to *resent* having to show *skin* for more *tips...*

You *said...*

That was *before* I kissed you for the first time...my whole *life* transformed at that instant, like it was my *first* boy-kiss...

You didn't *say...*

I tried to...would have if you'd...the *question on the stairs...* you said 'no.'

What *question on the stairs?*

*Blondie...*

You asked me to *forget...*

But you *didn't...*

How *could* I? That was the *first* time *any* woman had asked me *outright...*

That day I *wanted you so bad...*

And I failed you...

Anything *but,* in retrospect.

*Retrospect?*

*Yeah!* Shut up while I *soliloquize* myself. Up until that moment I'd thought I would always be alone because I only *knew* guys I didn't *want* to be with for the rest of my life...but *you* wanted more than a bump-and-tickle...and I *adored* you for it...

You didn't *look* like you *adored* me...

Well, I *did, even though* I had to *paddle* my *pink canoe* for the *first time* since...can't *remember...*

*Paddle* your...

How *girls* rub one out...

Ah...

*That night* I started working on my business plan, even if it *was* for school *and* a week *late...*

Because you *couldn't sleep*...?

Because I could barely *think* I was *so*...but I did *that*, and... I put all *the pluses* down on paper by two the next morning and *that* was when I decided to talk to Dad and Boss about *buying* the bar...

You did all this because *I wouldn't*...?

*YES. That* was when I started thinking of a future *beyond* my next *paycheck* or my next *date*...except the *bar*...

It's *not* what you see for *your* future anymore.

Not after *we* decided all those things about *us*. I *finally* figured out that *you* would fill the emptiness I felt. Before that, I wanted both you *and* to be free. Is *that* screwed up?

Girls complain they can't *find* a boy, then ignore us when we try to start a conversation or start talking about a second or third date. Hard to believe that one *kiss* led you to a *new* life, exciting and scary and filled with possibilities, in contrast to your *old* life, familiar and safe, barren and going nowhere...

Ain't *that* the truth? You made me *not* want to be single anymore. *C'mon*, babe; *make love* to me till dawn.

***

Across The State...?

Made an offer and said he'll *move* us.

Babe, I *can't* go just yet...Mom's pretty torn up.

She's tougher than she looks.

Yeah, but this has been a *tough* year. Between Idiot Brother, Dad, and Sister's divorce...the *major* work on the hall will be finished next month. I *don't* want to leave anyone in the lurch.

See what you can do to find a manager?

Yeah, *but*...

OK...well...*then*...regardless...*I've* got to talk to Big Boss... Good *luck*...

***

Big Boss says he *can't* meet that...

So...

So...*you* need to stay...?

Yeah; for *now*, yeah...

*Then...I've* got to talk to your *mom, now...*

About *what.*?

Business.

*Whose...*?

*Hers...yours...mine,* now...

I don't...

*Trust* me...

I *trust* you...I should get to the bar...haven't *been* there since the week before last...

*And...*

*Yeah...*?

They're coming for the *furniture* next Monday...

*Oh...*

# And Gets Answers!

---

*Hey, Blondie! What's...?*

*Deputy* wants to meet with me, my *lawyer* and *the investigator* in about *ten minutes...*

So why are *you...?*

Meeting *here*, in the bar...

*Why?*

It involves *you, too...*

Um...*OK*, you guys; *go* outside...I said *outside! Vamoose*, you *clowns!* I have *business* to discuss with my *husband...* come back *half an hour* from now...I don't *care* how *hot* it is outside...a *round* on the *house* in thirty minutes! Now *scram....!*

Expensive business meeting...

Naw...the round will be all rail booze...I SAID *GET...!*

*****

Your creditors are *forgiving all* your debts because of those *pictures* you took?

Yeah...The Guy worked for a credit reporting outfit; his gang of scammers has cost their customers—and *them—millions...*

*That's* how he knew *so much* about *us*. Huh. He's been working this scam for *how* long?

Investigator said two years in *this* state...at *least* three in the *country* that they *know* of...part of an interstate *ring*...the *feds* have been after *them*. That picture identified *who* rented that *truck* and *that* led to The Guy.

I can hardly *believe* it.

Me, neither...*and*...

And...that's *your* evil cat face. *What*...?

Your mom's moving all of your family business's marketing and advertising over to Big Boss's agency; all under one roof, as it were, for the *first* time.

The largest restaurant and commercial kitchen equipment suppliers in the state are now represented by *your* firm?

Yep. Would about *double* Big Boss' current revenues. Lets *me* get a 25% *bump* if I want it. Big Boss said he can't find *anyone* with my diverse talents *and* ability to work with *anyone*...

Ah; *that's* what you've been talking to Mom and Dad about all this time...?

*Bingo*...

Why the *secrecy?*

The ad game has more secrets than a romance novel shelf. If your parent's firm had approached Big Boss directly, their current-soon-to-be-former agencies would get up on their high horses and start suing over contracts and intellectual property secrets. Well, we'll be telling those agencies that their contracts will *not* be renewed, but the current work will continue—pretty *standard* in the business—until they *complete* the contracts. I've just been the *go-between* since last fall...

So, this means we're gonna stick around, cowboy?

We *are*, little lady...

Call me that *again*, Herman Melville Bartleby, and I'll *smack* you...

Then don't call me *cowboy* anymore, Chastity Prudence Wachowski...stick with *Blondie*.

Stick with *Red* from here on out. Let's try to *have* those beautiful *hypothetical* kids for *real* and let me manage *our* money so we won't have to quibble about it; we'll just argue about who gets to clean up after Scheherazade...

*My* cat who sleeps in *your* lap and pukes everywhere that *I* get to clean up...

You got a *problem* with *that?*

*No*, dear...marriage; where two people who love one another get to drive each other *crazy* for the rest of their lives...

And here I thought it was two people taking turns pushing the kitchen garbage down so we *don't* have to take it out...

*Yes*, dear; it's *that*, too...happy *wife*, happy *life*...

Just remember, *nothing* rhymes with 'happy husband...'

Honey, my life before *you* was a blank slate. Then *you* came along with buckets of fresh paint...and I'll *always* be happy with you around...

Me, too...

It's *not* who you can live *with*, it's who you *can't* live *without*.

Got *that* right, babe...let's let 'em back *in*...OK, everybody! *Next* round's *on the house...!*

Oh, *that* reminds me...Gal-Behind's *expecting*...

*Wow!* How did *that* remind you...?

*How* the hell would *I* know...?

You and your *funny* brain...want a *drink?*

Sure...*what* are my *choices?*

*Yes* and *no*...

*HA!*